Loretta Chase holds a B.A. [...] majored in English and [...] Her job history includes [...] part-time teaching posts at Clar[...] [...]ery and clothing retailers; and a Dicke[...] [...]ix-month experience as a meter maid. In the course of moonlighting as a corporate video scriptwriter, she fell under the spell of a producer who lured her into writing novels ... and marrying him. The books resulting from this union have won a number of awards, including the Romance Writers of America's RITA.

Also by Loretta Chase

Miss Wonderful
Mr Impossible
Lord Perfect

Not Quite A Lady

Loretta Chase

PIATKUS

Visit the Piatkus website!

Piatkus publishes a wide range of best-selling fiction and non-fiction, including books on health, mind, body & spirit, sex, self-help, cookery, biography and the paranormal.

If you want to:
- read descriptions of our popular titles
- buy our books over the Internet
- take advantage of our special offers
- enter our monthly competition
- learn more about your favourite Piatkus authors

VISIT OUR WEBSITE AT: www.piatkus.co.uk

Copyright © 2007 by Loretta Chekani

First published in Great Britain in 2007 by
Piatkus Books Ltd.,
5 Windmill Street, London W1T 2JA
email: info@piatkus.co.uk

This edition published 2007

First published in the United States in 2007 by
The Berkley Publishing Group, a Division of Penguin Group (USA) Inc.

The moral right of the author has been asserted

A catalogue record for this book is available from the British Library

978 0 7499 3795 9

Data manipulation by Phoenix Photosetting, Chatham, Kent
www.phoenixphotosetting.co.uk
Printed and bound in Great Britain by
Mackays of Chatham, Chatham, Kent

Acknowledgements

Thanks to:

Claudia Chartrand, Margaret Evans Porter, Myretta Robens, and Sue Stewart, for their wit and wisdom about horses.

Old Sturbridge Village of Sturbridge, Massachusetts, for its knowledgeable and wonderfully helpful interpreters, for keeping so vibrantly alive, and, of course, for the pigs.

My family and friends, with special thanks to:

Nancy Yost.
Mary Jo Putney.
Walter.
Cynthia.

Yorkshire, England
24 May 1812

"May I see him?" the girl asked. She was a girl in truth, scarcely seventeen. Her blue eyes enormous in a chalk white face etched with pain and fatigue, she seemed at present far too young to be a mother.

Hers had been a long labor, and she was not out of danger yet.

The two older women attending her—one, though modestly garbed, obviously a lady and one as obviously a servant—exchanged worried glances.

The lady had become the Marchioness of Lithby and the girl's stepmother scarcely a year earlier. Yet her manner was as compassionate and affectionate as that of a mother or sister. She bent over the fair head on the pillow. "My love, it would be better if you did not," she murmured. "Better to rest now."

"He's quiet," the girl said. "Why is he so quiet?"

Lady Lithby stroked her forehead. "The baby is . . . not strong, Charlotte."

"He's going to die, isn't he? Oh, you must let me see him. Only for a moment, Lizzie, please. I am so sorry to be so much trouble—"

"You are not to blame," Lady Lithby said sharply. "Never think that."

"You listen to her ladyship," the woman servant said. "It was that wicked man's fault. Along with the worthless creature who called herself a governess. It was her job to watch out for wolves in sheep's clothing. But she didn't, did she? She left it to you— and how's an innocent girl to know anything about the wickedness of men?"

The wolf in sheep's clothing was dead, killed in a duel—over a woman, naturally. Lady Charlotte Hayward was by no means the first or the last Geordie Blaine had wronged, though perhaps the youngest and highest born.

"There, you see?" her stepmother said. "Molly is on your side. I am on your side." A tear slid down her cheek and onto the pillow. "Never forget that, love. You can always come to me."

If only you had done so last summer . . .

Lady Lithby did not say this, yet the awareness hovered like a ghost in the quiet room.

"I'm sorry," the girl said. "I was so foolish. I am so sorry. But please, Lizzie, please may I see him? Only for a moment. *Please.*"

She spoke between ragged gasps. Her eyes filled, and her bosom rose and fell rapidly. The two women feared they would lose her, though they were careful not to let their anxiety show.

"I don't want her agitated," Lady Lithby murmured to the maid. "Let her see the child."

Molly went out and into the next room, where the wet nurse had taken charge of the babe.

All had been so very carefully and discreetly arranged: the midwife, the wet nurse, the carriage that would take the boy to his new parents. His mother's indiscretion had been well concealed.

The maid returned a few minutes later with the infant. Charlotte smiled and rose a little on the pillows, and Molly laid him in her arms. He made what seemed to be a feeble attempt to find her breast but gave up with a sigh.

"Oh, don't die," his mother said. She stroked over the white down on his head. She drew her index finger lightly over his nose and lips and chin. She touched her finger to his hand, and the tiny fingers curled about it. "You mustn't die," she whispered. "Listen to Mama." She whispered something else, too low for the others to hear.

She looked up at her stepmother. "They will take good care of him?"

"He goes to a good family," Lady Lithby assured her. "They have tried and tried to have a child. They will lavish all their affection on him."

If he lives.

This, too, went unsaid.

Too much went unsaid, perhaps, but Charlotte was too conscious of the wrong she'd done and the painful position in which she'd placed her stepmother—too conscious, in short, of all she owed these women, to say what was in her heart.

Perhaps, as well, the ache in her young heart went too deep and left her without words.

She only gazed at her baby and grieved as she had not thought it possible to grieve. She gazed at her son, her beautiful son, and thought of how she'd wronged him.

She'd believed Geordie Blaine had broken her heart, but that was nothing to this. She had brought an innocent child into the world. He was weak. He needed his mother. But she couldn't keep him.

Love.

Because of it, she'd wronged so many—and above all, the one innocent being she most wanted to protect.

Love.

It made one blind, truly. Blind to others. Blind to past, present, and future. Blind to all but one conscienceless man and the wicked feelings he inspired: desire . . . passion . . .

They were poetic words for simple animal urges. She saw that now, too late. Those feelings quickly faded.

What remained was the ache of grief, almost beyond enduring.

Love.

Never again. Her soul could not bear it.

Charlotte kissed her baby's forehead. Then she turned her glistening blue gaze to the maid. "You may take him now," she said.

Chapter 1

The trouble with Darius Carsington was, he had no heart.

Everyone in his family agreed that the Earl of Hargate's youngest son had started out with one. Everyone agreed that he had not, at the outset, seemed destined to be the most aggravating of Lord Hargate's five sons.

Certainly he was not so very different from the others in appearance.

Two of his brothers, Benedict and Rupert, had inherited Lady Hargate's dark good looks. Darius, like Alistair and Geoffrey, had Lord Hargate's golden brown hair and amber eyes. Like all of his brothers, Darius was tall and strong. Like the others, he was handsome.

Unlike the others, he was scholarly, and always had been. He'd commenced aggravating his father by insisting on going to Cambridge, though all the males of the family had always attended Oxford. Cambridge was more intellectually rigorous, he said. One might study botany there, and iron smelting, and other subjects of natural and practical philosophy.

True, he'd done well at Cambridge. Unfortunately, ever since he completed his studies, he seemed to have let his intellect gain the upper hand of his affections as well as his morals.

To put it simply, Darius divided his life into two parts: (1) studying animal behavior, especially breeding and mating behavior, and (2) devoting his leisure hours to emulating this behavior.

Item Two was the problem.

Lord Hargate's other four sons had not been saints when it came to women—except for Geoffrey, that is, who was monogamous from the day he was born. When it came to quantity, however, none of the others matched Darius.

Still, his being a rake was a minor issue, for his father, mother, and the rest of his family were far from puritanical. Since he drew the line at seducing innocents, they could not complain that he was a cad. Since he was astute enough to confine himself to the demimonde or the very fringes of the Beau Monde, they could not complain of scandals. Morals among those groups were lax anyway, and their doings seldom raised eyebrows, let alone appeared in the scandal sheets.

What infuriated the family was the methodical and impersonal way he carried on his raking.

The creatures he studied meant more to him than any of the women he bedded. He could list all the differences, major and minor, between one breed of sheep and another. He could not remember his last paramour's name, let alone the color of her eyes.

Having waited in vain for his twenty-eight-year-old son to finish sowing his wild oats or at least show a sign of being human, Lord Hargate decided it was time to intervene.

He summoned Darius to his study.

All of Lord Hargate's sons knew what a summons to his study signified: He meant to come down on them, as Rupert would put it, "like a ton of bricks."

Yet Darius strode into what Alistair called the Inquisition Chamber as he might stride to the lectern to present a paper: shoulders back, head high, the fierce intelligence burning in his golden eyes.

All arrogant certainty, he stood in front of his father's desk and met his gaze straight on. To do otherwise was fatal. Even a man of lesser intelligence would have learned this, growing up with four strong-willed brothers.

He made sure to give the impression, too, that he'd taken no special pains with his appearance, since that would look like an attempt to appease the monster.

The fact was, Darius always knew exactly what he was doing and the impression he created.

Perhaps he'd merely swiped a brush through his thick brown hair. But the observant eye would note how the cut emphasized the natural golden lights, which his time out of doors—too often hatless—had bleached to tawny streaks. The sun had burnished his chiseled countenance as well. Likewise, the deceptively simple suit of clothes drew attention to his powerful frame.

He did not look scholarly at all. He didn't even look civilized. It wasn't simply the brawny physique and golden glow of strength and health but the animal energy he exuded, the sense of something untamed lurking beneath the surface.

What many observers, especially female observers, saw was not a wellborn gentleman but a force of nature.

Women were either swept away or wanted to tame him. They might as well try to tame the wind or the rain or the North Sea. He took what they offered, caring no more about them than the wind or the rain or the North Sea cared.

He saw no reason to behave otherwise. These dealings with women were, after all, transient by definition. They would have no impact on society, on agriculture, on anything of significance.

His father saw it differently, as he made plain. He said that raking was common and a sign of vulgarity, and the quantity of paramours made Darius appear to be in competition with other idle, thoughtless men incapable of doing anything more meaningful with their lives.

The lecture went on at some length, in the pithily devastating style that had made Lord Hargate one of the most feared men in Parliament.

Reason told Darius the speech was an illogical diatribe. All the same, it stung, as he knew it was intended to do. However, the rational man did not let emotion rule his actions, even under extreme provocation. If refusing to let his emotions rule him was Darius's great crime, so be it. He had learned long ago that logic and a cool detachment were powerful weapons. They kept overbearing family members from crushing one with the force of their personalities, prevented manipulation—by women, especially—and won respect—from fellow intellectuals, at least.

Thus Darius retaliated by giving the most aggravating reply he could think of on short notice: "With respect, sir, I fail to understand what emotion has to do with such matters. It is the natural instinct of the male to copulate with the opposite sex."

"It is also, as you have reported in several articles regarding animal courtship, the natural instinct of several species to choose a mate and stick with her," Lord Hargate replied.

Ah, here it was, finally—and not altogether surprisingly. "In other words, you want me to marry," Darius said. He'd never seen the point of mincing words—yet another of his many aggravating traits.

"You chose not to pursue a scholarly career at Cambridge," said his father. "Had you pursued an academic career, naturally, one would not expect you to wed. But you have no profession."

No profession? At only eight and twenty years old, Darius Carsington was one of the most highly regarded members of the Philosophical Society. "Sir, if I may say, my work—"

"Half the aristocracy seem to be writing pamphlets and papers to impress one scholarly society or another," Lord Hargate said, with a dismissive wave. "For the most part these gentlemen have a source of income, however, and the source is not their fathers' purses."

The gesture rankled, and Darius wanted to retort.

What was I to do with my life instead? he could have said. *How was I to distinguish myself from the others: Benedict the paragon and philanthropist, Geoffrey the model family man, Alistair the war hero and incurable romantic, Rupert the lovable rogue and, lately, bold adventurer. How else was I to stand out than by cultivating my one advantage—my intellect? How would you get out from their shadow?*

Though these questions were more than reasonable, he would not ask them. He refused to be baited into defending himself against a rebuke so patently unjust and illogical.

Instead he pasted an amused expression on his face. "In that case, Father, perhaps you would be so good as to choose a well-dowered bride for me. My brothers seem satisfied with your selections for them, and it is a matter of complete indifference to me."

He truly was indifferent. This, he was sure, deeply aggravated his parent. This offered some consolation but not much, since Lord Hargate was an expert at not showing his feelings.

"I haven't time to search for a suitable bride for you," his lordship said. "In any event, I said nothing about marriage to your brothers until they were on the brink of thirty. In fairness, I must allow you another year. I must give you an opportunity as well to make yourself useful instead, as I have given the other younger sons."

The eldest son, Benedict, did not have to follow a profession or find a rich bride, since he would inherit everything. To date, the other younger sons had married money. They had married for love, too, but Lord Hargate knew better than to mention that subject.

Darius classified Romantic Love in the category labeled Superstition, Myth, and Poetic Nonsense. Unlike attraction, lust, and even familial love and affection, which one observed in the animal kingdom, Romantic Love seemed to him to be an emotion constructed primarily by the imagination.

He was not contemplating love at the moment, though. He was wondering what his Machiavellian father was up to. "What sort of opportunity?"

"A property has lately come into my possession," said Lord Hargate. "I will give you a year to make it produce income. Do so, and you are excused from marriage altogether."

Darius's heart leapt. A challenge, a true challenge. Had his father at long last realized what he was capable of?

No, of course not. That was impossible.

"It can't be that easy," he said. "Where's the trap, I wonder?"

"It won't be easy at all," said his sire. "The property was in Chancery for ten years."

Chancery was London's court of equity. It was far, far easier to get a case into Chancery than to get

it out again, as numerous parties had, to their grief,
found out.

"Ten years?" Darius said. "You must mean the
Cheshire property. The mad old woman's place.
What is it called?"

"Beechwood."

The "mad old woman" was Lord Hargate's cousin, Lady Margaret Andover who, by the time of her
death, had not been on speaking terms with any of
her family or her neighbors or anybody, apparently,
except her pug, Galahad—now long deceased—to
whom she left the property, in a codicil to a will
whose codicils went on for two hundred eighteen
pages. They contradicted one another, as did the
many other wills she made out during the later de-
cades of her life. This was why her estate had ended
up in Chancery.

The puzzle pieces fell into place. "Is the house
still standing?" Darius said.

"Barely."

"And the land?"

"In what state do you imagine it would be after a
decade's neglect?"

Darius nodded. "I see. You offer me a Labor of
Hercules."

"Precisely."

"You must be certain it would want not one but
several years to bring it into order," Darius said.
"That is the fly in the ointment."

"It once provided a handsome income and holds
the potential to do so again," said his sire. "Lord
Lithby, whose land adjoins it to the east, has coveted

it this age. If you feel unequal to the challenge, he will be happy to take it off my hands."

There—as he obviously knew, the manipulative devil—he caught Darius on his raw spot. And it worked, as the devil knew it would. Even the most powerful intellect rarely won a battle with masculine pride.

"You know very well I will not—cannot—refuse when you put it that way," Darius said. "When does my year start?"

"Now," said Lord Hargate.

Cheshire
Saturday 15 June 1822

The pig's name was Hyacinth.

She lay in her pen, patiently nursing her numerous offspring. The fattest and most fertile sow in the county, she was the pride of her owner, the Marquess of Lithby, and the envy of his neighbors.

Lord Lithby leaned on the sty fence, admiring his favorite swine.

The young woman standing beside him was thinking that she and the sow had a good deal in common, both being prize specimens upon whom his lordship doted.

Lady Charlotte Hayward was seven and twenty years old. Lord Lithby's only child by his first marriage, she was his only daughter and his pride and joy.

Society's sharpest critics could not fault her looks.

They agreed that she was neither too short nor too tall, neither too plump nor too thin. Pale gold hair framed a face that met all the standards of classic beauty: Wedgwood blue eyes, an elegant nose, and Cupid's bow lips, all of which a porcelain complexion set off most artistically. The many women who envied her found, to their exasperation, that it was impossible to hate her, because she was so good-natured, generous, and gracious.

They had no idea how much work it was to be Lady Charlotte Hayward, and would have been flabbergasted to learn she envied a pig.

She was wondering what it was like to roll about in the mud and root in the muck and not care what anyone thought, when her father said, "Charlotte, you really must marry, you know."

Her insides froze, and *I really must kill myself*, she thought.

Within, it was as though she looked down from a cliff edge into an abyss. Outwardly, she offered no sign of uneasiness. Concealing undesirable emotions was second nature, after all.

She turned an affectionate smile upon her father. She knew he loved her dearly. He didn't mean to make her desperate. He had no idea what he was asking of her.

How could she marry, and risk her secret being found out on her wedding night? The man whose property she'd become—how would he react if he realized his bride was not a virgin? How would *she* react? Could she lie well enough to persuade him he was mistaken? Did she want to begin her marriage with a lie? But how could she trust any man with the truth? How could she reveal her secret to him? How could she admit to all the betrayals she'd committed, and risk further betrayals of those she loved?

She'd asked herself these and many other questions long ago. She'd pictured all the possible outcomes in her mind.

She'd decided she'd better die a spinster.

She could not say so to Papa. It was unnatural for a woman to wish to remain single.

Since it was equally unnatural for a father to wish such a thing for his daughter, she could not be surprised at his bringing up the subject. Another father would have done so years ago. She ought to be grateful for the period of freedom she'd had. Yet she wondered, *Why now?* And she couldn't help thinking, unhappily, *Why ever?*

"A girl ought to marry, I know, Papa," she said.

But I can't, she thought. *I cannot marry with this secret burdening me, and I cannot reveal it.*

"You have been too unselfish for too long," her father said, innocently unaware how he stabbed her guilty conscience. "I know you have put off your own happiness in order to be of help to your stepmother during her confinements. I know you love her. I know you love your little brothers. But my dear, it is time for you to have a household of your own, and children of your own."

Oh, it cut deep then, the grief, deeper than it had done in a long time.

Children of her own.

But he didn't know the truth of what had happened ten years ago. He didn't know what he was saying to her. He didn't know how it hurt. He must never know.

"I blame myself," her father went on. "I have made a selfish habit of treating you like the son I thought I'd never have. Even now, though you've four brothers in the nursery, the habit is hard to break."

Her mother had died when she was not fifteen years old. To her shock, her father had wed again only a year later. Her stepmother Lizzie, a mere nine years older than she, was more like an older sister than a mother . . . though Charlotte had failed to grasp this at the time. Stupid, so stupid she'd been.

"You've spoiled me, that is the trouble," her father went on. "Not once since that terrible time when you were ill have you given me reason to worry or grieve. Instead, you've given of yourself—to all of us."

After bearing the baby he knew nothing about, she had been ill, truly, for a long time. After that terrible time, she'd vowed she never would again cause anyone she cared about a moment's anxiety or sorrow or shame. She'd done enough damage— damage she could never undo—to last a lifetime.

"Perhaps, too, I did not think any of the young men who swarmed about you could properly appreciate you," Papa continued, explaining his thinking as he'd always done with her. "Naturally, you are kind to all your admirers, though not overly so, for your behavior is always above reproach. Yet none, I think, truly engaged your affections?"

"None," she said. "It is merely fate, I suppose."

"I am not sure one ought to trust to fate," he said. "It worked in my favor, I readily admit. I was lonely after your mother died. I might have made a foolish mistake."

She, too, had been lonely after her mother died. When her father remarried, Charlotte had been—oh, she could hardly remember now, beyond a general recollection of a great misery. She had been vulnerable, at any rate. And Geordie Blaine had been there to take advantage.

Her father was too kind to remind her of the mistake he believed she'd *almost* made. He thought he'd sent Blaine packing before any real harm was done.

Even the two people who knew the truth never reminded her.

Charlotte didn't need reminding.

Her father turned to her, his grey eyes unusually serious. Lord Lithby was a cheerful man, and most of the time his eyes sparkled with good humor. "Life is unpredictable, my dear. We cannot be sure of anything, except that we will all die one day."

Not many months ago a fever had nearly killed him.

Her gloved hands tightened on the sty fence. "Oh, Papa, I wish you would not say such things."

"Death is inevitable," he said. "In the winter when I was so beastly ill, I thought of so much left undone. One of my great anxieties was you. When I was gone, who would look after you?"

Servants, she thought. *Lawyers. Trustees.* An heiress could always pay someone to look after her, and there would never be a shortage of people willing to take the job. The last girl in the world who needed a husband was a rich girl.

Charlotte was a very rich girl. Her mother's marriage settlement had included a generous provision for offspring. The marriage having produced only one child, Charlotte's portion was considerable even for the daughter of a marquess.

"I'm sorry to be a worry to you," she said.

He dismissed this with a wave of his hand. "Fathers are supposed to fret about their children. This is hardly a worry. It is simply a problem to be solved. Granted, I have never tried matchmaking before. I have given the business a great deal of thought, however. Once I was well again, I began to observe closely what went on during the Season."

The London Season was, among other things, the time for unwed aristocrats to find mates. Like the other unmarried ladies, Charlotte dutifully attended all the required social functions. Like the others, she put herself on display at the weekly subscription balls at Almack's Assembly Rooms, to which only the cream of Society was admitted—for the meritorious purpose, it seemed to her, of confining excruciating boredom to a small, select circle.

"Most girls find a husband during the Season," Lord Lithby said. "But you have had eight Seasons. Since one cannot fault your behavior, the fault must lie elsewhere. Having studied the matter, I have arrived at two conclusions: Firstly, the method is too haphazard. Secondly, London offers too many distractions. We must approach the problem scientifically, you see."

Lord Lithby was an agriculturalist. A member of the Philosophical Society, he was constantly reading pamphlets or writing papers on farming. He went on to explain that some of the principles employed in agriculture might be applied to human beings. What one needed was a system, and he had devised one.

He had no idea how careful his daughter had been not to achieve the desired result. He had no idea how scientifically she had approached the problem of How Not to Get Married. Charlotte had devised a system years ago and continued to refine it.

She had been blind once about a man. Never again.

Thanks to the prolonged illness—of spirit as well as body—resulting from that error, she had made her debut belatedly at the age of twenty. Long before then, though, she was studying the gentlemen of her social circle, gauging their characters as carefully as her father gauged the characteristics of his turnips and beans, his cows and sheep and pigs. As her father studied ways to make his livestock and crops thrive, she studied ways to make men's interest wane.

She learned to be stupendously boring with one, bland to the point of invisibility with another. With some she'd talk incessantly. With others, she was silent. Sometimes she became absentminded and easily distracted. Sometimes she persisted in failing to recognize a man she'd met time and again. And more than once she'd led her suitor to another woman.

This last maneuver wanted extreme care and subtlety.

They all did, actually. No matter what technique she used, she must always appear sweetly obliging.

It was uphill work for an attractive, rich girl not to get married and not get caught not getting married.

She ought to be ashamed of herself for deceiving him, but the shame of the truth was many times worse.

"Lizzie and I have made a list of fellows we believe you will find agreeable," her father said. "In a month's time, these gentlemen will arrive at Lithby Hall for a fortnight's stay. Naturally, some of your girl cousins and friends will come as well, to make up the numbers. In this way, you'll have a better chance to get to know the gentlemen. In turn, spared the distractions of Town, they will have a better chance to win your regard." He beamed at her.

Lord Lithby's beams were not confined to a smile but, like the sun's rays, seemed to radiate from his very being.

Charlotte smiled back. How could she not, when he was so pleased with his terrifying idea?

"If it does not work this time, we shall try again in the hunting season," he said. "It is not as though we would not be entertaining guests in any event."

Though he added no "buts," Charlotte heard one all the same.

He had his heart set on her finding a husband by this method, and whatever he said, he was confident it would succeed the first time. He would be dreadfully disappointed if it didn't.

It would kill her to disappoint him.

It would kill her to do as he wished.

"I am sure it will work, Papa," she said. "Of course I trust your judgment completely."

"There's a good girl." He patted her shoulder.

That settled, and sublimely unaware of the bomb he'd set off inside her, he went on to other topics: something about the adjoining property . . . Chancery suit settled with miraculous speed . . . but Lord Hargate always . . . his sons . . . Carsington's paper on salt . . . foot rot in sheep . . .

She tried to pay attention but the noise inside her head made it impossible. Her mind bounded from one panicked thought to the next, one unwanted memory to another. She stared at the pig and wished for porcine contentment. She wished for Hyacinth's utter certainty of her place and function in the world.

Then Lord Lithby set out to talk to his head gamekeeper, and Charlotte went her own way, taking her tumultuous mind with her.

Lord Lithby had been trying to tell his daughter about the property next door and its new occupant, Darius Carsington.

Because Darius made no scandals and Lord Lithby paid little heed to gossip, he did not know—and if he did, probably would not care—that his new neighbor was a rake, impersonal or otherwise. All Lord Lithby cared about was that Lord Hargate's youngest was a fellow member of the Philosophical Society who had authored several exciting papers on animal behavior and a number of remarkable pamphlets about livestock. Lord Lithby owned every one of these pamphlets. The one on pig farming, in particular, he considered momentous.

Naturally he was delighted to have this brilliant fellow in charge of the derelict property on his western border.

To his daughter Lord Lithby had explained about the Chancery suit and Lord Hargate's astonishing feat in getting the case settled after a mere ten years. He spoke enthusiastically of Mr. Carsington's studies of foot rot in sheep and his views regarding salt in livestock diets. He would call upon his new neighbor this day and invite him to dinner, he announced.

His lordship might as well have addressed his remarks to the pig.

Meanwhile, two miles away, Darius—who had as little to do with Fashionable Society as possible and would rather be gutted with a rusty blade than set foot in Almack's—knew nothing of Lord Lithby's plans, enthusiasms, or daughter.

Lord Hargate's aggravating son had arrived late the day before and spent the night at the Unicorn Inn in the market town of Altrincham, not three miles away. Though his mother had insisted on sending servants ahead to make the house, if not ready, at least habitable, Darius intended to ignore it.

Restoring the building was illogical. It would only cost money; it would not bring in any. Staying at the inn was cheaper and easier. He need only pay his bill. He needn't hire any servants in addition to his valet, Goodbody. He needn't repair anything. Servants, supplies, and maintenance were the innkeeper's problem. Furthermore, his land agent, Quested, had his office in Altrincham.

The land was the priority. Thus, first thing this morning, he and the agent had made a tour of the estate.

Matters were more or less as one would expect. With the property in dispute, nothing could be done legally to it or with it for ten years.

Insects, birds, and assorted small animals had invaded many of the outbuildings, which were in varying stages of disrepair. The gardens had reverted to wilderness, the plantings overgrown where the weeds hadn't strangled them. The wildlife seemed to be flourishing as well, although the vermin population was smaller than he'd expected.

The great surprise was the home farm. This was not the abandoned ruin he'd envisioned. Someone—his father, most likely—must have circumvented the red tape and hired men to look after it.

Nonetheless, when Quested left some hours later, he carried a long list of assignments, mostly having to do with hiring workers.

Letting his brain rest from the weighing, measuring, and calculating, Darius took a walk through the jungle that used to be a landscaped park and made his way along an overgrown path to a stagnant pond. Here, spying dragonflies, he paused.

One of the fellows of the Philosophical Society had written an article on dragonfly courtship that Darius considered fanciful. Insects, except for those

troublesome to livestock, were not a particular interest of his. Nonetheless, he spared a passing glance
for the dragonflies. Then, as so often happened, curiosity got the better of him.

In a moment he was stretched out on his stomach amid the tall weeds, all his fierce intelligence focused on the fairylike creatures skimming over the
water. Intent on trying to distinguish male from female without aid of a spyglass, he was deaf, dumb,
and blind to everything else.

A herd of stampeding bulls might have got his
attention at this point, if it happened to be an especially large herd.

Which explains why he was so slow to notice.

He was distantly aware of muttering before it
finally penetrated his mind. A moment later, he
heard a twig snap. He lifted his head and turned
that way.

It was a girl, not ten feet away, and when his head
came up out of the weeds, she shrieked and leapt
straight up off the ground. She stumbled, and her
arms flailed like confused windmills as she tried
to regain her balance, but the ground was slick
there, and she slid, heading straight for the mucky
water. He was already on his feet and hurrying toward her while the birds flew up from the trees,
their squawking drowning out the insects' gentle
drone.

He got his arms round her middle as she slid
downward, but she shrieked again when he touched
her and nearly dragged them both into the scummy
pond. He yanked her back, and the heel of her half

boot hit his shin. In spite of his own boots, he felt it, and had to struggle for balance. He swore.

"Calm down, curse you!" he snapped. "Do you mean to drown us both?"

"Stop squeezing my bosom, you—you—" She pushed at his hands, and they began to slide again, toward the water.

"I am not—"

"Let me go!"

He pulled again, hard, dragging her back toward level ground.

"Let go! Let go!" She squirmed, shoving her elbow into his stomach.

He let go so abruptly that she stumbled.

She flung out her hand and grabbed his arm to keep from falling. "You beast! You did that on purpose!" She bent over, gasping for breath, still clutching his arm.

"You told me to let go," he said.

She lifted her head then, and he found himself staring into an extraordinary world of blue that was her eyes. Everything else went away while he tried to take it in: the flawless oval face, as perfect as a cameo . . . the ivory skin brightening to pink along the delicately sculpted bones of her cheeks . . . the sultry pout of her parted lips.

He watched the endless blue world of her eyes widen, and for a moment he forgot everything: where he was and who he was and what he was. Then he dragged a hand through his hair and wondered if he'd hit his head without realizing.

She looked away quickly, down at her gloved

hand clutching his arm. She pulled her hand away, giving him a little shove as she did it.

He could have stepped back a pace, as she clearly wanted, but he held his ground, standing too close. "That will teach me to rescue damsels in distress," he said.

"You had no business hiding there and jumping out at me, like a—like a . . ." She put her hand to the tumbling mass of champagne-color hair piled upon her head and frowned. She looked about her. "My hat. Where is my hat? Oh, no."

Her hat, a silly bit of straw and lace, had tumbled to the water's edge.

He swallowed a smile and started that way.

"Don't trouble yourself," she said, and hurried toward the hat.

"Don't be ridiculous," he said.

His long stride easily overtook her nervous little trot, and they both bent and reached for the hat at the same time. Thanks to his longer arms, he captured it first, but as he came up, his head hit hers.

"Ow!" She sprang back, clutching her forehead. Her feet slid out from under her, and down she went, in a swirl of petticoats. She started to scramble up, but not too quickly for him to miss the handsome calf briefly on display.

This time he planted his boots firmly onto the sloping ground, reached down, caught her under the arms, and pulled her upright, then hauled her firmly against him as he backed up the slippery embankment.

Her round backside pressed against his groin.

Along with the smell of pond muck he detected a sweeter, distinctively feminine scent. He noticed a tiny spot of mud on the nape of her smooth white neck. He caught himself in the nick of time—half a heartbeat before his tongue could flick out to . . . groom her?

She stomped her heel on his boot and shoved with her elbow.

He let go. "If you persist in this behavior, I shall be obliged to summon the constable," he said.

That turned her around sharply. "The constable?"

"I could bring charges against you for trespassing," he said. "And assault."

"Tres— *Assault?* You touched my—my—" She gestured at her bosom, which was a fine one and which his hand had encountered during the tussle, perhaps not completely accidentally. "You put hands on me." Her face was quite rosy now.

"I may have to do it again," he said, "if you continue to blunder about the place, alarming the wildlife."

He had not thought her blue eyes could open any wider but they did. *"Blunder about?"*

"I fear you have disturbed the dragonflies during an extremely delicate process," he said. "They were mating, poor things, and you frightened them out of their wits. You may not be aware of this, but when the male takes fright, his procreative abilities are adversely affected."

She stared at him. Her mouth opened, but nothing came out.

"Now I understand why none but the hardiest

of the livestock remain," he said. "You must have either frightened them all away or permanently impaired their reproductive functions."

"Impaired their— I did *not*. I was . . ." Her gaze fell to the hat he still held. "Give me my hat."

He turned it in his hands and studied it. "This is the most frivolous hat I've ever seen." Perhaps it was and perhaps it wasn't. He had no idea. He never noticed women's clothes except as obstacles to be got out of the way as quickly as possible.

Still, he could see that the thing he held was an absurd bit of froth: a scrap of straw, scraps of lace, ribbons. "What does it do? It cannot keep off the sun or the rain."

"It's a *hat*," she said. "It isn't supposed to do anything."

"Then what do you wear it for?"

"For?" she said. "*For?* It's . . . It's . . ." Her brow knit.

He waited.

She bit her lip and thought hard. "Decoration. Give it back. I must go now."

"What, no 'please'?"

The blue eyes flashed up at him. "No," she said.

"I see I must set the example of manners," he said.

"Give me my hat." She reached for it.

He put the nonsensical headwear behind his back. "I am Darius Carsington," he said. He bowed.

"I don't care," she said.

"Beechwood has been turned over to me," he said.

She turned away. "Never mind. Keep the hat if you want it so much. I've others."

She started to walk away.

That would not do. She was exceedingly pretty. And the breast that had more or less accidentally fallen into his hand was agreeably round.

He followed her. "I collect you live nearby," he said.

"Apparently I do not live far enough away," she said.

"This place has been deserted for years," he said. "Perhaps you were unaware of the recent change."

"Papa told me. I . . . forgot."

"Papa," he said, and his good humor began to fade. "That would be . . . ?"

"Lord Lithby," she said tautly. "We came from London yesterday. The stream is our western border. I always used to come here and . . . But it does not matter."

No, it didn't, not anymore.

Her accents, her dress, her manner, all told Darius this was a lady. He had no objections to ladies. Unlike some, he was not drawn exclusively to women of the lower orders. She seemed a trifle slow-witted and appeared to possess no sense of humor whatsoever, but this didn't signify. Women's brains or lack thereof had never mattered to him. What he wanted from them had nothing to do with their intellect or sense of humor.

What did matter was that the lady had referred to her *father's* property bordering Darius's. Not her husband's.

Ergo, she must be an unmarried daughter of the Marquess of Lithby.

It was odd—not to mention extremely annoying— that Darius had mistaken her. Usually he could spot a virgin at fifty paces. Had he realized this was a maiden, not a matron, he would have set her on her feet and sent her packing immediately. Though he had little use for Society's illogical rules, he drew the line at seducing innocents.

Since seduction was out of the question, he saw no reason to continue the conversation. He had wasted far too much time on her already.

He held out the hat.

With a wary look, she took it.

"I apologize for startling you or getting in your way or whatever I did," he said dismissively. "Certainly you are welcome to traipse about the property as you've always done. It is of no consequence to me. Good day."

Chapter 2

Darius turned away, walked back to the pond's edge, told his reproductive organs to calm down, and once again settled onto his stomach to watch the dragonflies.

Since a mere female could not possibly throw an experienced rake into a panic, it could not occur to him that something about the encounter had caused him to panic and leap to a hasty conclusion.

However, Darius's most intimate companion, as his family often complained, was Logic. He was objective and rational to a fault. Thus, it was not too long before he detected the flaw in his reasoning.

As he was trying with limited success to return his mind to the dragonflies, his best friend and mentor, Logic, noted that unmarried daughters were not the only kind of daughters who might belong to Lord Lithby. An unhappily married daughter might be visiting. A widowed daughter might have returned to live with her parents.

Hope rose again.

So did Darius.

She was very pretty, after all.

She had vanished from view.

"Damnation," he said.

It was unlike his wits to be so sluggish. How long had he lain there, staring at the insects, before his mind had woken up?

He shook his head. He had spent too much time in London, that was the trouble. The country air had not had time enough to cleanse his brain.

Still, it was easy enough for someone to disappear in this wilderness. Perhaps she had not gone far.

He started down the path she'd taken.

He followed it to the stream that divided the two properties. He discerned no sign of his prey.

He kicked a pebble into the stream, then started back to his house—or the stables, rather. He wanted a wash and something to eat, and for that he must ride back to the inn. He'd counted at least two attractive and clearly willing maidservants there.

Either one—or perhaps both—would serve his purpose.

He'd wasted enough time on the lady.

Lithby Hall, a short time later

Her stepmother was coming down the stairs as Charlotte was going up. Both paused.

"Good heavens, Charlotte, what has happened?" said Lizzie.

"Nothing," said Charlotte.

"How can you be so absurd?" Lizzie said. "You

have mud on your nose. Your dress is soiled. Your gloves are unspeakable. Where is your hat?"

"I gave it to Hyacinth," Charlotte said. She had stopped at the pigsty on the way back.

"You *what?*"

"She ate it," Charlotte said. Contrary to Lord Lithby's cherished beliefs, Hyacinth could and did eat anything and everything, with no discernible ill effects. The sow had easily digested more than one book of sermons officious relatives had foisted upon Charlotte.

Lizzie turned and followed Charlotte up the stairs. She said no more, however, until they reached Charlotte's room.

"Good heavens, your ladyship, what's happened?" said her maid, Molly.

"Nothing," said Lady Lithby. "Leave us for a moment, Molly. We'll ring when we want you."

"But, your ladyship, she's all over mud," said Molly.

"It doesn't matter," said Charlotte. "I don't expect you to clean it. You can feed my clothes to the—" She broke off, wondering what was the matter with her. She ought to have better control of her tongue.

The stream separating Beechwood from her father's property was about two miles from Lithby Hall. Charlotte easily covered two or three times that distance and sometimes more in the course of a day's perambulations. Long walks helped calm her. On some days she needed more calming than on others.

Maybe she should have walked farther today.

Molly's gaze traveled over Charlotte, up and down. She shook her head.

"Later, Molly," Lady Lithby said firmly. "Close the door behind you."

The maid went out, still shaking her head. She closed the door.

"Charlotte," said Lizzie.

"It's nothing," said Charlotte. "I was walking next door. At Beechwood. I met the new resident."

"Mr. Carsington, do you mean? The neighborhood is abuzz. He arrived yesterday, I am told." Lizzie eyed her up and down. "Did you meet him before or after you fell into the pigsty?"

Charlotte, who had fallen into the pigsty more than once in her childhood, considered accepting the easy lie. The trouble was, her stepmother always knew when she was lying. Life was simpler when one told her the truth, albeit as little of that as was absolutely necessary.

"He was lying among the tall weeds," she said. "I did not see him at first. My mind was elsewhere. I was practically on top of him when he raised his head. Then I nearly leapt out of my skin. I stumbled on something . . . and I fell."

Charlotte saw no reason to describe in detail what had happened between the first time she'd stumbled and when she'd fallen on her arse.

She was trying very hard to forget what had happened.

He was so . . . big . . . and his hands . . .

For ten years her physical contact with men had

gone no further than a gloved hand lightly clasping hers, or, in the course of a waltz, a gloved hand touching the back of her waist.

He had not been wearing gloves, and her layers of clothes might as well not have been there, for all the good they did.

His hands, his hands. She could feel them yet . . . along with other disturbing feelings, too much like longing.

But that was impossible. She would never long for a man's touch, she told herself. She'd learned her lesson.

What had happened today was simple enough: She'd already been upset when she came upon him. Being upset, she'd panicked, which made her too irrational to comprehend that the man was simply trying to keep her from tumbling into the bog that used to be an ornamental pond.

She was upset because of Papa's brainstorm and the nightmare she foresaw of a marriage beginning in shame and likely destroying the happiness of everyone who cared about her: not only her father but Lizzie, who'd deceived him on Charlotte's account practically at the start of their marriage.

Without warning, while all this worry churned in her mind, she'd found herself caught in the arms of . . . a very large man.

Small wonder she'd behaved at first like a cornered animal.

Then, as she was struggling to reclaim her powers of reason, she'd looked up into his face. Under the onslaught of those brilliantly golden eyes and a deep voice that set her vibrating within like a tuning fork, her wits had shattered utterly.

For a moment it had seemed as though one of the Greek gods—Apollo, for instance—had accosted her, as they were known to do to unsuspecting women.

"I see," said Lizzie.

With a little start, Charlotte came out of her troubled reverie.

Her stepmother had a worrisome habit of seeing more at times than one could wish.

She was petite and dark-haired, the opposite of Charlotte's mother in looks, and far from the classic English rose her predecessor had been, objectively speaking. But a great many people, including her husband and stepdaughter, couldn't see Lord Lithby's second wife objectively. They saw the beauty of her nature and the brightness of her spirit. She laughed easily—at herself, especially. This easy laughter not only lit her face but brightened everything and everyone about her.

"She's full of life," Papa always said.

That was what drew him to her in the first place.

At the time he met Elizabeth Bentley, Lord Lithby was not looking for a replacement for the wife he'd loved so dearly. He did not believe anyone could take her place. Still, he was looking for something; and though, as he'd admitted, he had been too lonely to think clearly, Fate had smiled on him.

He could not have chosen better.

Charlotte knew this. She knew, too, that had her stepmother been a fraction less perceptive, Lord

Lithby's precious daughter would have been utterly
and irrevocably ruined ten years ago.

All the same, she did wish, this once, that her
stepmother would not study her quite so closely.

"No doubt you thought you would have your
favorite wilderness to yourself for a while longer,"
Lizzie said. "But how curious it is that your father
did not tell you about Mr. Carsington."

"He told me," Charlotte said. "But I fear my mind
wandered." She let out a small sigh and began to
peel off her dirty gloves.

"He told you of his matchmaking scheme first, is
that it?" said Lizzie. "That was a great deal for you
to take in. That would explain why you became distracted."

Distraught was more like it. Desperate.

"I was a little surprised, yes, though I should not
have been," Charlotte said. "It is perfectly reasonable for Papa to wish me wed. All of the girls I came
out with are married. With children."

Her child would be ten years old now, if he lived.
She felt the stab in her chest, the old ache. She still
wept sometimes for her lost baby. Only when she
was alone, though. Lizzie would grieve for her if
she knew, and Charlotte had long ago vowed never
to cause her another moment's trouble.

"I asked Lithby to let me tell you about his plan,"
her stepmother said, "but he said it was his responsibility."

Naturally, she had respected his wishes.

Only the once, very early in her marriage, had
Lady Lithby gone behind her husband's back. She

had done so because Charlotte insisted, because she was so sick with shame—over what she'd done, over deceiving him. She couldn't live with the disappointment and hurt she'd cause him. She was the center of his life, and she feared she'd break his heart.

Charlotte would never ask such a sacrifice of her stepmother again. She knew Lizzie deeply loved Papa and respected him. She loved Charlotte, too. At the beginning, his new bride had loved her stepdaughter mainly for his sake. Charlotte had soon learned that for Papa's sake his young wife would move heaven and earth.

If only Charlotte could have seen that. If only she had been mature enough to understand what a remarkable woman her father had married.

Had Charlotte understood, she would not have behaved so stupidly. She wouldn't have given Geordie Blaine a second glance. Then she might have had a chance at a marriage as affectionate and happy as her father and stepmother's.

If onlys were a waste of thought, she told herself for the thousandth—or ten thousandth—time.

Lizzie's voice interrupted her brooding. "Your father is right, you know. It is time, well past time, for you to make a life of your own. We cannot undo the past. You suffered two grievous losses, following close upon each other, when you were very young. Though it is natural to feel sadness about these matters, we must not let sorrow cripple us."

"I am not crippled," Charlotte said. "I think of—of him as dead, like my mother. One mourns, but life goes on."

"All the same, if you are at all uneasy, my dear, on account of that long-ago time—"

"I am not uneasy," Charlotte said. That was not a lie. She was so far beyond uneasy that she had no word for her state of mind.

Lizzie did not look quite as though she believed her. She didn't press the point, though. "Perhaps, after all, this is what we need," she said. "One who views the situation with a fresh eye."

"It is very good of Papa to bother about it," said Charlotte. "I know he would rather spend his time in the country attending to country matters. The livestock. Drainage. Turnips."

Lizzie smiled. "True, but consolation has arrived in the shape of Mr. Carsington. You know how Beechwood's decline has frustrated your father. Imagine his delight in learning it will be in the care of a fellow agriculturalist and kindred spirit."

Charlotte could easily imagine how her father felt.

He could not imagine how *she* felt. The wilderness next door was her refuge and had been for years.

Months after the baby's birth, when Charlotte continued ill and listless, Lizzie had taken her to Switzerland. There, walks along mountain paths, through Alpine meadows, and alongside rivers, waterfalls, and sparkling lakes, had gradually healed and restored her.

When they returned to England, Beechwood took the place of the Swiss countryside. At Beechwood, thanks to Lizzie's intervention, Charlotte was allowed a degree of solitude.

Whenever she was troubled, she went the same way, across the stream that separated the two properties. The groom in charge of her did not cross the stream but waited there for her to return, while she continued down the path that ran alongside the pond. She went that way because there wasn't—or hadn't been until now—anyone about to see her. Within that wild place, she might be wild, too. She might for a time set aside all the rules she'd vowed ten years ago never again to violate.

She'd vowed to be good, to do all that was right and proper and nothing that was wrong or even hinted of impropriety.

But when she was alone where what she did could not displease or hurt or shame or shock anybody, she loosened the stays of propriety and let herself breathe.

At Beechwood, with none but the wild creatures to look on, she might stride or stomp along, depending on her mood. She might wave her fists or give vent to long, muttering rants about whatever had most recently upset her.

She wouldn't dream of behaving that way along her father's manicured pathways, where the outdoor staff or touring visitors might see her.

Now her refuge was lost, forever.

She walked to the fireplace and dropped her soiled gloves onto the empty grate. She should have fed the gloves to the pig, too.

Good-bye, hat. Good-bye, gloves.

Good-bye, freedom.

She became aware of the lengthening silence. What had Lizzie said last? Oh, yes.

"Agriculturalist, perhaps," Charlotte said. "But as to kindred spirits—" She caught herself in the nick of time, before her wayward tongue got the better of her again. She made herself smile. "Naturally it is difficult for me to see any resemblance. I came across Mr. Carsington only a short time ago, and very briefly. One can scarcely call it a meeting, in fact."

Lizzie nodded. "Then I shall not call it one, and shan't mention it to your father. He is looking forward so much to introducing the famous Mr. Carsington to everybody."

Papa would want to do so this evening, of course, at the gathering with neighbors that always marked their return from London.

"This morning, as always, your father told me his plans for the day," Lizzie went on. "First he would speak to you about his matchmaking scheme. Then he would speak to his gamekeeper. Then he would call upon Mr. Carsington and invite him to dinner."

"It is typical of Papa to wish to make Mr. Carsington feel welcome," Charlotte said.

Oh, Papa, why must you always be so welcoming? she thought.

"There's more to it," said Lizzie. "I must speak plainly to you. Though the gentleman is merely an earl's younger son, the earl in question is Lord Hargate. That connection, as you know, is a most desirable one."

A weight settled in Charlotte's gut.

She'd thought she was done with Lord Hargate's sons.

Last year, both families had tried to promote a match between her and Lord Hargate's widowed heir, Lord Rathbourne. Charlotte had no difficulty with him. Though he was perfectly courteous, she could tell she might as well be invisible to him. She had only to make sure she did nothing to make herself more visible. To her relief, he had married someone else last autumn.

"Bear in mind, too, that Mr. Carsington is a man of considerable prestige in the Philosophical Society," Lady Lithby went on. "This well-regarded gentleman now has charge of the property next door, which your father has always wanted. Kindred spirit or not, in Lithby's eyes these factors combine to make Mr. Carsington an acceptable marital candidate. We must add him to the list of eligible gentlemen."

She went out, closing the door behind her.

Charlotte stared blindly at the door for a time.

Then she lifted her chin and squared her shoulders.

"It doesn't matter," she said under her breath. "I've contrived not to marry scores of men. I can not marry him, too."

Meanwhile, at Beechwood

Darius's hopes regarding the beautiful girl were dashed within moments of his reaching Beechwood's stables, for there he met up with her father, who'd come to welcome him to the neighborhood and invite him to dinner.

Though it took a moment to sort out a pig named Hyacinth from a daughter named Charlotte, Darius soon discovered that his lordship possessed only one daughter, who was not married, unhappily or otherwise, or widowed.

The other children were four young boys, the two eldest of whom were staying with cousins in Shropshire at present.

Darius promptly pushed the daughter to the back of his mind as not meriting further thought, and focused on her father, who did.

Being Logic's loyal servant, Darius had spent the fortnight before he came to Cheshire analyzing the problem he had to solve and gathering useful information.

He'd learned that, of all those hereabouts, Lord Lithby was the man most worth cultivating. Generations of his family had lived here. He was the largest landowner. But most important, he was an agriculturalist and a natural philosopher, like Darius.

Today came an especially agreeable discovery: Unlike Lord Hargate, Lord Lithby had a proper regard for Darius's work. He even quoted from the pamphlet on pig farming.

His mood improved by a generous dose of flattery, Darius happily accepted the invitation to dinner.

Normally, he avoided Fashionable Society, preferring those circles where morals were known to be loose. That way, a man didn't waste time pursuing women he couldn't have.

This time, though, Darius had to make an exception. His lordship was a valuable source of information and advice. Too, some if not all of the guests would be country folk—a breed Darius understood well and with whom he was fully at ease. And among these country folk he might even find an attractive widow or unhappy wife not overburdened with morals.

He mounted his horse and set out for the inn.

By the time he arrived, the beautiful girl had crept to the front of his mind again.

How on earth had he mistaken her for a matron? he wondered.

He was an intelligent and observant man. What had misled him?

He brought her image back into his mind's eye: the delicious face and figure . . . the trace of huskiness in her voice, with its expected cultivated accents and unexpected animosity. The hostility bothered him. To be sure, not all women melted instantly into his arms, but the few who didn't never put up more than a token fight, either.

What an absurd creature she was, as nonsensical as her hat. Tripping over her own feet. Squirming and kicking and elbowing when he tried to help her . . .

She was quite good at dislodging a man, actually. For some reason, that had aroused him.

Her haughtiness was provoking. Still, it had amused him to make a game of it, like flirtation—

which everyone knew was an early step on the path
to seduction.

Why had he failed to—

He slapped his head.

Idiot.

He'd sensed *experience*. That was what had
thrown him off course. He'd sensed and reacted to
it without articulating it to himself.

Though it was never easy to determine a woman's age precisely, any moron could identify a green
girl.

This girl was not fresh from the schoolroom.

Darius was surprised, however, when he found
out exactly how old she was.

He did so, he was sure, merely to satisfy his intellectual curiosity. This was no different than his curiosity about the dragonflies. He approached the matter as he would any other scientific inquiry, though
he was more discreet about it.

At the Unicorn, while his manservant, Goodbody,
sighed over the grass stains and mud on his trousers, Darius encouraged the pair of not-unattractive
maidservants to gossip.

This was how he learned that Lady Charlotte
Hayward was seven and twenty years old.

Seven and twenty and unwed!

Darius could not make sense of it.

She was the only daughter of a marquess.

She was beautiful.

Her father was no impoverished aristocrat but
a high-ranking, well-liked, and wealthy one. What
family in England would not wish for the connec-

tion? What gentleman seeking to fill his nursery would not wish to breed with such prime blood-stock? How was it that none had done so?

Darius was so perplexed—not to mention exasperated—that he forgot about bedding the maidservants. Instead, following a wash, shave, and change of clothes, he left Goodbody to brood over his boots and continued his investigation in the Unicorn's taproom.

Here he found that theories—or rather, rumors—abounded.

"A terrible tragedy, that one," said the innkeeper's wife as she served his pint. "Lady Charlotte had her heart set on an officer, but he got blown to bits at Waterloo."

"Nothing to do with Waterloo," one of her patrons insisted. "He was killed at Baltimore during that war with the Americans."

"Wasn't no officer," another argued. "A Count Somebody come to London with the Tsar of Russia for the victory celebrations. Caught a fever and died."

An argument ensued.

At the inn's stables, a less romantic point of view prevailed. Lady Charlotte had not buried her heart in any dashing officer's or foreign nobleman's grave. The reason she wasn't wed was simple enough: No one was good enough for her.

"I see," Darius said. "Her suitors were an inferior lot of fellows."

"Oh, no, sir," said one of the stablemen. "She had a duke after her. And a marquess."

"There was that earl's eldest son last year," said another. "The perfect one."

One of his fellows nudged him and muttered something. The man looked abashed.

Darius didn't need the hint. They referred to his eldest brother Benedict, Lord Rathbourne, also known as Lord Perfect.

"Well, if Lord Perfect wasn't good enough for her, perhaps she has an excessively high opinion of herself?" Darius said. She had been quite haughty with him, and perhaps made his pride smart a very little bit—because he wasn't used to that sort of nonsense, he told himself.

"Not proud at all, sir," said the first stableman.

"Sweetest lady in the world," said another.

"Never a unkind word for anybody."

"Always a smile and thanks, even for the smallest thing you do for her."

"All the servants say the same."

"The ladies, too. They all like her—and you know what cats they can be."

Then followed stories of Lady Charlotte Hayward's various kindnesses to her fellow creatures, from the great to the insignificant.

Darius tried to reconcile the picture they painted with the woman he'd met. It wouldn't reconcile. This couldn't be the same lady. Yet it must be.

He turned the problem over in his mind. He looked at it from first one angle then another. The conundrum remained.

This was annoying. He had more important things to do than puzzle over a woman he couldn't bed.

The trouble was, she *was* a puzzle, and whatever else Darius Carsington was capable of, he was no more capable of leaving alone an unanswered question than he was of resisting a challenge to his abilities. Which, after all, amounted to much the same thing.

"In short," he said with a trace of irritation, "the lady is a saint."

The men looked at one another. "Well, I dunno," said one meditatively, "as I'd say *that*."

Drawing room of Lithby Hall, that evening

Mr. Carsington had caught Charlotte unprepared the first time.

This time she was fully prepared. Her head was clear, her demeanor all it should be. She had her company smile in place and all eighty-three thousand six hundred fifty-seven rules of proper behavior in the front of her mind.

Nonetheless, when Mr. Carsington appeared, standing in the doorway for one perfectly timed dramatic moment, she felt a jolt, as though she'd touched one of those magnetic devices her boy cousins found so fascinating.

She was distantly aware that others were not unaffected. Every head turned his way, and many faces—especially the female ones—expressed more than simple curiosity about the newcomer.

The candlelight caught the gold in his hair and burnished his tanned countenance. Once again he seemed a golden god come among mortals.

Apollo, that was the one, beyond question. The sun god, all glimmering gold. His hair. His eyes.

And like a god, he seemed larger than life, his powerful frame filling the doorway.

But he wasn't a god, she reminded herself. Merely a man and, if she was not much mistaken, an all-too-common variety.

A rake.

The man who had destroyed her future was a rake. Among the many lessons she learned from that experience was the importance of learning to recognize the breed.

She could spot one at fifty paces.

Had she not taken leave of her wits during their first encounter, she would have immediately filed Mr. Carsington under the category "Rakes" in her private Encyclopedia of Men.

Still, better late than never, she told herself while she adjusted her expression to one of polite welcome.

Her poise faltered when he left the doorway and made straight for her.

Heart racing, she almost took a step backward. Then she became aware of her father at her shoulder.

"Mr. Carsington, welcome," Papa said. He introduced the man to Lizzie, and Mr. Carsington made her a graceful bow. Lizzie spoke to him, and he answered. Charlotte wasn't sure what they said. Her head was buzzing as though filled with bees.

"Charlotte, my dear." Papa's voice broke through the buzzing. "Here is our new neighbor Mr. Carsington." She heard the pride in her father's voice as he continued, "Sir, my daughter, Charlotte."

Inside her was a frantic flurry. She had all she could do to keep from trembling. She kept her muscles rigid while her heart beat so furiously that she couldn't swallow or catch her breath.

Yet she was aware, too, of Papa beaming at her.

He loved her so much. She wanted so much to be everything he wanted her to be.

She made her muscles relax.

Mr. Carsington bowed. "Lady Charlotte."

"Mr. Carsington."

A pause ensued. It was not a quiet pause. The air seemed to hum, as though the bees had left her skull and now hovered between them.

Mr. Carsington's amber eyes slanted toward her father, who had turned away to say something to Lizzie.

The gaze shifted back to her. This time she saw in his unusual eyes the same teasing expression he'd worn when he quizzed her about her hat.

"But I believe we've met before," he said in a rumbling undertone. Though he stood a proper distance away, the words felt like a secret breathed in her ear. Her skin prickled.

"I think not," she said, flashing him a warning look.

He lifted his eyebrows.

She lifted hers.

She thought, *Utter one word of what happened, and I'll wrap my hands around your throat and choke you dead.*

She knew no one could read minds. He must have read something, though, because the quizzical expression disappeared, and he blinked.

She watched his mouth curve slowly into a smile. "Have we not?"

Under that lazy smile, something inside her seemed to unfurl, like flower petals opening under the sun.

But that's what rake's smiles did, she reminded herself: They made women soft and malleable.

"No," she said. She glanced at her parents. The rector and his wife had claimed their attention.

"Perhaps you have a twin sister," said Mr. Carsington. He made a show of looking about the drawing room.

"No, I do not," she said.

"How strange," he said.

"It is not at all strange not to have a twin," she said. "It is more common not to have one."

"I could have sworn that we met, only a few hours ago, by a pond at Beechwood," he said, still in the We-Have-a-Secret undertone. "You were wearing—or rather, not wearing—a wonderfully frivolous hat."

He had teased her with the hat as a little boy might do, and for a moment she had wanted to play.

Experience came to her rescue. The mischief in his eyes was no more boyish than it was innocent. What she saw in those changeable amber eyes was a rake's guile.

"A lady and a gentleman may not know each other unless they have been properly introduced," she said coolly. "If they do not know each other, they cannot have met. Since we were properly introduced only a moment ago, we cannot have met previously."

"What a madly contorted logic that is," he said.

"It is a rule of behavior," she said. "It needn't be logical. There may even be a rule that rules of behavior must be illogical."

His eyes lit. At first she thought what she saw there was amusement, and she cursed herself, because she did not wish to entertain him. But then his gaze drifted from her face to her neck and downward, lingering upon her bosom before it swept down to the toes of her silk slippers. It came up again so swiftly that she hadn't time to get her breathing back to normal. She could hide that, but not the rest of her reaction.

Her face was hot. Everywhere was hot. Meanwhile, her tattletale skin was announcing the fact, she knew, spreading a blush over her neck and the extensive area of shoulders and bosom her gown revealed.

He was enjoying her agitation.

Anger crackled inside her.

Once, only once, she would like to do something, instead of silently enduring a man's insolent examination.

But a lady must pretend not to notice when a man disrobed her with his eyes.

It was not fair.

When a man took offense at something, he was allowed to react. He was *expected* to react.

If she were a man, she could push him into a piece of furniture or black his eye.

But she wasn't a man, and she could not summon another man to do the job for her. Creating a scene would be disastrous as well as ridiculous. She was not a child. She was a woman of seven and twenty, a nobleman's daughter with eight Seasons behind her. She was expected to possess complete self-control. She was expected to handle difficult or unpleasant situations with poise and courtesy.

She must not get even or punish him.

She must ignore it . . . and he knew she must, the beast.

She simmered helplessly for a time.

But Lady Charlotte Hayward was nothing if not resourceful. Even while she was fuming, her mind was working. She had dealt with scores of men. She could deal with this one, too.

Chapter 3

Mistake, Darius thought. *Stupid, stupid mistake.*

He couldn't believe he'd made it.

Virgins are out of bounds.

His eldest brother Benedict had thrashed the rule into him when he was fifteen.

Long after he'd outgrown the thrashing method, Logic had verified the rule. Virgins, said Logic, were a waste of time, too much work for too little reward. When the virgin was a gentleman's daughter, the price for this negligible amount of pleasure was marriage.

Move on, Logic told Darius. *Now.*

Darius always heeded Logic unhesitatingly.

This time, though, he hesitated, for three reasons.

One, she represented a puzzle.

Two, it was exceedingly difficult for a healthy male to turn his back upon a splendid physical specimen—and she was one of the finest physical specimens he'd ever seen.

Three, that dress. On her, the virginal white gown

was anything but virginal. He saw not Diana but Venus, not the maiden huntress but the goddess of love.

The thought brought into his mind the painting in Florence that Benedict had dragged him to see years ago. It was about the only work of art worth seeing on that long, boring Grand Tour, in which far too many churches and far too few women figured.

It was the famous Botticelli painting of Venus standing naked upon an overlarge seashell.

Naturally, Darius imagined Lady Charlotte naked, like the Venus she so strongly resembled. Any man would do the same, whether he'd seen the painting or not.

Imagining was reasonable. Letting his eyes wander was deranged. Even he knew better than to look lasciviously at an unwed lady in that way—in public, and under her father's roof, no less! It was a sure way to find himself (a) standing at the altar hearing the marriage service or (b) at the wrong end of a horsewhip, or (c) facing a pistol at twenty paces.

Fights to the death over females were common enough and all very well among the birds and beasts. Among reasoning beings, however, such behavior was absurd. Especially when the last thing a reasoning being wanted was to offend her father.

Darius hastily dragged his attention upward from the mouthwatering, maidenly pink blush spreading over her silken skin.

Too late. Murder, plain as day, stared back at him from her ice-blue eyes.

She'd looked that way a moment ago when he'd

started teasing her about their previous meeting. He'd thought, *She's going to throttle me*, and he'd wanted her to try to do it. That would be entertaining.

But she hadn't tried to strangle him then and didn't now.

To his surprise, she smiled a conspiratorial smile.

Then she leaned toward him, offering a better view of her perfectly rounded breasts, which the gown's narrow bodice, aided by the upthrusting corset, displayed more of than seemed proper for a virgin.

All of his self-protective instincts went on the alert, along with the reproductive ones.

"Mr. Carsington," she said huskily.

Trap! Trap! cried Logic. *Run away!*

"Lady Charlotte," he said warily.

"Let us not stand on ceremony," she said. "My parents are occupied with other guests."

Darius knew he should have become occupied with other guests right after the introductions. He started to turn away.

She touched his arm very lightly.

His pulse rate accelerated.

He looked down at the gloved hand barely touching his arm. He looked up into her far-too-beautiful face.

She still wore the conspiratorial smile. "I know you will wish to meet your neighbors," she said. "I shall be happy to stand in for Papa. I often do. We are quite informal here—and he does seem to be engrossed in his conversation with the rector."

While she talked, she led Darius away from her parents and toward a small group at the other end of the drawing room.

At the last instant, though, she changed direction, and steered him toward a curvaceous redhead who stood at the pianoforte, examining the sheet music heaped there. Her name, he learned, was Henrietta Steepleton. She was a young widow with a breathless voice—no doubt the result of her talking at great length without stopping to inhale.

As soon as Mrs. Steepleton began talking, Lady Charlotte left them.

In the instant before she turned away, Darius saw her vacuously polite smile sharpen into a grin.

Drawing room of Lithby Hall,
three and a half hours later

"It would have been kinder to strangle me," Mr. Carsington murmured.

Charlotte stopped short, and tea sloshed to the brim of the cup she was carrying. She took a steadying breath and willed her hands not to tremble.

She had not heard him coming up behind her. She did not exactly hear him now. She felt his voice vibrating along her spine. The skin on the back of her neck prickled as though he'd touched it.

"That would be discourteous," she said. She continued walking. The rector's wife, Mrs. Badgely, sat at the other end of the drawing room near the fire, which burned solely for her on this warm June evening. Mrs. Badgely was crippled with arthritis. Even if she hadn't been Papa's cousin, one must see to her comfort. One must always see to the comfort of one's guests.

Except for this one. There was a limit, after all, to what even the most dutiful of daughters would do.

"Strangling is discourteous," he said. "That is an interesting viewpoint. I suppose I cannot accuse you of discourtesy in leaving me to have my ears talked off."

She glanced at his too-handsome profile. "Please do not trouble yourself on that account. Your ears appear to be firmly attached to your head." She wished they'd been the sticking-out kind of ears. She wished she could find something wrong with him that showed. Providence was not at all fair in that way. What it ought to do was leave an indelible mark on wicked men. Preferably a scarlet A on their foreheads.

But no, he was unblemished, unmarked. She had searched in vain for a physical flaw. She would be happier with herself if she could stop looking . . . and if her breathing would return to normal.

"Then they remain in spite of Mrs. Steepleton's best efforts," he said. "She commenced talking the instant you concluded the introductions. She continued until dinner was announced. At dinner—and why does this fail to surprise me?—I found myself seated next to her."

Charlotte had tried not to look that way, but it was difficult, because he sat directly opposite her. At one point, he'd caught her eye and shot her an accusing look, followed by a martyred one, hastily erased when Mrs. Steepleton reclaimed his attention. Charlotte had wanted to laugh. She had found it unusually difficult to maintain a politely blank expression. She'd found it almost impossible to concentrate on the conversation about her.

"She talked," he went on, "throughout dinner. She did not stop until Lady Lithby signaled the ladies to leave the table."

"Think of the trouble she saved you," Charlotte said. "You were not obliged to devise clever things to say. All you had to do was appear attentive."

"I don't *devise* clever things to say, Lady Charlotte," he said. "I usually say what comes into my head. It makes life less complicated, I find."

"Less complicated for you, perhaps," she said. "You are a man."

"You are most observant," he said.

"Men seem to like candor in their own sex," she said. "They are not so enamored of the trait in women, I have noticed."

"Close-minded men don't like it, perhaps."

Charlotte smiled. If he liked candor in a woman, he was headed in the right direction.

They'd reached the fire, and the rector's wife. Charlotte turned her warmest smile upon the neighborhood's most feared harridan.

"Ah, Lady Charlotte, here you are," said Mrs. Badgely. She was tall and portly, with a correspondingly large voice. "I hoped you were only temporarily distracted and hadn't forgotten me altogether."

She eyed Mr. Carsington. "Yet it's no small distraction, I admit."

Charlotte delivered the tea. "Mr. Carsington very kindly accompanied me," she said. "It is not difficult to guess why he wishes to further his acquaintance with you. Being observant, he noticed your discomfort. Naturally he wishes to employ his vast knowledge in helping you. But first he will need information. I know he will wish you to describe, in detail, *all* of your symptoms."

She beamed at Mr. Carsington.

He blinked once. Then his golden eyes narrowed.

"You are an expert on arthritis, too, Mr. Carsington?" said Mrs. Badgely. "In humans?"

"I'm familiar with the ailment," he said. He turned his attention to the woman occupying most of the love seat.

When he turned his attention upon someone, Charlotte had noticed at dinner, he did so *absolutely*.

As she'd told him, dinners at Lithby Hall were quite informal. At times people did talk—or shout—across the table and sometimes—as when Papa and Lizzie had something to say to each other—down its length. She'd noticed how Mr. Carsington would turn his attention to one, then another, when his interest was caught, and it was easy to tell when that happened. He became completely fixed, to the exclusion of everything and everyone else. He'd reminded her of a falcon on high, sighting its prey.

Now he fixed on Mrs. Badgely, who had begun

enumerating in exhaustive detail her many symptoms and the treatments she'd tried.

Charlotte started to turn away.

"Are you not interested, Lady Charlotte?" he said.

"The poor child's heard it all scores of times, but she's too tactful to say so," said Mrs. Badgely.

Though excused, Charlotte hesitated. This was not because she did not wish to seem indifferent to the lady's troubles. Some devil inside her wanted to watch him suffer from Mrs. Badgely's arthritis as well as one of her inquisitions.

"Have you tried castor oil, Mrs. Badgely?" he said.

Castor oil? Was he joking? Charlotte tried without success to read his face.

"The trouble is in my joints, not my bowels, young man," said Mrs. Badgely. "My bowels are in excellent order—and I don't mean to disorder them with purging and such. A lot of quackery, if you ask me."

"I should have been more explicit," said Mr. Carsington. "Have you tried rubbing castor oil upon the affected joints? Not long ago a physician presented a paper describing his experiments with the remedy. I recommended it to my grandmother. Though she hates me, she admitted that the treatment succeeded."

"Your grandmother hates you?" Charlotte said.

She said it unthinkingly, surprise and curiosity taking the fore. The falcon's gaze swung back to her, and she wished she'd held her tongue. She wished, in fact, she'd made herself scarce as soon as she'd delivered him to the neighborhood crocodile.

"Yes," he said.

"Nonsense," said Mrs. Badgely. "Parents may find their offspring detestable from time to time, but grandparents always dote upon their grandchildren. I speak from experience."

"She hates me," he said, still watching Charlotte. "She sent for me a fortnight ago expressly to tell me so."

"If it is true," said Charlotte, "how strange that you should boast of it."

"I wasn't boasting," he said. "I merely wished Mrs. Badgely to understand that the remedy was deemed effective by a skeptic who was prejudiced against me. Do you wish to know *why* Grandmother Hargate hates me?"

Yes, desperately.

But he didn't want to tell her, Charlotte was sure. What he wanted was to make her guess. After eight Seasons, she had no trouble recognizing an invitation to flirt.

After eight Seasons, her heart ought not to beat so fast, and she ought not to feel a surge of anticipation.

"I should never expect you to discuss so private and painful a matter with a stranger," she said.

She made herself walk away.

Darius watched her go. A few blond tendrils had come loose from the pins to caress the graceful arch of her neck. He recalled the tiny spot of mud he'd been tempted to groom earlier. Even tonight, in a crowd of people, he'd not had the easiest time keeping his mouth from that neck.

He recalled the agreeable warmth of her breast against his hand.

His hands itched.

He should have kept away. He was not used to resisting temptation, that was the trouble. He'd always avoided situations where he'd have to resist it. He shouldn't have to resist it, drat her.

What a tiresome girl she was, not to be unhappily married by now!

"I can guess why," said Mrs. Badgely.

Swallowing an oath, he turned back to her. He could not afford to offend any of his neighbors. Rectors' wives often wielded considerable power, and this one, he'd perceived, ruled the roost. Moreover, she was Lord Lithby's cousin.

"I beg your pardon?" he said.

"Though I know it is impossible for your grandmother to hate you, I can easily imagine why she would have harsh words for you," she said. "If you were my grandson, I should be vastly disappointed in your sense of moral obligation, castor oil or no castor oil. I should certainly not have to tell you that it is your duty as a landowner to see to the welfare of your dependents."

"I am not, precisely, the landowner at present," said Darius. "My father is the legal—"

"Pray do not plague me with lawyers' gobbledygook," said Mrs. Badgely. "Beechwood is your responsibility."

"And I mean to bring it back into order as soon as possible," he said.

"But the house?" she said. "I have heard that you stay at the Unicorn in Altrincham, that only a small staff is at Beechwood House, and those are Londoners. Why have you installed London servants in a country house when local families who have served Beechwood for generations are in want of work? Have you any idea how many of the younger people have been forced to leave their homes and families in order to earn a living? All thanks to the Chancery nonsense."

She went on about Mr. Carsington's duty to Beechwood and to the neighborhood. She told him what others had done, how they'd tried to preserve the property and find work and homes for those abruptly cast out.

He tried to explain the economics of the matter: It was the land that supported the house; ergo, the land must come first. But Logic might have lived on the moon, for all she knew of it.

He glanced at Lady Charlotte, who had joined her mother and Colonel Morrell. He was a tall, dark, good-looking fellow of about the same age as Alistair, Lord Hargate's third son. From Mrs. Steepleton, Darius had learned that Morrell had a property to the south of Lord Lithby's. Though the colonel's family, like Lord Lithby's, had lived here for generations, he had spent most of his life abroad. He had settled here scarcely a year ago and would probably not stay for very long, since he was expected to inherit an earldom from an elderly uncle in Lancashire.

He meant to have Lady Charlotte as his countess, that much was plain. Though the man was not at all obvious about it, he was not too subtle for Darius. After all, mating behavior was Darius's pet subject.

Morrell wanted Lady Charlotte.

If she noticed, she gave no sign.

Is that what she always did? Was feigning indifference sufficient? It couldn't be. Males happily pursued females without any encouragement whatsoever, and sometimes despite clear signs of hostility.

She did not appear hostile. She merely wore a placid cow expression Darius knew was false. She was far from placid and definitely not so simple or innocent as she appeared. She was most certainly not so kind and considerate as everyone claimed. Had she not—for the second time in a few hours—abandoned him to one she knew would drive him mad?

"You know how it is when a property goes into Chancery," Mrs. Badgely was raging on. "One may do nothing, even in charity, for fear of being dragged into the lawsuit. Even Lord Lithby found his hands tied. He was not to 'interfere,' as they put it—even at his own expense! You know this is disgraceful, sir. Can you be so heartless as to perpetuate the outrage?"

The word *heartless* made Darius want to gnash his teeth. It was absurd enough hearing it from Father, but Grandmother Hargate used it, too. Hypocrites.

They said what they pleased, never minding anyone else's feelings.

"I have no wish to perpetuate any outrages," he said. "However, your well-meaning philanthropy fails to take into account certain rules of economics. The land supports the house. The house cannot support the land. Therefore, the logical way to proceed is to begin with the land and any outbuildings crucial to livestock and agriculture."

"Nonsense," she said. "Here is Lady Lithby. Let us find out what she thinks."

Darius wanted to shout that it was irrelevant what a lot of females—to whom logic was as foreign as Sanskrit—thought.

He told himself to calm down. It was irrational to become incensed over a female's irrationality.

He made himself smile benignly at Lady Lithby. Unlike Mrs. Steepleton and Mrs. Badgely, she would not talk him to death. He had noticed that Lady Lithby listened a good deal more than she talked.

Mrs. Badgely went on about the house.

Lady Lithby listened patiently for a time, then said, "Like other men, Mr. Carsington was not trained to manage a household. No doubt he has no idea where to begin."

Darius grasped at the lifeline. "Indeed, I haven't. What do I know of cooks and housekeepers and scullery maids? What do I know of proper furnishings? Should one paint the walls or paper them? What color goes with what? Is this piece of furniture too ornate or unfashionable? I hear women speak of these things and it makes me dizzy. I should rather tackle a hard problem in trigonometry."

"That is perfectly understandable," Lady Lithby said. "One cannot expect a man to deal with these matters."

"But they must be dealt with," said Mrs. Badgely. "Are we to excuse him on grounds that he is a man?"

"Yes, we must," said Lady Lithby. "You may put the house out of your mind, Mr. Carsington."

"Thank you," he said, resisting the childish temptation to stick out his tongue at Mrs. Badgely.

"I shall be happy to do what needs to be done there," Lady Lithby said.

Then Darius saw, too late, the pit yawning in front of him.

Ye gods, the Marchioness of Lithby, accustomed to a bottomless purse, renovating his house.

In his mind's eye, Darius saw ledgers with long columns of expenses, totaling in the thousands. He would have the devil's own time turning a profit as it was. How could he do it if he refurbished the house?

But only a madman would attempt to speak to women of money. First, the subject was vulgar. Second, ladies of the upper orders had no notion of basic rules of economics. He might as well try to explain Ampère's *Theory of Electrodynamic Phenomena* to Lord Lithby's pig.

Third, and most important, his pride would not permit it. He'd be hanged before he'd reveal anything of his financial or time constraints.

"I shouldn't dream of asking you to add this burden to your present responsibilities," he said. "You are expecting a large party of guests, I understand, next month."

"Entertaining guests is nothing," her ladyship said. "We do it all the time."

"But to take charge of another household, one that is in complete disorder, without adequate staff—"

"Your agent Quested is completely reliable," she said. "I shall apply to him for staffing. And you must not fret about how much work needs to be done. Work is what I seek. I recently redecorated Lithby Hall from top to bottom. We were obliged to make some architectural changes as well. While Lithby is happy with the result, he has made me promise not to do it again until the youngest boys are at university. I am at leisure, you see. Too much so, in fact. You would be doing me a favor."

"Beechwood House is in a ghastly state," he said, though he had no idea, having not yet darkened its door. "The rats—"

"I shall bring Daisy, my young bulldog," she said. "She will enjoy catching rats. Charlotte, too." She signaled to her stepdaughter.

"To catch rats?" Darius said. He watched the stepdaughter approach. She still wore the vacantly agreeable look.

Lady Lithby laughed. "Charlotte is not afraid of rodents. She's a countrywoman. She will enjoy the challenge, I don't doubt. Is that not so, my dear?"

"What challenge, Stepmama?" said Lady Charlotte.

"We are going to put Beechwood House to rights."

Lady Charlotte gave her stepmother one short, shocked look. It was so brief that Darius would have missed it had he blinked. A fraction of a second later, her placid cow mask was back in place.

"Are we, indeed?" she said coolly. "I should have supposed that the last thing in the world Mr. Carsington would want is a pair of women he hardly knows fussing about his house. He has so much work to do, and a great deal on his mind. I should think he would want a refuge. Instead of allowing him an island of calm, we shall turn his house upside down. We shall have bricklayers and carpenters and plasterers and paperhangers and such banging about. And scaffolding everywhere. Not to mention we must pester him about this, that, and the other thing—for after all, it is his house, and ought to be the way *he* likes it."

She met his gaze then.

For an instant he was lost in a vision of a beautiful someone making a refuge for him, a place of warmth and order, a place of his own where things were as *he* liked them to be.

Then his mind cleared, and in the cool blue eyes he saw the death threat once more.

The message was plain enough: *Agree to this, and I will kill you with my bare hands.*

That was amusing.

Logic told him he couldn't afford to be amused. He must decline the offer, and to hell with Mrs. Badgely. Lady Lithby's involvement would cost him thousands. He was supposed to turn a profit.

The trouble was, Lady Charlotte clearly wanted nothing to do with his house.

The trouble was, she had left him to Mrs. Steepleton's ear-numbing chatter, then Mrs. Badgely's scolding.

"When you put it that way, Lady Charlotte," he said, "how can I possibly say no?"

Charlotte really was going to have to kill him.

She smiled sweetly, and said, "If Mr. Carsington does not mind our destroying his peace, I shall be happy to help. It should be a most interesting undertaking. I do not believe Lady Margaret made any improvements to the house in all the time she lived there."

"A fossil of a house," said Mrs. Badgely. "The same as it was in your great-grandfather's time. Lithby Hall was a fossil, too, but not so ramshackle."

"A little old-fashioned," said Lady Lithby.

"Inconvenient," said Mrs. Badgely. "The rectory was more modern when I came, and that isn't saying much."

"It was a good while before I did anything of importance here," Lady Lithby said.

This was because she'd spent most of the first three years of her marriage saving Charlotte from herself, and several years after that giving Papa four healthy little boys.

"You are too modest," Charlotte said. "From the first day you came, you made us more orderly and comfortable."

All the same, it was naughty of Lizzie to give Charlotte no warning at all before dragging her into her Beechwood House scheme.

"Comfortable is all very well, but the recent work is splendid," said Mrs. Badgely. "I only wish you could have seen Lithby Hall three years ago, Mr. Carsington, to compare. You would hardly recognize it."

Being a man, he was unlikely to notice what was wrong and inconvenient, Charlotte thought. Certainly he could have no idea what he was in for once Lizzie took charge. Papa certainly hadn't realized.

Oh, but it had been great fun.

Perhaps, after all, Lizzie had done her a favor. A large project like this would offer Charlotte a happy distraction, if only temporarily, from the nightmare of the coming house party.

The project would certainly offer Mr. Carsington an unhappy distraction, and that would be fun, too. Meanwhile, she'd love to see his face when he began to understand what would happen when Lizzie took control.

Charlotte donned her most innocent expression. "I made some paintings and drawings before, during, and after the alterations," she told him. "We have architects' renderings and artists' paintings of the old house and property from various times, too. Papa keeps a portfolio containing estate plans and such. He has made a great many changes to

the property, as he may have told you. Perhaps you
would like to see these documents?"

Mr. Carsington arched an eyebrow.

"They're in the library," she said. "I'll be happy to
show them to you, if you are interested."

He glanced at Mrs. Badgely and quickly away. "I
should like nothing better," he said.

Chapter 4

Yes, Darius would do better to spend his time with the gentlemen.

Yes, he was asking for trouble, following Lady Charlotte out of the drawing room.

But he had to know: What was she up to now?

She led him across the great hall to the library.

The large and comfortably arranged room was obviously in frequent use. Books, covering every subject under the sun, filled the oak shelves lining the walls. In the room's center stood an orrery, a mechanical model of the solar system. Elsewhere Darius saw a pair of globes and a telescope, several more tables of various kinds, and a ladder. All the usual accoutrements, in other words, of the well-equipped library.

The rector sat snoring, his head resting upon the back of a sofa near the fireplace. A book lay open on the table in front of him.

"It seems I'm not the only one eager to get away from Mrs. Badger-Me," Darius whispered.

He received one sidelong glance from the cool blue eyes, too quick for him to read.

"Papa has always encouraged his guests to wander the public rooms as they please," she said. "He wants them to feel at home."

She continued across the room to a large table near the south-facing windows. Beyond the windows, the long summer day had ended early under a thickening blanket of clouds. Darius heard rain pattering on the terrace outside.

Inside, pier glasses hung between the darkened windows. In their mirrors danced the flames of the recently lit candelabra standing on the matching pier tables. In the nearest glass he saw, too, the open doorway behind them and servants passing in the hall outside.

Lady Charlotte opened the large portfolio that lay on the table.

Darius did not immediately join her at the table. He bent and looked under it. He walked around and looked behind it. He looked up at the ceiling, then at the windows.

"The plans are here, Mr. Carsington," she said, tapping a slim finger on the portfolio.

"I'm looking for the trap," he said, keeping his voice low. "First Mrs. S, then Mrs. B, then Lady L. What next, I wonder? A hinged door that opens up beneath my feet and drops me into a vipers' pit?"

"I've never seen a viper at Lithby Hall," she said.

"*Vipera talka-lot-icus, Vipera henpeck-us-to-death-icus, Vipera-bankrupt-me-remodeling-my-house-icus.*"

Her lips quivered. To his disappointment, though,

the placid cow expression swiftly settled back into place.

"Here is a drawing of Lithby Hall at the end of the seventeenth century," she said in the dispassionate tone of a lecturer. "Here it is a century and a half later. This is more or less how my stepmother found it when she first came."

Darius drew nearer. "Is that a moat?" he said, sliding one of the larger drawings toward him.

She nodded. "It's less obvious now. Grandfather turned a section into an ornamental lake. An orangery once stood where the kitchens and servants' hall are. In this one you can see how they closed in the kitchen court. Stepmama added the vestibule, there." She pointed. "But the greatest changes were inside. This house used to be gloomy and oppressive and cold—or so it seemed to me, as a child. She brought light and warmth."

He gazed at her, surprised, as he had been earlier, at the way her voice softened when she spoke of how her stepmother had transformed Lithby Hall.

"You are fond of your stepmother," he said.

"Yes," she said. "I know it is abnormal. I am supposed to hate her."

"It's certainly unusual," he said. "Females can be more viciously territorial than males."

"Can we, indeed?" She looked at him, and he had the distinct sensation of being assessed or tested in some way. "Have you made a study of women, then, too, Mr. Carsington? I'm surprised I haven't heard of it. Papa quotes you all the time. I envisioned you as a sage." She looked away, her brow knit. "I saw you with sparse, white hair and a stoop. And spectacles. People must be shocked the first time they come to hear you lecture."

Oh, she was good. She'd turned the conversation smoothly from herself to him.

She ought to know how to do it, at her great age!

And he ought to know how to press on, at his age. "I have not yet lectured on familial relationships," he said. "I have studied them, however." *In self-defense*, he could have added. "Your case is most intriguing. You had already emerged from childhood when your father remarried. You had to give way to a woman merely nine years older than yourself. This same woman has borne your father four sons so far, the eldest of whom will inherit the title and property. Yet you seem neither jealous nor resentful."

"It is like having an older sister," Lady Charlotte said.

"One might resent or be jealous of a sibling," he said.

"One might," she said. "You speak from experience, I daresay, having four older brothers."

Damnation. She was too good.

"I don't have to live with them," he said. "Boys are usually sent away to school. We don't have to live under the same roof for years on end. Women do. They are usually eager to have homes of their own."

"This is my home," she said.

She took some sketches out of a portfolio, clearly wishing to put an end to the subject.

Perhaps he had become too personal. He was not

used to conversing with Society maidens—but it was maddening not to know why she *was* a maiden still.

Though Mrs. Steepleton had talked endlessly, she'd added only one more rumor to those surrounding Lady Charlotte.

This one concerned a mysterious illness in her youth: For a time it was believed that Lady Charlotte would soon follow her mother to the grave. However, after her stepmother took her for an extended stay in the north, then another in the Swiss Alps, she'd recovered from the ailment and made her debut belatedly, at the age of twenty.

The illness, Mrs. Steepleton whispered, was the reason Lord Lithby allowed her more freedom than some people thought proper.

Not much of an explanation. A debut at age twenty still left Lady Charlotte eight Seasons to get a husband.

Darius would find out the answer, eventually. He always found out the answer.

"Not all of the changes Stepmama made are merely aesthetic," she said. "It was more than decorating. She made important repairs and improvements."

He drew closer to her and tried to fix his full attention on the sketches.

"New floorboards for certain rooms," she said. "New airholes cut for ventilation . . ."

She went on about chimney pots, windows, and tiled floors, about water closets and washstands and calling bells, about painting and plastering and carpentry.

He was soon left in no doubt that bringing Beechwood House into order would cost a king's ransom. Simply maintaining it at a minimum level would be costly. He couldn't afford it.

He didn't want to think about money.

He didn't want to think about pipes and drawer pulls and stove bottoms.

He couldn't, even if he wanted to. He'd come too close, and he'd caught her scent. She spoke of ventilation, and he was aware mainly of the light scent of flowers or herbs wafting about her—the soap she used or the herbs stored with her clothes. He bent his head and drank it in.

The soft skin of her neck was inches away from his mouth.

You are three and a half inches from serious trouble, said Logic.

Darius made himself straighten.

What he couldn't do was keep his mind on house maintenance.

When she talked of stoved feathers—cooked first, she explained, to kill vermin—to fill mattresses, he saw himself lifting her off her feet and tossing her onto a bed.

He saw her grinning wickedly up at him, the same wicked grin she'd worn when she delivered him to Mrs. Steepleton.

She's playing with you, said Logic. *Maiden she may be. Naïve she isn't.*

He firmly banished the pictures from his mind. "It seems a great deal of work," he said. "I wonder at Lady Lithby's undertaking it. Though others will

do the actual labor at Beechwood, she must supervise and keep track of everything."

"Not if you hire a competent house steward."
Lady Charlotte tipped her head to one side and
studied the sketches with a critical eye. The movement set her eardrops swaying. One lightly touched
her cheek. "Your land agent Quested will find the
right man for you."

"He's finding me a land steward," said Darius.
At two hundred pounds per annum. "I understood that
the steward would manage the household as well
as the land."

"That is how Lady Margaret arranged matters,"
she said. "And that is how my grandfather did it.
But it is an old-fashioned system. Not at all efficient.
Ask Papa."

"Beechwood is not like Lithby Hall," Darius said.
"It is a more modest dwelling, and my needs are far
more modest than those of a convivial peer with a
large family and an extensive acquaintance."

She turned her head toward him. Captivated by
the teasing eardrop, he'd drawn closer, so very close
that he could feel the warmth radiating from her
body. Her clean scent was everywhere, it seemed.
His mouth was mere inches from hers.

Her gaze lowered to his mouth.

Her breath came a little faster.

He leaned in a little closer.

She turned away. "Colonel Morrell," she said.
"What is your opinion regarding house stewards?"

Darius swore silently, casually eased away from
her, and looked in the same direction.

The colonel crossed the threshold and quickly covered the length of the room.

She must have spotted him in the pier glass. But how long had she known he was there?

How long, before she noticed, had Morrell stood in the doorway, watching and listening?

"I should think a butler sufficient for a smaller property, particularly a bachelor's abode," he said. "But we soldiers are accustomed to spartan living. I should consider a housekeeper and valet and perhaps a few day servants more than sufficient. However, I am told that this is a disgracefully nipfarthing, cheeseparing way of getting on, not at all in keeping with my consequence."

He did not say who had told him this, probably because the critic's husband snored nearby.

Morrell joined them at the table, taking a position on the other side of Lady Charlotte.

"I was ordered to come and look at the pictures and discover ways to make my house grander," he said. "Is this your work, Lady Charlotte? Your draftsmanship is very good."

In the process of taking up the picture, he contrived, without being obvious about it, to draw nearer to her.

She edged away from him, which brought her closer to Darius. He ought to move away, too, to give her space. But he knew that Morrell hadn't closed in merely to be near her. He knew she would back away, and he thought Darius would retreat to give her room. This would push Darius to the very edge of the table. One more such maneuver would force Darius to the other side of the table, where he must view the material sideways.

A territorial move, in short.

One could be amused, and let the fellow have the lady to himself. After all, Darius had no use for her.

However, he had grown up as the youngest of five aggressive males. He never gave up ground without a fight.

He moved not an inch.

Morrell reached out to pick up another sketch, moving nearer still to Lady Charlotte as he did so.

She backed away, and since Darius stood with his hip against the table, this brought her rump against his breeding organs. They instantly took notice of her.

As did she of them, with a sharp intake of breath.

Though his own breathing wasn't steady, Darius casually reached for another picture. "Ah, the dairy," he said. "One thing—one of many—I miss in London is fresh country cream and butter. City cream doesn't taste the same at all."

"You will need cows, then," said Lady Charlotte. She set her heel down on his toe.

She put some weight on it, and though he was wearing thin evening shoes rather than boots, it was not enough to make him yield. "I'm a countryman," he said. "I know where milk and cream come from."

She shifted her weight onto the one foot. Hers was no great weight, but his toes, unlike his upper body, were not constructed to bear it. He swallowed a gasp . . . and withdrew.

"I thought you were a London man," Colonel Morrell said as he perused a plan. "You lecture there often, I believe."

Careful to keep his toes out of danger, Darius picked up another document. A crayon sketch, which must have been stuck to the bottom of it, fell to the table.

Lady Charlotte reached for the sketch, but Darius got it first.

"I lecture in London," Darius said. "I learn in the country. In Derbyshire—not very far from here, in fact. My brother Alistair lives in the Peak, near Matlock Bath. Who is this sweet creature, Lady Charlotte? I cannot read the inscription."

In the picture, a woman sat on the doorstep of a cottage, dandling her infant.

Lady Charlotte snatched the picture from him. "It must have fallen on the floor," she said. "One of the maids must have picked it up when she was cleaning and put it with the others. It doesn't belong to this lot. It's one of the villagers with her child. Merely the sort of rustic scene ladies are expected to draw. Well, I will leave you gentlemen to debate the finer points of dairy farming."

She hurried out of the library.

That was odd, Darius thought.

Morrell must have thought so, too, because his brow knit as he turned and watched Lady Charlotte go. But neither man remarked on it. With stiff courtesy they exchanged opinions about dairies, brewhouses, and bakehouses. They agreed that Lithby

Hall's kitchen court was conveniently situated and arranged. Then Mrs. Badgely came in and woke her husband, after which they all returned to the drawing room.

Darius kept away from Lady Charlotte. He could not believe he'd taken such risks in the library. He was not a boy of fifteen. He knew better. Now of all times he needed to keep a clear head. He was going to prove his father wrong. He was going to revive Beechwood. He was not going to get into trouble with a nobleman's unwed daughter.

He was already in trouble, and he'd no one to blame but himself. How in blazes was he to finance Lady Lithby's refurbishing of his house?

He wasn't. He couldn't. He had to get out of it somehow.

He was still trying to determine the "somehow" as the party began breaking up. Then, as he was taking his leave of his hosts—and looking forward to a long night of kicking himself—rescue came, all unexpected.

"My lady tells me she means to take charge of your house," Lord Lithby said. "I advise you to have a care, sir. She looks dainty, but she will run roughshod over you if you let her."

"I hope I am not as bad as all that!" said Lady Lithby with a laugh. "I only want to make a refuge for Mr. Carsington, as Charlotte said: a comfortable place to come to after his labors."

"Your and his notions of what is comfortable are not likely to be the same," said Lord Lithby. "Mr. Carsington is a man of science. I have not received the impression that he wishes, as we do, to entertain multitudes. Certainly he is not interested in following the latest fads and fashions."

His genial grey gaze returned to Darius. "You must stand up for yourself, sir. Tell my lady plainly what you want."

Don't touch my house, Darius wanted to say.

That wasn't the politic answer, and even he knew better than to utter it.

"I merely wish to make the place habitable for the present," he said. "At a later time, I shall consider beautifying it."

"Clean and in order," said Lord Lithby. "That's all, Lizzie. Then let the man do his work, which is of somewhat greater importance, as you well know, than the latest fashion in curtains."

As he spoke, Lady Charlotte joined them. Darius didn't linger. He took a polite leave of them all and made his escape.

He couldn't escape her.

She plagued him during the ride back to Altrincham. Along with the first mystery, he had another puzzle to wrestle with: the strange reaction to her drawing of the woman and infant . . . the odd expression he'd so briefly glimpsed in that beautiful face, an expression he hadn't expected.

Grief?

And why not? he asked himself impatiently. She had been on the brink of womanhood when she lost her mother. Why should a picture of a mother and child not remind her of the loss, even many years later?

Dogs were known to pine when their master died. Sometimes the pets died of grief. Certain species of birds mourned their mates' deaths and would not mate again.

Why shouldn't a woman—of any age—continue to mourn the loss of her mother?

Still . . .

"Plague take her," he muttered. "What the devil is it to me?"

Balked lust, obviously.

That neck. That bosom. That round, warm derrière. He could almost feel it still, pressed against his groin.

"Stop it," he said. "Stop thinking about it. Nothing's going to come of it. Virgin, remember? Put it—her—out of your mind."

He couldn't.

It was maddening. Beautiful and wellborn and rich and seven and twenty and *unwed* . . .

It was unnatural was what it was. That sort of thing ought to be against the law.

He turned his mind to the inn and its comfortable bed and the two willing maidservants, either or both of whom might join him in the comfortable bed.

And yet, in the end, he spent the night alone.

Eastham Hall, outskirts of Manchester
Evening of Sunday 16 June

Now that Colonel Morrell had returned from London, he spent his Sundays with his uncle, the Earl of Eastham, at the ancestral pile on the outskirts of Manchester.

He arrived in the morning in time to escort the cantankerous old man to church and did not leave until late in the evening or early on Monday morning.

Colonel Morrell didn't do this out of affection. He'd always loathed his uncle. Lord Eastham's only redeeming quality was the misogyny that had kept him from marrying. Thanks to his failure to produce a son, his eldest nephew, the colonel, would inherit an old title, several large properties, and heaps of money.

A year ago, Lord Eastham had decided that his nephew must give up active service abroad for an administrative post at home, in order to concentrate on finding a wife and filling his nursery. Without consulting the nephew, his lordship had used his considerable influence to arrange matters.

Though accustomed to taking orders, the colonel was not accustomed to having his life rearranged at the whim of an irascible civilian. He'd come back to England in a state of mind very close to homicidal. Then, one of the military superiors who'd connived with his uncle took him to a ball in London. There Colonel Morrell met Lady Charlotte Hayward.

This did not make the colonel hate his uncle any the less. It went a good way, however, in reconciling him to dawdling about England, bored witless, instead of doing what he'd been born to do.

Lady Charlotte was not boring. On the contrary, she was fascinating. He'd never seen anything like the way she managed men. He couldn't stop watching her. How did she do it? Why did she do it? He saw instantly how useful such a wife could be to an ambitious soldier with limited experience of the Beau Monde. Unlike the typical eldest son of a nobleman, Colonel Morrell had not been groomed for the title. But she knew what to do, and she knew everybody. She would smooth his way into the highest reaches of civilian life. She would bring him into the exclusive heart of Fashionable Society.

Naturally, since she was beautiful, he looked forward to bedding her. But he looked forward quite as much to mastering a woman who had so effortlessly mastered so many men.

Since the colonel needed to spend his time near the elusive target, and since her family lived near to his own family's old place, this brought him closer than he liked to his uncle, who lived not ten miles away from them.

However, the old wretch was a prodigious gossip, and Colonel Morrell was willing to sacrifice Sundays in order to learn everything he possibly could about everyone in Lady Charlotte's sphere.

At present, the two men sat at dinner.

"The family is back at Lithby Hall, I hear," Lord Eastham said. "I'd have thought you'd have the banns called by now. I don't understand this shilly-shallying. You ain't a bad looking fellow, you know. If she won't have you, there's plenty others not so finicky."

Colonel Morrell was a fine-looking man. He was tall, dark, and well built. Moreover, his magnificent military bearing drew looks of envy from men and looks of admiration from women, even when he wore civilian attire.

His uncle swallowed some wine and frowned. "Better try for a young female, fresh from the schoolroom. Easier to train."

Colonel Morrell didn't want an easy-to-train girl. Where was the challenge in that? He wanted someone worth conquering.

He said, "Youthful good looks quickly fade. Intelligence, manners, and personality are of more lasting value, especially in one who will be Lady Eastham one day. I have never seen Lady Charlotte fail in cordiality or courtesy."

Except for Friday night, he thought.

"She's amiable to other women, which is rare, as you well know, sir," he went on. "She's kind and attentive to the elderly and frail. She's unfailingly cheerful and gracious. She always knows exactly what to say and do to put others at ease. If she's ever out of temper, she conceals it so skillfully that it's impossible to detect."

And she rejects her many suitors so cleverly and courteously that they go away with no idea she's done it, he could have added but didn't. He was quite sure he was the only one who understood what she was up to, and he intended to keep it that way.

He added, "Her temper is so mild and agreeable that I believe you would not at all mind having her under your roof, sir, even for long periods of time."

If anyone could manage the overbearing old brute, it was Lady Charlotte. She could even manage Mrs. Badgely, who was as provoking as Lord Eastham: no mean feat.

"I need a wife who is sophisticated," the colonel went on. "A young girl is not likely to be sophisticated, and I should have no notion how to make her so."

Training Lady Charlotte would be much more interesting and worthwhile. She was accustomed to too much freedom—always dangerous for a woman—and she would not give it up easily. But Colonel Morrell had no worries in that regard. He'd dealt with the army's spoiled aristocrats as well as the scum who filled the bottom ranks. He could deal with an overindulged young lady, no matter how clever she was. He had no doubt she'd be grateful. She was intelligent enough to appreciate the comfort of being looked after properly, of leaving all the care and worry and decision-making to him.

"If by sophisticated you mean old, I'll agree," said his uncle. "Should have been wed ages ago. Something wrong there, but it's no use telling young men anything." He drank, frowning. "Speaking of flies in the ointment, I hear Darius Carsington has moved in next door to them. I should watch out for him was I you. Them younger sons of Hargate's have a knack for marrying fortunes."

"Do they, indeed?" Colonel Morrell recalled the cozy scene he'd interrupted in the library. The unflappable Lady Charlotte had appeared flustered. That was not a good sign. "I met his two eldest sons during the Season, but I know next to nothing about the others. I daresay you do, sir."

Of course his uncle knew, and he was happy to tell it and a great deal more. This, after all, was why Colonel Morrell spoiled an otherwise perfectly good Sunday.

His uncle talked, and he listened, noting every tidbit and putting it aside for future use.

On Sunday, after thinking it over, Darius decided to move into Beechwood House. While he could not mark his territory as animals did, he could place his belongings about at strategic points, to help the ladies remember whose house it was and what the rules were.

Lady Lithby wasted no time in setting to work. On Monday she and her stepdaughter arrived bright and early. She promptly sent the London servants back to Lady Hargate—to their obvious joy—and let loose hordes of local men and women, who swarmed over the house like an army of busy ants. They scrubbed, dusted, polished, repaired, and mended. They carried out a fair number of corpses, too, although these were mainly insects.

In spite of Chancery, someone had made sure the house was sealed. Someone must have let a cat patrol it regularly. It was dusty and musty and crumbling in certain places but it had not become home to much wildlife. Or, if it had been their home, the rodents and other small animals had the good sense to flee when Lady Lithby arrived.

While Darius did not flee, he did stay out of the way.

Until late on Friday afternoon.

He was at the home farm with his new land steward, Purchase, when his manservant Goodbody arrived, breathless and in a sweat.

To see the magnificently patient, quiet, all-but-in-
visible valet venture beyond the safety of the once-
formal gardens was amazing enough. That he'd obviously run most of the way was shocking.

"What's happened?" Darius said. "Is the house
afire? Or did the laundress put too much starch in
my neckcloths?"

"Sir," Goodbody gasped. "Your books."

Darius felt a chill.

He had brought with him from London only
the books he would need to consult immediately.
He'd stored them in his bedroom, from which he'd
banned everybody but Goodbody.

This was because Darius did not trust Lady Charlotte any farther than he could throw her. He could
easily imagine a hundred torments she could inflict
upon him, especially with the bulldog's help.

Daisy seemed to be a well-trained and good-
natured canine. Still, bulldogs, especially young
ones, could be busy animals. With no rats to catch,
she would find something to chew.

Had she sneaked—or been let—into his bedroom?

"What about the books?" he said very calmly.

"Several crates of them were delivered this morning," said Goodbody. "I was not informed, sir, or I
should have told you the instant they arrived. As it
was, I only discovered it but a short time ago when
I happened to pass the library. I saw that the crates

had been opened, and Lady Charlotte was putting the books away." He paused. "It was not my place to say anything to the lady, sir, but I was not sure whether you had informed her of your system."

Darius had brought with him fewer than two dozen volumes. They had fit in one trunk.

"Crates of books," he said, as a cold foreboding swept over him.

"Yes, sir. Judging by the number of them, it appears that your collection has arrived," said Goodbody. "All of it."

Darius's collection comprised several hundred volumes. Many were rare, some irreplaceable.

"But I never sent for them," he said. "I am sure I—Devil take it!" His mother. This was her doing.

Against his wishes, she had sent servants to ready Beechwood House. Those unwanted servants had returned to London early in the week. From them or her numerous correspondents she must have learned that Lady Lithby had taken charge of Beechwood House's refurbishment.

Mother had simply decided to send his books after him.

Without consulting him.

As usual.

From the day he was born, practically, he'd had to assert himself—forcefully—or be pushed into the shadows or crushed by the formidable personalities about him. If he wasn't on the spot to stand up to her, his mother would decide what was best for him.

Now his precious books were in the hands of a

woman who had apparently decided that his life was lacking in trials and tribulations, and was determined to correct the deficiency.

He mounted his horse and galloped back to the house.

Chapter 5

Darius burst into the library, then stopped short.

Lady Charlotte stood halfway up a set of library steps, a book in her hand.

Dust and cobwebs clung to her. Her lacy cap must have been white once. It was grey now, and the hair it was meant to protect was escaping its confines, the blond tendrils sticking to the back of her neck. The strings of her apron dangled over her magnificent bottom, whose outline was tantalizingly visible, thanks to the undergarments clinging to her damp skin.

A small ball of dust had caught on the button of her footwear—those short boots that looked too fragile to be boots. He had no idea what they were called. All he knew was that they revealed the shape of her ankles, and he could see a bit of stocking when she reached up to push a book into place.

At his entrance, she gave him a quick glance before taking up a book from the top of the steps. "Is something wrong, Mr. Carsington?" she said. "Has the brewhouse caught fire? Or perhaps you have at last discovered where all those vast hordes of rats you promised us are hiding. Poor Daisy is bored."

Darius dragged his gaze away from the lady's arse and ankles and focused on the dog. Lying near the foot of the steps and busy with some object, she looked up hopefully when her name was uttered.

He stared at the article between her paws. "Is that—*was* that—a book she's eating?" he said.

"Fordyce's *Sermons,*" said Lady Charlotte.

Darius sucked in air and let it out, then advanced into the room through a narrow path between crates. "That's not one of mine," he said. "There are no sermons in my collection."

"And why does this fail to surprise me?" she muttered.

Though his hearing was sharper than most, he feigned otherwise. "I beg your pardon?" he said, drawing closer to the steps.

"Certainly it isn't yours," she said more distinctly. "I should never let Daisy chew one of your books. That would be discourteous. The book is one of mine. But Daisy gets so much more enjoyment out of it, you see."

Something clicked in the back of his mind, but the shapely bottom practically under his nose was muddling his thinking processes.

"Then is it safe to assume you'd consider it discourteous as well to let her piss on any of my books?" he said.

She made a small, choked sound. Laughter? Or had she merely inhaled dust? He moved a little to one side of the steps, trying for a better view of her face. He detected no sign of amusement.

"I should never permit that, either," she said.

He let his gaze sweep upward again. He could not make her out—but then, his brain was not working very well. He saw how pink her cheeks were. He saw a few wisps of blond hair stuck to her temple. He saw the sheen of perspiration slicking her face and neck.

It was not unusual for a gentleman to see a high-born woman in a sweat. But most usually he saw her—above him or below him or beside him, as the case may be—in such a state during a lively bout of lovemaking.

Darius's temperature climbed, and a jolt of not-unfamiliar sensation shot to his groin.

Don't waste your time, he told his reproductive organs.

They weren't listening. They were fixed on a warm, moist female. His mind wasn't helping matters. It conjured images of this female, hot and tousled, amid tangled sheets.

"What are you doing on those steps?" he said irritably. "There seem to be a thousand servants in the house. Aren't you supposed to be sitting in a chair, sipping lemonade and ordering them about?"

"I did supervise them," she said. "The London servants merely swiped the room with a duster and called it cleaning. I had our lot do it thoroughly while I sorted your books. But cleaning is one thing and putting away books is another. The servants cannot all read very well, some very little. It was simpler to do it myself." She rubbed her forehead with the back of her hand, leaving a streak of grime there.

"It is hard work," he said. "Your face is red, and you are sweating."

"Gentlemen do not notice such things," she said.

"Where did you get that mad idea?" he said. "That is precisely the sort of thing men notice."

"I said *gentlemen*," she said.

"Gentlemen are men, too," he said. "But I believe you meant that I should have pretended not to notice. One of those absurd social rules."

"And you do not believe in rules," she said.

"No more than you do," he said. "I know it is against the rules for a lady to perform any sort of manual labor. Yet you are putting away all these books by yourself."

"I wanted it done properly." She came down the steps. She held a volume of Homer's *Iliad*. He wondered if she knew what it was.

He doubted she'd been taught Greek. Except in rare cases—such as his sister-in-law Daphne's—the classical languages tended not to be included in a lady's education. In his experience, the higher a lady stood upon the social ladder, the less erudition—or even intelligence—mattered. There was an easy way to find out.

"Where is the right place to file the erotic Greek poetry, I wonder?" he said.

She glanced down at the book, and her reaction told him she could no more read Greek than he could read ancient Egyptian hieroglyphs: Her flushed face deepened from pink to rose. So did her neck.

She wore a high-necked dress with a great many

ruffles about the upper part. However, she'd undone several fastenings in front, leaving a narrow
line of her throat and an area below plainly visible.
The bodice material, once crisply starched, hung
limply. She pulled this droopy cloth away from her
skin and fanned herself with the damp fabric. The
action revealed the swell of her bosom, and the fine
line of sweat trickling between her breasts.

"Under F," she said.

"F," he said blankly. At the moment he could
think of only one topic belonging under that letter.

He was aware of a musky fragrance, not at all un-
pleasing. Quite the contrary. It was precisely the sort
of thing that, in the animal kingdom, drove male
dogs to burrow under fences and bound over tall
walls: the scent of a heated female.

He pulled out his handkerchief. "Perhaps you'd
like to wipe off the—er—*not*-sweat," he said.

"Thank you." She took the handkerchief.

He turned his gaze to the shelves behind her. He
saw something wrong, very wrong, but his brain
was too sluggish to name it.

He tried desperately to concentrate. "F," he said.
"Greek begins with a G. Poetry with a P. Erotica
with an E."

She dabbed her forehead with his handkerchief.
"F for foreign," she said.

"F for foreign," he repeated.

She nodded.

He looked about him. He blinked once, then
stalked to one of the shelves and stared at the
books.

"You've put them in alphabetical order," he said hollowly.

"Yes," she said cheerfully.

"By title," he said.

"Yes, except for the foreign ones. I considered doing the others by author, but I thought you'd remember titles more easily."

He turned to look at her. Apparently thinking him otherwise occupied, she had pulled the bodice open and was mopping the space between her breasts with his handkerchief.

I have to kill her, he thought.

This was beyond anything. This was diabolical.

He set his jaw and focused on the shelves.

"There are a great many books under T," he said levelly. *"The Elements of Law, Natural and Political. The Practical Husbandman and Planter. The Sceptical Chymist."*

"Yes, it is amazing how many there are," she said brightly. "But you will find a prodigious number under A, as well." She moved away to a set of bookshelves and read: *"A General System of Nature. An Enquiry Concerning the Principles of Morals. A Treatise on Ruptures."* She waved at another set of shelves. "There are a fair number of O's, too. *On* this or that. *Observations* of something or other."

"And F for foreign," he said.

"Yes." She beamed at him.

"Lady Charlotte," he said.

"Pray do not thank me," she said. "It was my pleasure, I assure you." She gave him back the handkerchief, set the volume of Homer on top of a crooked stack of books nearby, and left him.

He watched her go, hips swaying, dress clinging.

When her footsteps had faded, he looked about him. Open crates, some empty, some partially filled, crowded the room. A few of the empty crates stood upside down. On top of them teetered towers of books. In the A, F, and T sections, books crammed the shelves. Elsewhere, they held only a volume or two.

"Her pleasure, indeed," he said.

He looked down at Daisy, who had remained. At the sound of his voice, she looked up from her chewing.

She was not pretty. Bulldogs were not bred for looks but for ferocity and fearlessness. One of the bulls or bears she was bred to bait must have sat on the face of one of her ancestors. Bowed legs projected from her barrel-shaped—and overweight—torso and crooked teeth from her drooly mouth. On the other hand, her brown and white coat was sleek and clean, and her temper was sweet—perhaps because she was small, even for a young female. The runt of the litter, he guessed.

Yet runt or not, young or not, she must be fast as well as fierce to catch rats. Despite appearances— the mashed-in face and the crooked teeth protruding from her drooly mouth—she was intelligent.

Sweet and well behaved. More intelligent than she appeared. Yet dangerous.

Like the lady who'd departed a moment ago.

"F for foreign," he said.

Daisy gave a little grunt—and returned to her chewing.

Darius looked at the damp, crumpled square of linen in his hand. "Plague take her," he said. He brought the handkerchief to his face and drank in the scent of hot female.

Blindly hurrying down the hall, Charlotte nearly collided with her stepmother.

Though what Charlotte wanted to do was run out of the house and all the way home, she stopped and made herself very, very calm.

Lizzie's gaze went from the top of the dirty cap to the dusty toes of her shoes. "I am afraid to ask," she said.

"I was putting away Mr. Carsington's books," Charlotte said.

"By yourself?"

Charlotte nodded. "The servants had more important things to do." The truth was, she couldn't resist the temptation to examine his belongings. A man's books told a great deal about the man, Papa said. That applied only to the men who actually read the books they owned. Some merely bought them by the cartload to fill their libraries, in order to impress visitors. She knew Mr. Carsington wasn't that kind of man. He was not in the least unsure of himself, he was not a parvenu trying to climb the social ladder, and he did not seem to care what impression he made on others.

She had hoped his books would offer clues about him. Usually, she had no trouble assessing a man and determining the quickest way to direct his interest elsewhere without appearing to do so. She was having a great deal of difficulty with him.

This, she supposed, was because he'd caught her unawares at the very beginning. Unprepared, she'd reacted unthinkingly. Ever since then, she couldn't seem to find the correct way to deal with him.

"Since he is a scholar," she told her stepmother, "I supposed he'd care a good deal more about having access to his books than about the state of the chair covers."

"I saw the crates," said Lizzie. "He owns a great many books. No wonder you're so rumpled and hot."

Charlotte was a strong girl, a countrywoman, as her stepmother understood. She walked a great deal more than other ladies of her social position did. Even on a sultry day like this, several hours of climbing up and down a short set of steps and putting away books, while warm work, hardly overtaxed her.

It most certainly didn't do to her what Mr. Carsington did when he burst through the library door. He was hatless, his gold-streaked hair windblown. He was breathing hard, his big chest rising and falling.

Then she started breathing hard.

Then her temperature shot up, and she began to sweat as though she'd been breaking rocks under the midday sun.

She would like to believe she was flustered because he'd caught her misbehaving. But she'd had fun misbehaving, and being caught merely meant she needed to use her wits, which was even more fun.

As to her playing the innocent idiot—why should her conscience take notice? Falsehoods and make-believe were central to a lady's repertoire. Pretend to be in complete control. Pretend not to notice an insult or a faux pas. Pretend not to be hurt. Pretend to be amused. Pretend to be interested. Pretend to care. Pretend not to care.

"Ye gods," she said under her breath. "When am I not pretending?"

"Charlotte?"

"Ye gods, I do need a bath," Charlotte said more audibly, tugging at the half-undone bodice. All of her clothes stuck to her. She wished she were a boy, and could tear them all off and leap into the nearest lake.

Mr. Carsington must have done that when he was a boy.

Very likely he still did it.

She could picture it: the broad shoulders and narrow hips and long, muscled legs . . .

Don't, she told herself.

Too late.

A wave of aching loneliness washed through her, and in its wake came longing. She saw his face as he took in her joke. How she'd wanted to laugh! She'd wanted to put out her tongue at him. She'd wanted him to pull her off the ladder and into his arms.

Feelings, too many . . . old, wicked feelings

she thought she'd killed and buried long ago.

She had to get away—from him, from this house. She tried not to look impatient.

"I'll be ready to leave in a minute," said Lizzie.

"I'll wait for you at the dog cart." Charlotte started down the hall.

"But Daisy is not with you," Lizzie said. "Where is she?"

Only then did Charlotte realize the dog had not followed her. "She must be in the library." She kept walking.

"Alone?" Lizzie's voice rose. "With valuable books?"

"Oh, no, Mr. Carsington is with her."

"He is here, in the house? Charlotte, will you stop? You will oblige me to shout."

Charlotte did not look back. "Don't worry," she called. "He won't leave Daisy alone with his books."

She recalled what he'd said . . . about her letting the dog relieve herself on his books. Only he hadn't used a euphemism, and she'd very nearly giggled, as she used to do when she heard her boy cousins use naughty words.

Oh, he was wicked . . . and so was she.

The look on his face when he comprehended her joke. She covered her mouth and hurried on to the dogcart.

Then, when none but Belinda the mare could hear her, Lady Charlotte did laugh . . . and cry a little, too.

* * *

Twenty minutes later

Between the trees, Charlotte caught glimpses as she drove of Beechwood's lake, its waters glistening in the sunlight.

In one secluded corner of Lithby Park's lake was a dock from which visiting boy cousins and, lately, the two older of her little brothers would leap naked into the water, as girls were not allowed to do.

She saw in her mind's eye Mr. Carsington, naked, running down the dock and jumping into the water, the way her cousins and brothers did, and laughing the way they did.

"Charlotte, you had better let me drive," said Lizzie. "You are not paying atten— Look out!"

Two hours later

After fuming for a time, Darius put Goodbody in charge of restoring order to the library. With a superfluity of servants about, the valet would have all put to rights in no time. It would give the housemaids something to do, now that Lady Lithby wasn't here to keep them busy.

Darius knew there was a pecking order among servants. Certain maids were trusted with certain areas of the house and certain tasks. Furthermore, even the most high-ranking maids were not allowed to wield so much as a feather duster in areas reserved to certain menservants. But sorting out precedence was best left to Goodbody, who understood and cared about such things.

Darius might have cared more had any of the maids been pretty. Since they weren't, he left the valet in charge and went to the stable, where he had only one groom, Joel Rogers, to deal with.

Darius had promised to evaluate the paving today, and decide whether to repair or replace it, along with the antiquated drainage system.

As he neared the stable, the groom hurried out. "You heard, then, sir?" said Rogers. "I saddled the mare, thinking you'd want her."

"Heard what?" Darius said. The back of his neck prickled.

"About the accident, sir. Along your road."

The world blurred and chilled for a moment, as though a cold fog had swept in. "What accident?" Darius said levelly.

"Lady Charlotte, sir, and Lady Lithby," said the groom. "I heard they caught in a rut and broke a wheel."

In his mind's eye, Darius saw Lady Charlotte's mangled body carried home on a ladder. To block out the nightmare image, he asked questions. The groom had little additional information. He'd heard the news from the blacksmith, who'd recognized the damaged vehicle when he passed it on his way here.

Within minutes, Darius was upon his horse.

It did not take long to find the place, though, thanks to the ruts, he had to make his way slowly. He found the dog cart on its side at the edge of the road. The wheel was badly broken, and one of the shafts was damaged.

Then he saw spots of blood. Logic told him this didn't necessarily bode calamity. Logic pointed out that if anything truly disastrous had happened, the news would have flown through the neighborhood. Since it was his road, people would have been pounding on the door to tell him, Logic said.

Logic might as well have spoken to the nearest tree.

Darius made for Lithby Hall with as much speed as the crater-filled road would allow.

The house appeared normal enough when he arrived. No weeping or wailing issued from any of the open windows. The outdoor servants had not gathered nearby, as they would during a catastrophe, to await news.

He looked toward the first-floor windows. He remembered Lady Charlotte dabbing at her damp breasts with his handkerchief. He recalled the potent woman-scent he'd inhaled.

He imagined the drawn curtains at one west-facing window abruptly pulled open, revealing the lady risen from her bath and as naked as the Botticelli Venus, her fair hair streaming over her shoulders, the late-afternoon sun gilding her silken skin.

Are you insane? he asked himself. *You'd better hope no worse has happened than her needing a bath. You'd better hope that body is in one piece.*

As he reached the stables, he heard shouting.

Not a good sign.

One of the stablemen hovering in the doorway, avidly taking in the dispute, looked round at Darius's approach. He left the door and hastened to attend to the visitor.

Darius dismounted, gave over his horse, and was about to ask for news when a familiar female voice pierced the snarling and snapping of the males: "No, it must be cleansed with warm water! Give me that cloth, Jenkins. No, Fewkes, do not interrupt. Wait. I need to think."

Darius went to the stable door.

Her back to him, Lady Charlotte stood two stalls away, murmuring to the horse whose shoulder she was gently washing.

Relief surged through him, as powerful as a blow. His knees buckled. He set his hand on the doorframe and pretended to lean there casually. Not that anyone heeded him.

The two men inside were too busy arguing, chests out, chins jutting. Their attire told Darius their positions. The older and larger fellow with the red hair and vinous red nose must be the coachman. The smaller, wiry man must be the head groom.

"Listen to him and that mare'll be the worse for it, your ladyship," said the coachman. "With a wound like that, the natural spirits is oozing out and taking down the heat. You wash it, and you takes the heat down more again. It's the black ointment what you want, to fire her spirits."

"An ointment on a scrape like that?" the groom said scornfully. "She'll take a fever for sure. It wants a poultice first, lest you want to kill the creetur."

"I worked for his lordship boy and man, and never kilt no horse—"

"They died all by themselves, did they?"

"Your ladyship—"

"Her ladyship knows a poultice is the proper—"

"You'll bring that mare down and no coming back!" the coachman roared. He took a step closer to the groom and swelled his chest. His face grew redder still. It was a threatening display, but the groom wouldn't back down.

"Why not bleed her as well, then?" the coachman demanded. "Why not draw off what little spirits is left in her? This is what comes of *some* people not knowing their place. I been looking after the horses here, boy and man, since you was a girl, your ladyship. This mare belongs to the coach house to be tended to."

"If her ladyship liked your way of tending cattle, she wouldn't've brought her to me, now, would she?"

"Enough!" Lady Charlotte snapped. "What is wrong with you? Belinda had a fright, and she is hurt—and now you are shouting and upsetting her. You ought to know better, the pair of you."

Darius straightened away from the doorframe. "Ahem," he said.

The two masculine heads swiveled toward him. Lady Charlotte turned sharply round and stood, sopping rag in hand, staring at Darius as though he'd sprung up direct from Beelzebub's hot parlor.

In the process, she dribbled water—or whatever solution she was using—over the front of her dress.

Though now fully buttoned, the dress looked more thoroughly disreputable, having acquired a good deal of dirt and several grease stains since last he'd seen it.

Darius walked farther inside, inhaling the familiar aromas of horseflesh mingled with manure and hay. The stalls were airy, well designed, and neatly organized. His stable was a much smaller affair, not a fraction so grand as this, with its screens of Ionic columns dividing the stalls. Small as his was, though, he'd want a good while to bring it to this pitch of cleanliness and order.

He took in his surroundings with a glance. Most of his attention, though, was upon the lady. She did not seem to be broken. Nor had she oozed away any spirits, by the sounds of it.

"Mr. Carsington," she said.

"I heard you had an accident," he said. "I saw your dogcart at the side of the road, and the broken wheel. I was . . . concerned."

Panicked was more like it. He never panicked. Ever. About anything. Even when his father summoned him to the Inquisition Chamber.

A state of panic was a state of total irrationality.

What the devil was the matter with him?

"The wheel stuck in a rut and the cart tipped," she said tightly. "It was no great matter, but Belinda took fright and jumped, and the shaft caught her in the shoulder."

"But you are unharmed," he said. "And Lady Lithby?"

"Oh, we are well," she said impatiently. "She and

I have taken worse tumbles. Colonel Morrell came along and helped us."

Darius did not snarl at the mention of the colonel. Animals snarled at enemies and rivals. He was not an animal but a rational being who had no logical reason to view Morrell as either enemy or rival.

Yet while Darius stood listening calmly, he was unhappily aware of a primitive, possessive part of him pacing restlessly in a shadowy corner of his being.

"He freed Belinda from the harness and pushed the cart out of the way," Lady Charlotte went on. "But Belinda has a nasty gouge—"

"And if you please, sir," the coachman broke in, "the mare belongs in my care, only her ladyship being in a taking—"

"What, you'll say my lady's out of her senses, will you?" the groom said, chin jutting out as he took a step toward the coachman. "She's got better sense than you."

"Jenkins, I will not have an altercation," Lady Charlotte said firmly.

The groom backed away, but he wouldn't be quelled. "Black ointment, in a case like this," he grumbled. He looked at Darius. "I ask you, sir—"

"Since you do ask, I should recommend that you first apply a poultice," Darius said briskly. "Fine bran mixed with boiling water and linseed paste."

Jenkins threw a triumphant look at the coachman. The latter's flush darkened to maroon. "Your ladyship, meaning no disrespect to the gentleman, but we always uses the black ointment," he said.

"We shall use the poultice the gentleman recommends," said Lady Charlotte, returning her attention to the mare. "You may not be aware, Fewkes, that this is the famous Mr. Carsington who wrote the treatise on pigs. We all know how Lord Lithby feels about that pamphlet. Whatever Mr. Carsington says regarding livestock must be considered holy writ."

Fewkes muttered something. He bestowed one murderous glower upon Jenkins, then stalked out.

"Maybe the gentleman will be so good as to explain to her ladyship how it's safe enough to let me tend the mare," Jenkins said, "now as matters is settled and old Quack-'em and Burn-'em won't be putting his fat, warty hams on her?" His affectionate glance at his mistress stripped any hint of disrespect from the speech.

Darius deduced that Jenkins, too, had known Lady Charlotte since she was a girl.

She thrust the rag into the groom's hand. "In future, kindly carry on your disputes outside of the stables in a place where others cannot hear you instead of upsetting the horses and setting a bad example for the other staff."

Jenkins apologized, and she walked out, spine stiff.

Darius followed her. "A troublesome coachman, I gather," he said.

She turned into a graveled path. "I don't know what's got into Fewkes," she said.

"Drink, I should say, judging by the condition of his skin as well as his behavior," Darius said.

"He never used to drink," she said. "Or not so much as to seem so . . . dangerous. I have never known him to be so belligerent as he was today. But then, I never have to deal with him directly. If my father had been here—but he wasn't—and I am merely the young lady of the family, qualified only to judge fashion and fripperies."

"That is no excuse for bullying," Darius said.

"I was not firm enough," she said, "because I did not know what to do. One ought to defer to Fewkes, as the superior in rank, but one could not, because he was . . ."

"Wrong," Darius said. "And filthy drunk in the bargain. My father would never tolerate that sort of behavior. Fewkes would find himself tossed out on his arse before he could say 'black ointment.'"

"You're right. I had better tell Papa." She paused briefly before adding, "I must thank you for intervening."

"Ah, well, I was glad to learn my word is holy writ for somebody," Darius said.

She gave him a sharp glance.

He wished the words back, but it was too late. "Your stablemen don't take you seriously," he said. "My father doesn't take me seriously. Or my work, rather. Mere scribblings, in his view." He recalled the way his father had waved his hand, dismissing years of laborious investigation and careful experiments, disregarding the care taken to render the fruits of these labors into simple, lucid prose, so that any farmer who could read could benefit, not only men like Lord Lithby.

Though Darius had borne it stoically at the time, the recollection made his face burn.

He knew she saw his color change, betraying him.

His fault. He'd let himself become agitated. This was what happened when one's feelings were allowed to overcome one's reason.

During the ensuing long silence, he told himself it was illogical to feel embarrassed, since neither her opinion nor his father's signified, in the great scheme of things.

Then she said, "Perhaps your father makes no great matter of it because it is no more than he expects of you."

Darius gave a short laugh. "He expects nothing. He's certain I can do nothing right."

"No, he expects great things of you," she said.

He regarded her perfect profile. He saw no doubt there at all. "What a sentimental imagination you have," he said.

"I am not in your family," she said. "I view it from outside. I am well acquainted with Lord Hargate. I am an objective observer, as you cannot be."

The something again clicked in his mind, and he realized what it was. He'd found a clue. He put it away for later study. "And what do you observe?" he said.

"He holds his sons to higher standards than most noblemen do," she said. "If he appears dissatisfied with your accomplishments, it is because he believes you are capable of greater things. He is exacting, yes, and some people find him terrifying. But everything is so clear, is it not? If you have erred or displeased or disappointed him, he says so, plainly."

"Plainly and at length," Darius said. "If he hears about the state of my road and your accident—" He broke off with a short laugh. "Why do I say 'if'? He's bound to hear of it. If no one else tells him, my grandmother will. She hears everything—and I'll never hear the end of it."

"That's very likely," she said. "But you must not mind what they say. The accident was not your fault but mine. The road is bad, yes, but it is not as though I've never driven on rutted roads before. This is the country, after all. The trouble is, I let my attention wander."

Being so fair-complected, she colored easily. He was not surprised to see her blush this time, but he was surprised to see the rosy tint swiftly drain away, leaving her ghostly white. Her lips compressed in a tight line.

"You're upset about the horse," he said.

"Yes, yes!" Her eyes glistened, and she blinked rapidly, refusing to weep. She clenched her fists. "I cannot believe I was so stupid and careless. I failed her, poor thing. They trust us because we teach them to do so. We make them our responsibility. Belinda trusted me to look out for her, and I betrayed her trust. I was not paying proper attention—and now she is h-hurt. And Fewkes might have hurt her worse."

"A small hurt," Darius said, surprised at this outpouring of emotion. "And your groom would not have let Fewkes hurt her. Jenkins would risk his position to protect the animal, I have no doubt. You must not fret about what might have happened. You know what ifs are pointless."

"What ifs," she repeated. "Yes, yes. Futile." She swatted at her eyes and essayed a smile. "Never mind. I feel like a fool, and I hate that." She looked about her. "Where am I going? The house is the other way."

"I wondered about that but said nothing, on the chance you were leading me astray," he said.

"Astray?" Her voice climbed in pitch.

"A man can always hope," he said.

Her color came back, a delicious pink. "I knew it," she said. "I *knew* it."

"Knew what?"

"Never mind."

She turned abruptly—too abruptly, because she stumbled, her heel catching on the hem of her dress. Trying to pull her foot free, she tore the hem. Her boot snagged on the torn cloth, and she tripped, pitching sideways toward the gravel.

He moved to catch her, but her flailing arms got in the way and, trying to avoid getting knocked in the eye, he trod on her skirt, ripping it more. She shrieked and jerked away, throwing him off-balance, but he managed to grab her as they both went down. He hit the gravel, and she landed on top of him simultaneously, her weight thrusting him harder against the small, sharp rocks.

For once, thanks to Goodbody's patient obstinacy, Darius was wearing a hat. Though it tipped over one eye, it stayed on, sparing him a bruise to his head and perhaps a concussion.

Not that he had time to care about bruises or concussions or the gravel digging into his backside.

They'd scarcely hit the ground before she was struggling frantically to get up. She'd fallen crossways on him, and when she tried to get off, he heard a ripping sound.

"Get up," she snapped. "You're on my dress."

"I can't get up until you get off," he snapped back.

"Move your leg, you idiot!"

Impatient, she yanked at the dress at the same instant he shifted his weight. The dress came free abruptly, throwing her off-balance. She toppled backward, legs waving comically. Her dress slid back, revealing not only dirty boots but a good deal of stockinged leg.

He had no time to admire the view—or even to laugh at it, though she reminded him of an overturned turtle—because he was too busy trying to protect himself from those flailing limbs. He grabbed her fist before it could hit his face.

"Let go!" She kicked and squirmed. "Don't touch me!"

He clamped his free hand over her mouth. "Stop shrieking, you idiot!" he said. That was all he needed: to be caught with her in a compromising position. "Someone will hear."

She wasn't listening. She was too busy wriggling this way and that, blindly kicking and hitting.

Fed up, Darius let go and tried to push her off.

She flinched at his touch and hastily struggled up onto all fours. She ended up straddling him—and that sent her into another flurry. In her clumsy haste to crawl off him, her knee landed on his groin.

He doubled up, gasping one short, very old English and most ungentlemanly word.

Through the miasma of pain he heard, "Oh, sorry. Sorry." He felt more movement as she shifted her weight. Then the knee, carrying all her weight, landed on his thigh.

He said the word again, with more feeling.

"Sorry," she said. "Sorry."

He really had to kill her.

He untangled himself from the skirts and frenzied limbs and staggered to his feet. He didn't wait for her to stand. He hauled her upright, grasped her upper arms, and shook her. "Calm down, curse you!" he snapped.

She stilled. She flashed him one of her murderous looks. She opened her mouth to say something.

He let go of her arms, clasped her face between his hands, and clamped his mouth on hers to silence her.

She froze.

He froze.

Then, *Oh, hell*, he thought.

And he kissed her.

Chapter 6

Don't touch me don't touch me don't touch me.

Don't touch him don't touch him don't touch him.

In the instant they fell together onto the path, an image flashed in Charlotte's mind, a picture from another life. She, so young, so happy for a time, tumbling with Geordie Blaine onto the grass, laughing.

And in the next instant, *Get up get up get up,* was all she could think—as far as she could think.

After that, it was all chaos and panic and trying to get away because she couldn't trust herself with this man.

The world had lit up when Mr. Carsington strode into the stable like a golden god, so tall and beautiful and so utterly sure of himself. Even the uneasy horse quieted at the sound of his voice.

Charlotte hadn't quieted. Her heart had leapt at the sight of him, lightening with relief because she knew he'd know what to do. He'd settle everything and save the horse.

Her heart had pounded, too, and not with relief

but with something less innocent, because he was beautiful, and she wasn't a good girl.

He was bold and improper and he made her want to laugh.

And now he was too close. He smelled like a man, and the scent was maddening. He felt like a man, and she ached for a man's body against hers.

Hold me. Touch me.

Don't don't don't.

Don't kiss me don't kiss me don't kiss me.

She beat her fists on his sides, then his back, but it was a sham, a joke. His big, capable hands were warm on her face. It had been too long since a man had held her so, her face cupped in his hands.

Turn your head away.

How could she?

He kissed her, and she tasted summer and freedom and the youth she'd lost. One tantalizing taste of him, and a place inside her opened, a great emptiness she hadn't realized was there.

She clenched her hands, trying not to touch him, but his mouth gentled on hers, and she tasted a sigh, or felt it. Her inner tumult began to quiet, and she felt a quieting in him, too, as he seemed to hesitate, to slow and pause. It was as though he'd felt something, too, something surprising.

It was his hesitation, perhaps, that made her heart give way. She felt it unfurling, even as her fingers uncurled and she rested her hands on his chest.

Only for a moment.

Only to feel it a little longer, the sweet wash of pleasure, the warmth of wanting and being wanted.

She wanted to pretend for a moment that all was right again, and this was the forever she'd dreamed of long ago: to be held so, in strong arms, where she was cared for and safe. To be kissed as though she were the only girl in the world.

To be loved.

She felt his hands slide from her face, felt him start to pull away, and she wrapped her hands about his upper arms.

Not yet, please, not yet.

Only a little more, another moment. It had been so very long a time she'd done without this. She'd forgotten how sweet it could be, a kiss, merely a kiss. She'd forgotten how perfect the beginning could be, before everything turned cold and ugly.

She held on and pressed her mouth to his.

Come back. I'm not done.

She coaxed him with all the sweetness she could find within her.

She coaxed him with all the dreams she'd given up dreaming.

She coaxed him with all the longing she'd stifled, all the wishes, all the loneliness.

Ten years.

It spilled out of her, as though an inner dam had broken.

Ten years' boredom, frustration, and anger.

Ten years' lying and evasion and manipulation.

Ten years' suppressed laughter, too.

It spilled out of her, all of it.

It was only a kiss, a mere kiss, but she kissed him with everything she had in her.

And at last he kissed her back.

He wrapped his arms about her and kissed her as though she were the only girl in the world and this was the last kiss in the world and all that was left in all the world was this kiss.

Only this kiss, so sweet.

... and wild.

... and hot.

... and devastating.

Her knees buckled. Her mind went dark.

The world shook and changed. Became unrecognizable.

The taste of him poured into her and swept everything before it. She was lost, tumbling along like a twig in a torrent.

She saw herself tumbling again, down to the ground, careless, laughing fool. Lost, lost, again.

No.

She couldn't. Not again.

She wrenched her mouth away. She planted her palms on his chest and pushed. He didn't move but only regarded her through eyes narrowed to slits of molten gold. The big chest under her hands rose and fell, fast and hard.

"You started it," he said. His voice had dropped to a rumble. She felt it low in her belly.

Her breath was short and she struggled to form words. "*You* started it," she managed to say.

"You didn't stop it," he said. "I was ready to, but you . . ." He trailed off. She watched a slow smile transform his face, making him more impossibly handsome than ever. "You know how to kiss. Well, well."

He was right on every count.

She wanted to kick him for being right, and for what he'd done to her, so easily, oh, so easily.

Ten years, and she was as great a fool as ever.

She ought to kick herself.

He shrugged and looked about him. His hat must have fallen off during the tussle. She watched him pick it up, brush off dirt and gravel with the back of his hand, and put it on, tipping it at a typically rakish angle.

As though she needed the reminder. A rake. She *knew* he was a rake. She *knew* the consequences. She'd borne the consequences for ten long years.

One kiss, and she'd surrendered.

Another minute and he'd have had her on the ground, her skirts up and her legs spread, like all the rest of his strumpets.

Yes, it was her own fault, but she couldn't bear it: the knowing rake's smile, the cool confidence— when she felt as though she, and the world she'd so carefully constructed over ten long years, had shattered to pieces.

She snatched the hat from his head and struck him with it. She hit his upper arm, then his chest. Then she flung down his hat, kicked it, and stormed away.

Darius remained where he was, waiting for his breathing to slow and his breeding organs to settle down.

That kiss.

He did not like to admit it, even to himself, but his legs were the slightest bit . . . wobbly.

On account of a kiss. A mere kiss. Nothing more. He hadn't put his mouth anywhere but on hers. He hadn't put his hands on her breasts or between her legs. He hadn't tried to unhook or unbutton or untie anything.

He couldn't. He'd had all he could do to keep up with her, with that kiss.

It wasn't supposed to happen, that kiss.

He knew better.

"*Moron*," he said between his teeth. "Did you leave your brain in London?"

He closed his eyes but opened them immediately again because the sight in his mind was too painful to contemplate. One insane act after another.

He, a man of science, whom other men of science looked up to. He, who devoted himself to reason.

Yet he'd panicked over her damaged dogcart, practically fainted with relief to find her unharmed, then whined to her about his *father*, of all things!

"This is unacceptable," he said. "This is . . . absurd."

He searched for his hat and found it eventually, under a shrub. He brushed off dirt and leaves. "Idiot," he growled. "Numskull."

He shoved the hat onto his head. It was the celibacy, he tried to tell himself. A fortnight at least, perhaps as much as a month or even more since he'd last bedded a woman. He couldn't remember when it was exactly, or who she was.

Celibacy was the trouble.

No, it wasn't.

The trouble was Lady Charlotte Hayward.

The trouble was his inexperience with blue-blooded virgins. They were a species he did not understand and didn't want to or need to understand. They were like . . . like an infectious fever. The only intelligent way to deal with them was to have nothing to do with them.

"You know that," he told himself. "You've always known that. *Keep away.* How difficult can it be?"

By the time Charlotte reached the house, she had herself under complete control. She walked past the servants in the same calm and self-possessed way she usually did, and they did not betray by the smallest change of expression any reaction to her mangled coiffure and cap or the ragged hem of her dress trailing behind her.

When Charlotte entered her bedchamber, Molly simply stared, her mouth open, while her wide brown gaze traveled from her mistress's head down, then up, then down again.

Before Molly could think of what to say, Lizzie came in. She, too, surveyed Charlotte more than once. "Did you have another accident?" she said.

"I fell," Charlotte said. "I caught my heel on the hem of my dress and tore it and tripped."

"Oh. I thought perhaps Belinda had stepped on you. Several times." A pause, then, "I was told that Mr. Carsington was here."

"Oh, yes. He was." Charlotte looked away from her stepmother's too-keen gaze and addressed the maid: "I need a bath, Molly. The sooner the better."

"He's downstairs, then?" Lizzie persisted.

"No. He heard about the accident and came to inquire after us. Then he left. That is to say, he left after settling a dispute in the stables about treating Belinda's wound."

Lizzie's dark eyebrows went up. "A dispute? Is that what took you so long?"

"I dared not leave," Charlotte said, and that at least was the absolute truth. "Lizzie, Fewkes was horrible. Mr. Carsington said he was drunk. Thanks to Mr. Carsington, Fewkes lost the argument, but he was furious, and now I'm worried he'll make the grooms or the horses suffer for it. Papa must be told as soon as he comes home."

As always, Lizzie understood what was important. "Of course, my love. But have your bath and leave it to me. I'll tell your father."

She left then, and Molly went out to order Charlotte's bath.

Alone at last, Charlotte walked to the looking glass.

It was worse, far worse, than she'd imagined, though she had painted a far from pretty picture in her mind.

Her cap was filthy, some of the lace torn. Her face was as dirty as a London street urchin's. Her hair hung down in clumps, with bits of hay stuck to it. One of her bodice hooks had torn off, leaving a hole, and the ruffles were soiled and limp. Dirt and grease spotted bodice, sleeves, and skirt. The rows of flounces at the hem hung in tatters.

It was too ridiculous. Even the sharp sting of shame could not withstand the ludicrous sight. She was a fool, yes, but . . .

"Ye gods," she whispered. "He kissed . . . *that?*"

And then she began to laugh, helplessly.

Sunday night 23 June

When Colonel Morrell came home after a long evening at Eastham Hall, he found his manservant Kenning awaiting him as usual. The colonel's faithful attendant was a small, wiry man of nearly forty with a head as round and hairless as a cannonball. He was not, in fact, completely bald. However, being perfectly neat and orderly, he could not abide straggling tufts of hair, and shaved it.

It might be said that Kenning shaved his fellows mighty close as well, down to the minutest speck of information.

Colonel Morrell gave the man his hat and gloves.

"I hope you had an enjoyable evening, sir," said Kenning.

This was a good deal too much to hope, but his commander did not say so. He didn't need to. Kenning had been with him since they were very young men. Their minds were as one. "His lordship's gout is troubling him," he said.

"I'm sorry to hear it," said Kenning. Their minds being as one, he did not have to add that he was sorry because he thought his lordship's gout did not trouble him nearly enough—to death, for instance.

Colonel Morrell started up the stairs, his manservant following.

"I heard that after church today, Mrs. Badgely was praising Mr. Carsington's cure for her arthritis," Kenning said.

The colonel said nothing, merely absorbed this information as he usually did. Carsington was ingratiating himself with the neighborhood. Any reasonably intelligent man would ingratiate himself with Mrs. Badgely. She was disagreeable enough when she liked you.

"Seems like he got a cure for everything," Kenning said. "Including the trouble at Lithby Hall's stables."

Colonel Morrell looked over his shoulder at the servant. "You're not referring to the coachman?" he said.

"Yes, sir. The one that took a fancy to the lady's maid Molly, who sent him off with a flea in his ear."

"I recall very well," said the colonel. "He's been treating his wounded feelings with large doses of gin. He should have been sacked before they left London."

One would have thought the officious Mrs. Badgely would have called Lord Lithby's attention to the problem. Since she hadn't—or his lordship had ignored her as he usually did—the colonel would have to find a way to get rid of Fewkes before he killed the future Lady Eastham in a drunken accident.

Bad enough she'd almost killed herself, driving

on that abominable road of Carsington's. Ladies had no business driving vehicles. They ought to be driven. But Lithby let his wife and daughter walk all over him.

"Fewkes is gone now, sir," Kenning said. "There was some wrangling at the stables Friday after the accident with the dogcart. Mr. Carsington stepped in. Fewkes didn't like it and went off in a temper. Mr. Carsington told Lady Charlotte the man ought to be sacked and she told Lady Lithby and she told his lordship."

And now Carsington was the hero.

It shouldn't matter. He was merely a rake. Colonel Morrell had guessed as much, and his uncle had confirmed his suspicions. Everyone knew the average rake was interested in conquest, not marriage. A rake who did not want to get his head shot off might steal kisses or take certain liberties with a wellborn girl, but he'd do nothing that would force him to the altar. The average rake, then, ought not to be a worry, especially in Lady Charlotte's case. She was remarkably astute about men.

The colonel recalled what Lord Eastham had said: *Them younger sons of Hargate's have a knack for marrying fortunes.*

The wise officer never underestimates the enemy.

Colonel Morrell had devoted much time and care to the challenge of winning Lady Charlotte. He wouldn't lose her to a worthless libertine.

He entered his bedroom. He thought the matter over as he undressed.

As Kenning helped him into his dressing gown,

the colonel said, "Fewkes was with them for a long time, I believe."

"More than twenty years," said Kenning.

"He'll feel ill-used," said the colonel. "He'll want a sympathetic ear."

"Yes, sir," said Kenning. "And I've got two of 'em."

During his Monday morning meeting with his agent, Quested, Darius learned that Lady Lithby had hired plasterers, carpenters, plumbers, stonemasons, slaters, and the devil only knew who else.

The devil knew, too, that it was necessary. The ornamental plasterwork in some places was crumbling, and on Sunday, a large section had fallen in his bedroom, narrowly missing Goodbody.

Though the house had been sealed against intruding wildlife, someone had missed a leak in the kitchen scullery. Over the winter—or perhaps several winters—water had seeped in, rotting the floorboards in a corner of the room.

The good news was, Beechwood had abundant timber and underwood that, according to Quested, would bring in a significant sum. Whether the profit would cover all of Lady Lithby's "improvements" was another matter.

But Darius could hardly tell her to stop. She had so far limited herself only to the most urgent repairs and refurbishments. It was up to him to find the funds.

For the first time in his life.

He'd had years of experience with country estates, at his father's as well as his brother's place in

Derbyshire. But someone else always paid for Darius's experiments and improvements. He'd never had to think about money.

His ignorance about costs was perhaps the most humbling aspect of this devil's bargain he'd made with his father.

Not that Darius would ever admit it.

He spent Tuesday and Wednesday searching the property for potential sources of income. This would have been easier could he have put Lady Charlotte completely out of his mind, but she plagued him, despite his staying far, far away from her.

On Wednesday, he was riding to Altrincham to look over the local timber merchants when he met up with Colonel Morrell.

They exchanged the usual civilities.

"I was on my way to call upon you," said the colonel. "I heard you had need of milk cows. I thought you would wish to know that Lattersley is selling his herd. It's a good lot, a dozen in all. I should take them myself had I room or use for them."

This was the first Darius had heard of his needing milk cows. He would rather be hanged, however, than appear not to know anything this man knew.

"A dozen?" said Darius. "Well, well."

"Not a moment too soon, I believe," said Morrell with a thin smile. "Lady Charlotte is hard at work upon your dairy."

Darius could easily imagine what Lady Charlotte was hard at work doing to his dairy. Digging a viper pit, perhaps. Planting explosive devices.

He was frantic to run to the dairy and make her

stop whatever she was doing. He made himself look nonchalant, and said, "I'm much obliged to you for the information. I'll send Purchase to see about those cows."

"A good man, your land steward," said Morrell. "I was glad to see that your road improves daily."

Being a man of reason, Darius could not knock the colonel from his horse, jump down from his own, and pound the fellow senseless as he fantasized doing.

No one—especially a dark and dashing war hero who was idling about waiting for his uncle to die and leave him a title and fortune—needed to tell Darius his road was a disgrace. A letter would come all too soon from Lord Hargate, who'd have more than enough to say on the subject.

Since Morrell had said nothing overtly insulting, Darius had to answer calmly, "I wished to avoid any more accidents."

Morrell nodded wisely. "Naturally you would. Lady Charlotte was much distressed about the cob. But the wound is healing quickly."

Had she confided her anxieties to Morrell? Had she wept over her horse with him? Had the great war hero comforted her? Not that Darius cared.

"I'm glad to hear it," Darius said stiffly.

"You're a hero at the Lithby Hall stables, it seems," said Morrell. "The coachman gave his notice before Lord Lithby could dismiss him. The rest of the stablemen are celebrating." Another thin smile. "Rumor has it that Fewkes has been crossed in love. Men can be strangely unforgiving when that happens."

Was the fellow warning him off? Did he think Darius needed to be warned off or that the warning would set him all atremble?

"I thought his trouble was spleen," Darius said. "He could do with bleeding. And sobriety."

"Perhaps, perhaps," said Morrell. "It is all servants' gossip, at any rate. My valet Kenning is too talkative, I daresay, but he was my batman, and accustomed to using his eyes and ears. His information saved me a good deal of trouble on more than one occasion. But I keep you from your errand."

They took a rigidly polite leave of each other, and Darius rode on toward Altrincham for a while. Though he told himself not to let the obnoxious colonel make him uneasy, he could not shake off the image of Lady Charlotte doing mischief in his dairy.

Never mind that the dairy was a ruin, its interior as gloomy as anything in Matthew Lewis's *The Monk* or Mrs. Shelley's *Frankenstein*.

Darius waited until Morrell was out of sight before turning into a lane. There was more than one route back to Beechwood and no reason for Colonel Busybody to know Darius took it at a gallop.

Cautiously Darius opened the dairy door. To his surprise, it opened smoothly and silently.

The last time he'd looked in—shortly after he decided to move into Beechwood House—he'd promptly shut the sticky, creaking door and gone elsewhere. He would not require much in the way of milk, cream, butter, and cheese, he reasoned. He could easily buy these commodities. Many families,

including great ones, did so. Lady Margaret must
have bought hers, certainly, given the state of the
dairy.

What he'd found the first time he looked in was
a dark, dank place, filled with broken furniture and
other rubbish, and apparently untouched by human
hands since sometime in the last century.

What he found now, first, was Lady Charlotte
Hayward.

She stood in the center of the room, turning about,
surveying the place, her hands clasped upon her
bosom. When her circuit brought her round to face
him, she jumped and let out a little shriek.

He would have laughed at the sound, so typically female, but his attention had swung from her
to their surroundings, and for a moment he was
dumbstruck.

He came inside and found himself turning in a
circle, too. "Great Zeus!" he said at last. "What have
you done?"

Whatever he'd been expecting, it wasn't this. He
would have been less astonished had he found the
dairy filled with unicorns.

He stood in an airy and elegant room. A yellow
and green flower design bordered sparkling white
tile walls. A checkerboard of black and white marble covered the floor. Light filtered through stained-
glass windows whose design and color comple-
mented the tiles' flowers. A broad marble shelf ran
round the room. A square table with a matching
marble top stood in the center.

Upon the table lay a bonnet, carelessly tossed

there, he could see, for it lay on its side, the ribbons dangling over the table's edge.

From ceiling to floor, not a speck of dirt or dust or mold or rust remained. Everything about him glistened and gleamed.

"What have you done to my dairy?" he said. "What happened to the Black Hole of Calcutta I was saving for the setting of the Gothic horror play I was going to write one of these days? Where are all my beautiful spiders? Where are my gloomy corners, where ghoulies might lurk? What have you done with the six inches of dirt on the floor? That was good dirt. I was saving it."

Her lips quivered and a small sound escaped. She made her face blank but not quickly enough.

What she tried to hide was mirth. He'd made her laugh.

She was happy, too, he thought. This was not the sly grin he'd seen when she'd delivered him to the talkative Mrs. Steepleton or the badgering Mrs. Badgely or when she'd made chaos of his library. This time she was truly pleased.

A truly pleased Lady Charlotte was a sight to behold. She seemed to glow from within. At this moment she was so beautiful—almost ethereally so—that it hurt to look at her.

There was another hurt as well, one he chose not to investigate too closely. He tried to persuade himself that he was . . . surprised, and it was the overall effect that struck him so forcibly.

Today she did not look at all disreputable, as she'd done the last time he'd seen her.

Kissed her.

Don't think about that.

It was nigh impossible not to, when she might as well have been wearing a nightgown. Yes, it was a pristine white dress garnished with layers of lace and ruffles, nothing like the plain gowns that respectable women wore to bed. All the same, it made him think of beds, and the thought made him want to muss her and make her look disreputable again.

What a sapskull he'd been to come here!

"I know what you're thinking," she said.

"I doubt it," he said.

"You do not believe you need a dairy," she said. "You need only feed yourself and a few servants."

"You have strange notions of what constitutes 'a few,'" he said. "At last count, thanks to Lady Lithby, I had sixteen million servants."

"Yes, but fifteen million, nine hundred eighty-eight of those are temporary," she said.

"I am all agog," he said. "You can add *and* subtract. Without using your fingers." He put his hand to his temple. "The blood is rushing to my head. Perhaps I'd better sit down."

He saw something in those blue eyes—was it disappointment? Then her expression hardened, the glow faded, and he wanted to cut out his tongue.

"Perhaps you'd better," she said coldly. "I wish to explain a matter of practical economics. You may find it heavy going."

Hold your tongue, he told himself.

"Practical economics?" he said. "You know what that is, do you?"

She looked away. "Sarcasm and mockery. How mature. What on earth possessed me to try to help you?"

"You've decided to help me?" he said. "That's novel."

Her blue gaze came back to him, scornful now. "Yes, it was the novelty. That must be it. Now, perhaps you would be so good as to allow me to explain my thinking?"

"I beg your pardon," he said. "I had no idea that elegant females thought—about anything other than bonnets and ribbons and shoes, that is. Pray do explain. I'm all ears."

She moved away, to stand by a window. She set her hand on the marble shelf and assumed the stance of a lecturer.

He should have found it amusing.

Instead, he was angry. She troubled him, and he was not used to being troubled by women. He didn't want to be here, looking at her: the impossibly beautiful countenance, its perfect oval framed by silken curls the color of champagne . . . the layers of ruffles and lace and ribbons covering her shapely body.

Her body, pressed against his.

His arms around her.

The kiss that had left him bewildered.

She'd walked away from it, from him, and now it was as though it had never happened.

Exactly as it ought to be, Logic told him.

"No doubt you believe it more economical for you to buy what you need for a household as small as yours," she said.

"Whereas repairing a broken-down dairy and hiring dairymaids is the less costly route?" he said. "Oh, and we mustn't forget the dozen cows I'm supposed to purchase or the cowshed I must rebuild to house them. Not to mention that I've yet to see the dairy scullery, where the real work goes on—as opposed to this playroom for ladies."

The dairy was used for very light work: separating cream from milk and setting cream and junkets. In the last century, fashionable ladies had played at being dairymaids, in the same way Marie Antoinette had played at being a shepherdess.

Her Ethereal Ladyship refused to be baited. "Perhaps you would be so good as to let me make my point without your sarcastic interruptions?"

Perhaps he could stop acting like an ass. Or if he couldn't, perhaps he'd better leave.

He gave an impatient wave, imitating his father's provoking style. "Say on."

She colored a little but went on coolly enough, "I know what I'm about. I've had your dairy scullery scoured, too. As you can see, there is no door to it from here." She gave a sweep of her hand to indicate the walls about them. "There will be no danger, therefore, of the scullery's heat and steam leaking into this room and spoiling the milk. You will be relieved, I'm sure, to learn that most of the equipment is in good order. You will need to replace the wooden gutters, but the vats and churn and coppers and such need only minor repairs. By the time you have acquired the cows you need, we shall be ready for the dairymaids to commence their work."

"And I need to hire dairymaids—yet *more* servants—because . . . ?"

"Lithby Hall has fifteen milk cows," she said in the patient tone usually reserved for small children and village idiots. "When the family is here, we use vast amounts of milk and butter. This leaves no cream to spare, nor milk for cheese making. As a result, for most of the summer and autumn months we buy our cream and cheese from others. We buy in large quantities. I can find out the exact figures if you wish. But it should not be difficult for a genius like you to do the reckoning. I have four younger brothers, two of them still in leading strings, and my parents are fond of entertaining. Now, we can buy our cream and cheese elsewhere or we can buy these articles from you. Which would you rather?"

Mortification ignited the smoldering embers of his temper. He'd told no one of his money troubles. He'd let wolves tear him to pieces before he did.

And here she was, in her ruffles and ribbons and lace that must have cost five years of a dairymaid's wages. Here she was, her nose in the air and her pale gold hair lit like the Botticelli Venus, lecturing him on finances.

"Thank you, Lady Charlotte, for telling me my business," he said tautly. "I wonder why I troubled to hire a land agent and a land steward, when I had only to seek your advice—in between your visits to the milliner." He glared at the ridiculous bonnet. "How foolish of me not to seek your counsel sooner. I blame it on my misguided upbringing. I was taught, you see, that it was vulgar to discuss money except with one's man of business."

Vulgar be damned. It was his pride she'd struck.

It was bad enough learning how ignorant he was about the costs of maintaining a property. To have her know it as well, and tweak him with it, was intolerable.

Her eyebrows rose. "I thought you did not care for rules," she said. "I had not thought to find you so close-minded."

"*Close—*"

"But I see what it is," she said. "I have wounded your masculine pride. My mistake. I had not thought to find you so childish as to reject sound advice merely because it came from a woman. How foolish of me."

"Childish?" he said. "*Childish?*"

"Yes." She moved away from the shelf and brushed past him, walking to the door. "I beg your pardon for wasting your valuable time. I humbly apologize for disturbing the perfection of your dairy. Tomorrow I shall tell the servants to restore the dirt."

He grabbed her bonnet from the table and stomped after her. "Don't forget your hat," he said. He held it out.

She took it from him and looked at it, then up at him.

She threw it at him. He caught it and flung it aside onto the marble shelf.

She turned away, head high, back straight.

Well.

He pushed the door shut before she could go out.

Her face went pink, but she looked back over her shoulder, the blue eyes flashing defiantly up at him. "Oh, now you are going to become all masterful," she said. "If you think you can intimidate me with your—with your great size and—and swaggering arrogance, I recommend you think again."

He was far beyond thinking. Logic, common sense, calculation, along with all the other components of the reason he prized so highly, jumbled into a useless tangle in his mind. He watched her perfect skin change, the pink washing over her face and neck. He stood near enough to discern the greenish tint in her blue eyes. He could see how long her lashes were, and how much darker they were than her hair.

Her lips were soft and pink and glistening, slightly parted as her breath came faster. He remembered the kiss that had all but brought him to his knees. He stared at her mouth and heard her sharp intake of breath.

Back away, said Logic. *Now*.

He grasped her arms and turned her toward him and lowered his head. She turned her face to one side.

That's a no. What could be plainer? Let her go. Give it up.

He clasped the back of her head and turned her back.

"No, you don't," he said.

He held her. She didn't struggle at all, but murder looked up at him from those blue eyes.

"Kill me, then," he said. "Go ahead."

Then his mouth covered hers, and Logic gave up.

Chapter 7

She didn't move a muscle. She remained stiff and haughty and angry, her mouth firmly shut.

Darius lifted his mouth from hers and regarded her stony countenance. He remembered how she'd glowed, only minutes ago, before he'd ruined everything.

He remembered how warm and yielding she'd been the other day, the sweet surrender that had made his heart ache, his tiny, hard, reputedly nonexistent heart. He could almost feel again the coaxing touch of her mouth on his, drawing him back when he knew he ought to pull away. Her gentle persistence had stripped away all his defenses, all his better sense.

Ah, well, then.

He brushed his lips against her cheek.

I'm sorry.

He heard her breath catch.

He lightly kissed the corner of her mouth.

Please forgive me.

A tremor went through her.

He kissed her nose.

Her eyes fluttered closed.

He brushed feather kisses at the top of her eyebrows.

"Oh," she said softly.

He kissed her temples and the corners of her eyes. He kissed the top of her ear and made a path of featherlight kisses along her jaw and kissed her chin and continued up to her other ear.

She made a half-stifled sound, suspiciously like a giggle.

He covered her face with butterfly kisses, and the stoniness melted away. Still, he didn't stop. He teased, he played, until at last her hands came up and grasped his shoulders. She turned her head to capture his mouth, and even when her soft mouth touched his, he held back, kissing her as though they were children, as though he'd never kissed before, and this was the first time, and it was all new, a discovery.

It was.

Her lips trembled under his gentle kiss, and something within him trembled, too.

He brought his arms around her, so carefully this time, as though he held an armful of delicate blossoms. He inhaled her scent, sweeter and lighter than any flower. He wasn't sure what he felt; he only knew he didn't want it to stop. He deepened the kiss but again by the slowest degrees . . . holding back, holding back, even while he felt the pull of desire, as sure and inevitable as the tide. Her tongue met his, and the taste of her was sweet and light and

inevitable, too, as natural as the clash and mingling of waters at the sea's edge.

It was a kiss, only a kiss, and everything in a kiss.

He wrapped his arms more tightly about her, giving more to get more, of the warmth and lightness and the strange sense of beginning. Her body yielded, pressing against his while she played with the deepening kiss, exploring, learning, taking it as slowly as he did, surrendering, as he did, a heartbeat at a time.

By the same slow degrees, feeling welled inside him. It came from someplace deep, unfamiliar. He had no defense ready for it, no protection now against it, and it built into a surge of longing so powerful that he staggered back under its impact and braced himself against the marble table.

He dragged his mouth from hers to press kisses upon her cheek and upon the arch of her brows and the perfect shell of her ear and the smooth arc of her throat. She caught her breath and let it out in a sigh. Then she lifted her hands from his shoulders and wrapped her arms about his neck.

He tightened his hold, pulling her closer. His hands moved over her back, along her straight spine and down to the sweet place where her waist curved out to her bottom. Down his hands slid, shaping to the voluptuous curve of her derrière, then pressing her against his arousal. She stiffened, but in the next instant she yielded, and pushed against him.

His control unraveled.

He reclaimed her mouth, and this time the kiss was deep and fierce. He grasped her bottom, turned, and lifted her onto the table. She clung to him, and he let his hands slide down over her dress to the hem. He slipped his hands under dress and petticoat, and slid them up over her feet, and clasped her ankles. Slowly, he drew his hands up the sweet curve of her legs while the silk stockings whispered under his hands.

Up, up, he moved, to her knees, the dress and petticoats moving up with him, rustling as they bunched up over his forearms. He let his fingers trace the shape of her garters but he didn't stop to untie them. He drew his hands up and up, and all the while, they kissed, no longer like children but like lovers, hungrily. Every pore of his body came alive with pleasure and with something else, something he didn't recognize, couldn't name.

He skimmed his hand over the thin cloth of her drawers to the place where the garment opened between her legs. His heart raced like a steam engine, as though he'd never before touched a woman intimately. And, as though he never had, and was almost afraid, he only drew the back of his index finger against the downy curls. He felt her sigh against his mouth. Then her mouth left his, and she kissed him as he had done her: lightly over his cheek, and to his ear. He felt her tongue lightly tracing the outline of his ear, then her lips along the angle of his jaw.

His intimate touch was equally delicate. He coaxed and teased until he felt her push against him for more. Then he brought the heel of his hand against her, and pressed. She rocked against his hand, her breath coming faster and faster.

His own breathing matched hers; her quickening pleasure excited him almost beyond bearing. He was aware of nothing but needing to be inside her and have her completely. Yet he let her pleasure herself until he felt her shudder of release. She gave a little gasp and moan, and buried her face in his neck.

He held her, his heart pounding so hard that everything seemed to be vibrating around him. His mind was thick, a haze of heat and excitement and triumph and need. Too thick for reasoning, let alone caution.

He hardly knew he was reaching for his trouser buttons. It was instinctive. But she caught hold of his neckcloth, forcing his face up to look into hers, and gasped, "For God's sake, *think*. Look at me. *Look at me*. I'm not one of your lightskirts."

He looked up into that ethereally beautiful face, and the last words lashed as sharp as any whip. He drew back abruptly and took a step away from her.

She pushed down her skirts. "Oh," she said. "Oh, I cannot believe this. You are—you are . . ." She let out a huff of air. "Curse *me*, why do I blame you? But you do not make it easy for a woman, do you?"

Darius barely comprehended. All he heard, ringing in his ears, was the one sentence: *I'm not one of your lightskirts.*

The warmth and longing and triumph and pleasure died under the icy blight of those words.

He stood appalled, ashamed.

This was a nobleman's daughter.

A nobleman's only, *unwed* daughter.

This was beyond stupidity. This was dishonorable, despicable.

And deeply disturbing. He was the servant of Logic, not of Lust. Never, never before in all his life had physical desire made him forget himself as he'd done a moment ago.

She slid down from the table and straightened her skirts. Then she shot him a scornful glance. "You needn't look so frightened," she said. "I won't tell anybody."

She caught him unprepared. He was stunned by his own behavior, far too shocked to notice the elevated pitch of her voice. He understood only the words, and these made him wonder if he'd lost his hearing along with his mind and sense of honor.

"Frightened?" he repeated incredulously. *"Frightened? I? Of you?"*

She lifted her perfect chin. "My bonnet, if you please," she said in precisely the tone she might have used with a lackey.

He was all but trembling with the turmoil within, almost sick with it. Yet he picked up her frilly bonnet from the shelf and gave it to her. He pulled the door open.

She did not put the bonnet on her head, only held it by the ribbons, as though he'd contaminated it by touching it.

"I won't tell anybody," she said with a small, scornful smile. "It is hardly worth mentioning, after all."

She sailed through the door, nose in the air.

He slammed it behind her.

* * *

As the door slammed shut, Charlotte let out a whooshing breath.

"You bloody damned *idiot*," she gasped. "How *could* you?"

How couldn't she?

He was infuriating, and she'd felt so sure of herself: no question she could stand up to him, no doubt in her mind of how she'd deal with his obnoxiousness. He thought all he had to do was act the conquering male and her heart would flutter and she would surrender.

She'd show him, she'd thought. How easy it had been to turn herself into a stone statue!

And then, and then . . .

. . . the light touch of his lips upon her skin, the tenderness that took her all unawares and made her heart ache.

Guile. It was nothing but the guile of a practiced rake. And she'd succumbed. Instantly.

Oh, but for a moment, a lifetime of a moment, it had been sweet, unbearably so. For that small lifetime she'd felt young again and could believe again. For that time it seemed a bud of true happiness was growing in her heart and blossoming in the warmth.

Warmth, indeed.

A euphemism for lust.

Yet for a time, for that small lifetime, she'd felt warm and cared for and safe. For that time, desire was a joyous blossoming of tenderness.

How could she be so deluded?

Easily, too easily.

She put two fingers to her lips. They were swollen and tingling. She was swollen and tingling down below, too, where no hand but her own had touched for more than ten years.

How gently he'd touched her. She remembered the way he'd gathered her in his arms, and made her feel precious. She'd even imagined his hands trembling . . . but it was she who'd trembled, fool that she was, with anticipation and hope and girlish excitement.

She could scarcely remember the girl she used to be or the excitement she'd felt so long ago when a man first gathered her in his arms.

She'd worked so hard to forget how wanton she'd been. She couldn't bear to think of it: the blind foolishness of a moment and the shame afterward, at what she'd given up so thoughtlessly, the most precious thing a woman had to give. The shame cut so deep she'd thought it would kill her. At times she'd hoped it would.

She doubted she and Geordie Blaine had had time for tenderness, even if he were capable of it, which was most unlikely. Their few couplings had been so furtive and hurried. She had loved him madly—or thought it was love—and she'd been ignorant. She had felt pleasure—or the madness of infatuation— simply to be with him, to be daring and defiant.

So there, Papa. Forget Mama so quickly, will you? Marry again, as though she never mattered, as though I never mattered? Forget me, too, will you?

Anger, loneliness, fear of losing her father as well

as her mother: She understood all the whys now.

She'd churned with feelings, far more than a spoiled, sheltered girl could manage, certainly.

She must have forgotten a good deal, though, because nothing she could recall of that time resembled what she'd experienced minutes earlier with Mr. Carsington. If he hadn't been holding her, she would have tumbled from the dairy table and melted into a puddle on the floor.

Wicked man. He was too curst skilled by half.

And she was the greatest ignoramus of a woman who'd ever walked the face of the earth.

Another minute and he'd have had her, there on the table of the dairy, like the sluttish dairymaids in those lewd prints her boy cousins had tried to shock her with.

Another minute and—

But it hadn't happened. She was not sure where or how she'd found the presence of mind to stop him, but she had.

Then—and again she had no idea where salvation had come from—she'd said the first thing that came into her head, and it turned out to be exactly the right thing, finally.

Hardly worth mentioning.

She glanced back at the closed door.

It was a wonder he hadn't thrown her out of the dairy bodily.

He could do it, too, easily.

He was not only large but he had the muscles of a blacksmith.

"Oh," she said, and she ached, because she could

feel it yet, the warmth of his big body, the strength of those muscled arms.

She pressed her fist against her mouth. She had to get away. Far away.

She hurried down the footpath, putting on her bonnet and tying the ribbons as she went.

Thunk. Thunk. Thunk.

This was the sound Darius's head made as it struck the dairy door, about ten minutes after he slammed it behind Lady Charlotte.

He needed to hit somebody, and the logical target was himself.

"You *moron.*"

Thunk.

"Half-wit."

Thunk.

"Imbecile."

Thunk.

He stepped back from the door and sank onto a stool. There he sat for a time, clutching his head.

The pain was a relief from the stew in his mind.

So close he'd come, so close.

Another minute and he'd have ravished her. And then . . . and then . . .

It didn't bear thinking of.

He saw it in his mind's eye all the same: a hasty trip to the altar, and everyone knowing why, because there was no other reason on earth the likes of Lady Charlotte Hayward would suddenly become wife to Lord Hargate's youngest and least impressive son, whose sole asset was a ramshackle property whose house was tumbling down about his ears.

There was no way out of marriage in such a case, no way even Darius could excuse himself. No matter how unjust and illogical he deemed Society's rules, he couldn't change them. Gentlemen expected their wives to be virgins. If they were not, they would suffer either public disgrace or private misery. He couldn't change Nature, either, who'd designated the female as childbearer.

Whatever else he was, he was a gentleman who understood that to deflower her and abandon her was out of the question.

He would have to marry her, which meant that, henceforth, her father would view Darius Carsington as a fortune-hunting debauchée.

Henceforth his own father would perceive him as an unprincipled incompetent. Darius could hear the deep, scornful voice: *You decided it was easier to seduce an innocent girl and live off her portion, I see.*

His brothers would despise him. His mother would be disappointed. His grandmother would be disgusted.

And the woman forced to wed him would hate him, of course, for the rest of her life, for ruining her life.

"Errgh." He clenched fistfuls of his hair. "Errrrrgh. No. Don't think about it. Just . . . stop. It didn't happen. It's not going to happen."

To blot out the nightmare in his mind, he opened his eyes and gazed about him.

Sparkling white. Elegant.

He sighed. The dairy was . . . beautiful, really.

Not merely immaculate but arranged exactly as it ought to be. If she'd found no fatal flaws in the scullery, that, too, must be . . . right.

"Damn me," he said. If he had only listened to her in a calm and rational manner, the situation would not have become emotional and he would not have acted like a cliché.

She was Lithby's daughter, after all. Hadn't she told him how her father quoted Darius's writings? Doubtless Lord Lithby shared his agricultural enthusiasms with his wife and daughter. Hadn't Lady Lithby said that Lady Charlotte was a countrywoman? Why should she not know how a dairy worked?

And why should she not assume he'd be interested in increasing his income? What responsible landowner would not wish to improve the productivity of his property?

"Besides, you gave her a hint, you know you did," Darius muttered. "Trying to be so witty. *Viperabankrupt-me-remodeling-my-house-icus*. Perhaps she was quick enough to realize it wasn't entirely a joke."

Not that her motives mattered.

She was right, more than right.

He dragged his hands through his hair.

Now what?

Tomorrow I shall tell the servants to restore the dirt.

Had any other woman uttered the threat, he would have laughed.

But *she* . . .

After what had happened here?

She'd do it.

He thought and thought.

He got up and paced the dairy.

He stared at one stained-glass window, then another.

He tapped his fingers on the marble shelf.

He set Logic to work on the problem. He looked at it this way and that way, inside out and upside down.

And in the end, being a servant of Logic, he knew he was doomed. He must go to her and endure the unendurable, a fate worse than torture, maiming, plague, pestilence, famine, or death.

He must APOLOGIZE.

Darius hurried back to his house, only to learn that the ladies were long gone. He'd left it too late.

He debated whether to go to Lithby Hall.

But what were the chances there of speaking to her privately? Even if he weren't in her bad books, how could he contrive to be alone with her? The only time parents would leave a gentleman alone with an unwed daughter was when they believed a marriage proposal was imminent.

He must wait until tomorrow, and it must be at Beechwood. While privacy was difficult here, too, this at least was his property. He wasn't at the mercy of someone else's servants. It only wanted ingenuity to devise a way to get her alone for the thirty seconds he needed to say what must be said.

Since he could do nothing productive today, and as long as he was mortifying himself, he returned to the dairy, found the separate door opening into the dairy scullery, and inspected that.

It was exactly as she'd said.

Thunk.

The next morning, after shocking Goodbody by changing his clothes four times, Darius was in place, guarding the dairy door, well before the ladies were due to arrive.

He waited for half an hour, and no one appeared.

He waited another half hour, and no one appeared.

Another half hour passed while he tugged at his neckcloth and took off his hat and put it on again, flicked dust from his boots with his handkerchief, frowned at the dust on his handkerchief, frowned at wrinkles in his trousers, and drove away several confused spiders who didn't understand that their eviction from the dairy was permanent.

Finally, he gave up and went to the house, watching all the way for any servants Lady Charlotte might have sent to put the dirt back in the dairy.

He found Lady Lithby first. She was talking to the plasterer—a man named Tyler, Darius recalled. Having received his orders, the workman was leaving as Darius joined her.

After the usual civilities, Darius said, casually, "I wonder if Lady Charlotte is about. I wanted to consult her about the dairy scullery gutter."

Lady Lithby's dark eyebrows went up. "The gutter? You've found out her secret, then."

"Do you mean the secret about her being far

more intelligent than she lets on?" he said. "Or the one about her knowing as much about estate management as a man? Or is there another secret I'd better find out in a hurry if I know what's good for me?"

Lady Lithby laughed. "I should have realized you'd find her out," she said. "The average gentleman would not. If she did let on how much she knew, he'd humor and patronize her."

As I did, Darius thought.

"Poor Charlotte must let them talk about agriculture and never venture a remark, though she is as knowledgeable as any of them."

"She ventured a number of remarks to me," Darius said. "I was . . . surprised." Not to mention obnoxious, childish, close-minded, and generally despicable.

"It is not so surprising when one considers her father's character and the circumstances of her childhood," said Lady Lithby. "Charlotte was the son, you know, for rather a long while."

"The son," he said, and the pieces instantly fell into place. Thanks to the talkative Mrs. Steepleton, he knew Lady Charlotte was the only child until she was nearly twenty, for the first Lady Lithby had become an invalid soon after giving birth. Apparently, then, seeing no prospect of having a son and heir, Lord Lithby had made his daughter a substitute of sorts.

She'd viewed Darius's dairy as a man would have done, assessing its potential, weighing costs versus profit.

No wonder she'd looked so pleased. She'd seen through the filth and accumulated rubbish to its potential, and gone to work. When he'd found her, she'd been proud and pleased with herself, as she'd every right to be, because she'd judged correctly.

Darius's conscience stabbed hard, and Logic did nothing to ameliorate the pain. He, who prided himself on his intelligence, on his objectivity, had behaved like the stupidest, most immature of men.

Was this what his father saw in him? Intellectual conceit? Immaturity? Close-mindedness?

At that moment a fair-haired boy—one of the workmen's apprentices, apparently—ran up to them, cap in hand. He stopped short, his face reddening. He bowed to them separately. Then, tightly clutching his cap, he looked about him. Clearly he was lost. Clearly, too, he was not bold enough to address his superiors without leave.

"Yes?" Lady Lithby said with a kindly smile.

Thus invited, he spoke, the words spilling out in a rush: "Begging your pardon, your ladyship, but I'm Mr. Tyler's apprentice, Pip. They told me he was looking for me, and he was here with you."

"He went upstairs a moment ago," she said. "To the master bedroom." She explained how to get there. The boy bowed again and ran off in the direction she'd indicated.

"The master bedroom?" Darius said. He'd given orders that no one was to enter that room. "I thought—"

"I know, I know," Lady Lithby said. "We were to

leave it alone. But you had not realized the plaster was so bad."

Darius recalled—and he shouldn't have needed a reminder—how a piece of ornamental plasterwork had nearly killed Goodbody. "Of course. It had slipped my mind. Naturally it must be repaired."

"Your manservant has removed your belongings to the south bedroom," she said. "Charlotte is upstairs as well, in the corner guest chamber. She's sorting the contents of that curious trunk."

Darius searched his mind. Nothing about a trunk there. "What trunk?" he said.

"Oh, did no one tell you? They found it when they were clearing out the dairy, under a lot of broken chairs and tables."

Within the top layers of the trunk's contents, Charlotte found an assortment of elaborate masks, half a dozen exquisite fans, a hooded cloak of a deep blue silk, a linen stomacher embroidered with birds of paradise, and an old-fashioned corset. There were a few letters and books, too, including a copy of Alexander Pope's *The Rape of the Lock*, its pages filled with pressed flowers: ancient roses, violets, daisies, pansies, and forget-me-nots.

Last, she found a small black silk bag that tied with ribbons.

Charlotte was kneeling on a cushion in front of the open trunk, the various contents she'd unearthed neatly sorted and arranged about her. She frowned over the mysterious bag in her hand. It did not seem sturdy enough to serve as a purse of any kind. What did it hold? Handkerchiefs? Was it an old style of pocket to wear under one's skirts? But why would it need such large ribbons?

From somewhere to her right a deep voice said, "A wig bag. I haven't seen one of those since Cousin Hector died."

Her heart instantly sped to triple time. She made herself turn calmly in the direction of the voice. Mr. Carsington stood in the doorway, leaning against the doorpost, his arms folded over his big chest.

How long had he stood there, watching her?

And wasn't "stood" a completely inadequate word for what he did? He not only seemed to take over the room even before he entered it but made the space seem too small to contain him. This was probably because he occupied her, completely.

She was aware with all her being of the arrogant Apollo on the threshold, his hair and eyes glinting gold. She was aware, too aware, of the broad shoulders and chest, the taut waist and long legs. She could almost feel those powerful arms wrapping about her as they'd done yesterday. She could almost feel the warmth of his hard body . . . the touch of his mouth on her cheek . . . those teasing kisses that had made her giggle, made her feel like a girl again . . .

Don't forget how near you came to doing exactly what you did when you were a girl, she told herself.

"A wig bag," she repeated calmly, while she rose calmly, too, while every pulse point of her body seemed to be jumping against her skin.

"A gentleman would wear it to tie up the queue of

his wig," said Mr. Carsington. "Cousin Hector was one of my mother's relations. An old-fashioned fellow." He paused, frowning. "As I seem to be. Lady Charlotte, I must speak to you."

"Are you not doing so?" she said.

He entered the room, closing the door behind him.

"You must open the door," she said.

He closed his eyes, made a growling sound, opened his eyes, then opened the door a crack. "Very well, if you insist on having witnesses."

Her heart sped up to quadruple time. "Witnesses?"

"I have come to speak to you about what happened yesterday," he said.

She was sweating. Why had she not thought to have a servant open the windows?

"Nothing happened," she said.

"Something did happen," he said. "I may be a blockhead but I do understand my duty."

He advanced and, to her horror, sank down on one knee.

She retreated a pace. "No! Get up! You must get up."

"If I stand I won't be abject enough," he said. "By rights I ought to crawl on my belly."

"Mr. Carsington, really," she said. "How can you be so medieval?"

"Medieval?"

"Yes. It was—it was nothing. Good heavens, I am twenty-seven years old. Really. You must get up. If you do not, I will not listen to you." She edged around him and started toward the door.

"You must," he said. "I have been tormented like—like—well, I'm not sure what, but it's deuced unpleasant and it's either this or hit my head against the door, repeatedly, until I'm unconscious."

She stopped and turned and stared at him. "What on earth are you talking about?"

"I'm here to apologize," he said. "For my stupidity and ingratitude and—and close-mindedness. Instead of fussing about curtains and wall coverings, you undertook a project of economic value to Beechwood. A great many men would not have seen the potential of that pit of filth on my property. You did. I most humbly beg your pardon for my childish, ungentlemanly behavior. I should have gone on my knees to thank you, instead of mocking and spurning your work and care in my dairy."

A wave of relief and happiness flooded through her. It was even better than the happiness she'd felt yesterday when the servants left and she could stand back and simply enjoy the satisfaction of a job well done. She had felt so proud of herself . . . and so disappointed in his reaction.

If only she'd had the good sense to walk out then, instead of trying to explain herself, trying to win an acknowledgment, a sign of approval.

She'd learned her lesson, though. She would keep her distance from now on. "The dairy," she said. "Oh."

He rose. "Yes, the dairy." His golden eyes narrowed and focused, falconlike, on her. "What did you think I came to say?"

What else but "Marry me"? To answer yes was out of the question. He'd find out she wasn't the innocent he thought she was, and he'd hate her for deceiving him. Naturally she must say no . . . but oh, it was a great relief not to have to deal with that wretched business at all.

"Nothing," she said brightly. "Thank you. I accept your apology. I must be going." She continued toward the door.

He swiftly overtook her and blocked her exit. "You thought I was offering matrimony," he said. "That was why you looked so frightened."

"I was not frightened," she lied. "I was shocked. I could not believe that a man of your—of your progressive inclinations would believe it necessary to—to . . . propose marriage." She swallowed. "Because of . . . a minor incident."

His eyebrows went up. "A minor incident like a kiss," he said, his voice very low. "And an orgasm. But do you know," he added meditatively, "marriage did not strike me as an appropriate course of action."

And why does this fail to surprise me? she thought. What rake would ever consider marriage appropriate?

"Good," she said. "Because it would be silly." She remembered the right thing she'd found to say yesterday, the way to make him hate her.

She lifted her chin and put her nose up and said, "I told you that the episode didn't signify."

"The episode," he said. "You mean when I put

my tongue down your throat and lifted your skirts and put my hand on your pudenda in that hardly-worth-mentioning way."

"It would be good of you not to mention it," she said.

"I'm not good," he said.

"That much I have ascertained for myself," she said. "And now if you would be so good—I mean to say, if you would refrain from blocking the door, I should like to take myself someplace where you are not."

He pulled the door fully open. She marched through it, her chin so high that her neck ached.

"Just one thing," he said.

"Yes?" she said without turning around.

"You won't put the dirt back in the dairy?" he said.

"Certainly not," she said. "That would be childish. Good day, Mr. Carsington."

She sailed away in all her haughty state, back poker straight, nose aloft.

"Look out!" a young voice called.

Too late.

She felt the bucket before she saw it. Her foot struck it at the same time she heard the warning, and the bucket toppled over, spilling water. She stopped short, but her thin-soled shoes slid on the wet floor. She tottered first one way then the other, trying to get her balance, but she couldn't. One foot went out from under her, and she saw the floor coming up to meet her . . .

Then strong arms lashed about her, pulling her

up and back. She fell back against Mr. Carsington, her heart beating too fast, her breath coming too quick and shallow.

It all happened quickly and could have ended quickly. As soon as she became aware of the strength and warmth of the body bracing hers, as soon as she realized she was sinking there, her brain softening, she started to pull away.

Then she saw him.

A boy looking up at her, eyes wide.

He was saying something and Mr. Carsington was saying something but she couldn't make out the words through the drumming in her ears. She saw the child, then she couldn't see him because everything was blurry, suddenly.

She drew in a long, unsteady breath and let it out. She closed her eyes and opened them again.

He was still there and it wasn't a dream. It wasn't a fancy.

Pale gold hair with a wayward curl and the world's most obstinate cowlick.

Her hair.

But the eyes weren't hers.

One was blue, one hazel.

Geordie's eyes.

Don't faint, she told herself. *Whatever you do, don't faint.*

Chapter 8

Darius expected Lady Charlotte to break away from him, with an elbow to his ribs for emphasis. Instead she went still, very still. In that strange stillness he became too aware of his hands on her waist and the scent of her and the smooth skin of her neck, inches from his mouth.

His hands itched to move upward—and downward and sideways and everywhere. He could draw her back into the room and close the door and . . .

Oh, yes, there was a brilliant idea.

Let go. Now. And go away. Far away.

Before he could do so, he felt a tremor go through her. Had she twisted her ankle when she tripped? Sprained it?

"Are you all right?" he said.

The boy spoke at the same time: "I'm so sorry, your ladyship. I saw that bucket when I came by the first time. I knew it oughtn't to be left there." He looked ready to cry.

"Never mind, never mind—Pip, is it?" Darius said.

The boy nodded, his worried gaze on Lady Charlotte. "It's actually Philip, your ladyship. Philip Ogden. But everyone calls me Pip. I knew that bucket oughtn't to be left there, but Mr. Tyler was shouting for me. I meant to come right back but I didn't get here quick enough."

"No harm done," Darius said. "Her ladyship isn't hurt." *I hope.* "Still, the floor is slippery, and someone else might take a tumble. Find a maid, as quick as you can, to mop it up."

"Yes, sir." The boy was off like a shot.

"Are you all right?" Darius asked her.

"Yes, yes."

"You can stand on your own? You haven't sprained an ankle?"

"No."

He let go of her waist but as he moved to one side of her, she grasped his arm. He looked at her. Her face was as pale as death. His heart pumped harder. "What's wrong?" he said. "You look as though you've seen a ghost. Did you see your life flash past you? I should have thought you'd be accustomed to falling on your face. Really, you are the clumsiest woman I've ever met."

"I need some air," she said.

No flash of the blue eyes, no cutting answer. Truly alarmed now, he swept her up into his arms.

She didn't object. She did not beat on his shoulders or slap him or box his ears or even try to crush his vanity. She closed her eyes and rested her head on his shoulder. "I need some air," she said.

He carried her back into the room where he'd

found her, crossed to the nearest window, and deposited her on the window seat. He flung open the window. She leaned on the sill, facing outward but with her eyes closed.

He sat beside her, anxiously studying her face. By degrees, the color began to return.

Finally, she opened her eyes, turned away from the window, and met his gaze. "How odd," she said. "For a moment I felt quite lightheaded. Perhaps it was from poking about in that musty trunk. Though today is cool enough, I should have had the windows opened. Or perhaps the dizziness was a delayed reaction to the shocking sight of you on bended knee. And the shocking sound of you apologizing."

"You couldn't be half as shocked as I was, having to do it," he said. Her color was returning but all was not well. The tautness at the corners of her eyes bespoke pain. Her voice was thin and fragile.

"I should have sent the lad for a glass of water," he said. "Shall I summon a servant? It's not as though we've a shortage of them." He looked about the room. "Are the bellpulls working?"

"I don't need a glass of water," she said. "It was nothing. A momentary dizziness. I'm quite recovered."

He didn't think she was.

He wasn't, certainly. His gut was in knots.

She had been very ill at one time, for a long time, he remembered. Had the ailment returned?

"It must have been a combination of events," he said. He had to concentrate to keep his tone light.

"My shocking apology following all your hard work of emptying the trunk. I shall not ask why you didn't let a maid do it while you sat here, supervising."

"You should not have to ask," she said. "Can you not see how boring it is always to have someone else do everything, even the lightest tasks? Can you not understand how tiresome it is, always to be looking on, never to be *doing*? But you would not understand, because you are a man, and you do not have someone hovering over you constantly and doing for you and watching you as though you were completely helpless and brainless."

"You are out of sorts, I see," he said. "Perhaps it is the menses."

She shot him one of her I-must-kill-you-now looks.

A promising sign.

"Many women become weakened during the menses because of the loss of blood," he said. "That would account for your lightheadedness. The imbalance this loss of blood causes to the bodily system no doubt explains the irritability that is so often a symptom as well."

She gazed at him for a long moment. "Have you any idea," she said, "how aggravating you are?"

She was definitely recovering her spirits.

A weight lifted from his. "I should like to know how I could fail to have an idea of it," he said, "since everyone in my family tells me, repeatedly. My grandmother in particular. She says that of all the aggravating men in the family—and that includes *Rupert*, she always takes care to remind me—I am the most aggravating. That, according to her, is my most remarkable achievement."

Lady Charlotte looked away from him and out of the window. She folded her hands in her lap and gave a little sigh. Then she turned her gaze to the trunk.

"You might soften your grandmother's feelings if you gave her one of the fans," she said. "They are splendid."

"Grandmother Hargate cannot be softened," he said. "Melting granite would be easier. Still, she does like fripperies."

He left the window seat and went to the trunk. "What a curious conglomeration of artifacts," he said, squatting to take up one of the masks. "Lady Lithby said you found it in the dairy, of all places."

He heard her light footsteps approaching. He didn't look up. Out of the corner of his eye he saw the hem of her dress, and the thin-soled, soft kid shoes, tied with ribbons and water-spotted. He remembered putting his hands on her feet and following the rise of her instep. He remembered the feel of her legs under his hand and the whisper of her stockings. He remembered the miraculous softness between her legs . . . and the way she'd trembled under his touch.

He felt a stab of something. Regret? Frustration? Who could say what it was? Feelings of some kind. Exactly what he didn't need.

Resolutely he gathered his wayward thoughts, shoved them into a distant recess of his mind, and planted his full attention on the chest's contents.

"I've no idea how it ended up there," she said. "We found a great deal else that didn't belong, but those were all discards: broken furniture and such. When the servants opened the trunk, I expected to find a nest of mice or a lot of decayed rubbish. But it was supremely well made, as you see. The lid fits snugly. The mice didn't get in, and nothing seems the worse for damp."

"It looks like a seaman's chest," he said. "Made to withstand abuse and wet."

He noticed the letters. "More of Lady Margaret's mad wills, do you think?" he said. "Or love letters?"

"I don't know," she said. "There may be a story in that trunk. I shall leave you and your brilliant mind to get to the bottom of it."

The light footsteps moved away, the door closed, and when he looked up, she was gone.

Don't look for him, Charlotte told herself when the door closed behind her and she stood in the corridor.

The bucket was gone and the floor was dry. A maid had come, done her work, and departed speedily.

The maid the boy had run away to summon.

Don't look for him.

How many fair-haired women did Great Britain hold? How many women had Geordie Blaine bedded and abandoned? How many bastards had he left behind? And what of his family? He had siblings, cousins. Any number of others, the most distant relations or no relation at all, might have those eyes. Others might have left their by-blows through-out the length and breadth of England—and Wales, Scotland, and Ireland besides. And who was to say the child was anybody's bastard? For all one knew, one of the boy's parents, properly wed to the other, had those eyes.

The cowlick needn't be Charlotte's, either: the obstinate tuft at the back of her head, the bane of Molly's existence. The boy's cap could have made indentations that appeared to be curls and a cow-lick.

The boy needn't be ten years, one month, and fif-teen days old. He might be eight or nine or eleven or twelve. Some children looked younger than their age, some older. Eight was not too young for an ap-prentice. Boys went to sea at that age and younger.

Don't look for him.

Put it out of your mind.

Even if it is he . . .

But it isn't. Put it out of your mind.

She looked down at her hands. They were shak-ing again.

It had taken a supreme effort of will to keep from trembling all that long while she'd made herself stay in the room with Mr. Carsington. She'd made herself stay and speak calmly because she knew that if she didn't take time, didn't make herself calm, she would run out and look for the boy.

She could not have trusted herself with anyone else. Anyone else she might have ignored.

She couldn't ignore Mr. Carsington. He called her mind away from the boy—at least a part of her mind—and he annoyed and worried her and kept her feet planted on the ground.

He called her mind to the trunk and its odd assortment of mementoes. She couldn't shake off the feeling that it meant something. She knew so little about Lady Margaret. She was one of the numerous daughters of the Earl of Wilmoth, who'd gambled away a great fortune. She'd married Sir William Andover, who came of an old and wealthy Cheshire family.

Charlotte had tried to search her mind for more—fact or rumor—about mad Lady Margaret. She might have stayed and told Mr. Carsington what she knew. The two of them might have tried to piece together the puzzle.

She couldn't, not so soon after seeing the child. As strong as Charlotte's self-control was, she doubted it was strong enough. In speculating about Lady Margaret's secrets, she was too likely to give away her own.

Mr. Carsington was a typically thickheaded male in so many typically male ways. In so many other ways, however, he was exceedingly quick and observant.

She'd stayed with him only until she was sure she could trust herself not to hunt down the boy.

Don't look for him, she told herself. *Nothing can come of it but grief.*

And so she continued down the hall and down the stairs, and in time, out of the house, looking nowhere for nobody.

* * *

Though the trunk offered a glimpse into times long gone, it was not intriguing enough to take Darius's mind off Lady Charlotte.

The boy Pip and his worried look, however, nagged at Darius even more insistently.

Any of scores of people might be responsible for a bucket forgotten in the corridor. Workmen crawled and climbed, scraped and hammered and carved and sawed throughout the house. Servants filled the remaining spaces. Any one of these hordes might have set a bucket of water down and forgotten it.

And any one of them would be happy to blame someone else, like a young apprentice. Any intelligent young apprentice would look worried, too, in such a case, seeing a beating in his future.

True, Darius had had his share of beatings and did not consider himself much the worse for it. He'd deserved his punishments, however. So far as he could determine, Pip did not. Yet the lad must have been beaten undeservedly or badly in the past to look so anxious.

The concern was sufficient to make Darius abandon the trunk for the time being and seek the boy's master.

Since others were at work in the master bedroom, Darius summoned Tyler to his study and shamelessly adopted his father's intimidating mode. He sat behind the desk, a letter in front of him, and looked up at the plasterer from under his eyebrows.

"You wished to speak to me, sir?" Tyler said, tightly clutching his cap.

"Regarding the boy Pip," Darius said.

"I told him not to run about the house, sir," said Tyler. "I hope it weren't on his account her ladyship got hurt. He don't mean to be ill luck but he's like a black cat. People see him, and it makes 'em leery."

Darius merely lifted his eyebrows, as his father might have done.

"On account his eyes, sir," said Tyler. "Them queer eyes of his that don't match. It takes some people funny. They say her ladyship fainted when she saw him."

If only one could devise a vehicle that traveled as quickly as gossip did through a community, Darius thought. Artillery fire was slower than news racing through a household.

"Lady Charlotte tripped over a bucket," he said. "The boy had nothing to do with the accident. On the contrary, he tried to warn her. I wished to make certain he would not be blamed."

"I can't help him being blamed, sir," said Tyler. "Everyone blames him for everything. On account them eyes."

"Superstition," Darius said.

"I dunno, sir. I never guessed the trouble them eyes would be. But I was needing a boy to help me. Me and the missus, we've six girls and no lads. Pip's healthy and willing, I'll say that for him. Don't find many such, in or out of the workhouse."

"You found him in the workhouse?" Darius said, astonished. Pip bore no resemblance to the wretched creatures typically consigned to the parish workhouse.

"Me and my missus used to live in Manchester,

near the Salford side," said Tyler. "I looked all over Manchester for a lad. Finally found Pip in the Salford workhouse. Weren't there long, which is why he was healthy. Clergyman he lived with died, winter before last. If you spoke to him, sir, maybe you noticed as he was educated."

Darius had noticed. He'd had too much else on his mind to wonder at it, though. Now he recalled the voice, with no trace of dialect, and the bow, the gentlemanly bow.

"Don't I wish I'd had my missus with me that day," Tyler said. "She saw quick enough what a trouble it would be, them eyes and him being educated like a gentleman. But he was healthy, sir, and willing and cheerful, and I hated to take him back and start looking again."

"It's unusual for a gentleman's child to end up in the parish workhouse," Darius said.

"He don't know who his father was," said Tyler. "Nor his mother, neither. He's somebody's bastard, that's all we know. Yorkshire clergyman and his missus, name of Ogden, got him when a infant. Then they died, and he went to the other clergyman in Salford, name of Welton. Then *he* died."

This sad story was one of thousands, Darius knew. It might have been sadder still. At least this boy had been given a good home to start. Many unwanted children were simply abandoned. Many ended in orphanages, living in far worse conditions than those of the workhouse.

He could do nothing for them, however. He could do something for Pip.

"His parentage is not his fault," Darius said. "The color of his eyes is a quirk of nature. I do not hold with superstition and will not allow a child to be tormented or persecuted on account of it."

"Oh, no, sir, I only meant—"

"I wish to make myself quite clear," Darius said. "No one in my employ is allowed to beat a child who has done nothing wrong. In the matter of Lady Charlotte's accident today, Pip did nothing wrong. On the contrary, his behavior was exactly what it ought to be. I should be greatly displeased were anyone to give the boy reason to believe otherwise. Children ought to be encouraged to do what is right. Do you understand me, Tyler?"

"Yes, sir."

"Then you may return to your work."

Though the matter of Pip was settled, Darius continued unsettled for some time after Tyler left his study.

He doubted Lady Charlotte would faint because a boy's eyes didn't match. He also doubted that the menses explained what had happened. Though she'd seemed to recover herself, he was sure she was not altogether well when she left him to puzzle over Lady Margaret's belongings.

He recalled the illness everyone talked about, the so-called "wasting sickness" Lady Charlotte had suffered years ago. They all said it was like her mother's ailment. But "wasting sickness" was merely one of those exasperating terms that covered a multitude of ailments. Consumption, cancer, diseases of the heart, and many others all qualified.

Brooding in his study would not answer the question, he told himself. He might as well do something productive with his day, and go to Altrincham, as he'd intended to do yesterday before the provoking encounter with Morrell.

In the entrance hall, Darius found Lady Lithby conversing with a woman of neatly unexciting appearance who appeared to be not much older than she was.

"Ah, here you are, Mr. Carsington," said Lady Lithby. "I was told you were in the study with a workman. I did not wish to disturb you when you were busy."

Now what? "Disturb me with what?" Darius said.

"Good news this time," said Lady Lithby. "Mrs. Endicott is your new housekeeper."

His new housekeeper was plain and whippet thin, but her unremarkable brown eyes were bright and intelligent. Her curtsy was as crisp and neat as her attire.

"She comes not a moment too soon," Lady Lithby went on. "Our guests arrive in a fortnight, and Charlotte and I shall not be able to come to Beechwood so often or stay so long as we've been doing. But all is in hand. By the end of the day I shall have brought Mrs. Endicott fully up to date. Then we may leave a great many matters to her."

At that moment, the boy Pip hurried into the entrance hall, the young bulldog at his heels.

"Good heavens, I'd altogether forgotten her,"

Lady Lithby said. "I hope she hasn't been up to mischief."

"She wanted to play in the master bedroom, your ladyship," the boy said. "Mr. Tyler told me to take her out because it isn't safe there. Something could fall on her, he said. He told me to stay out, too, until he got all the broken plaster taken down and cleared away."

"She is not allowed in the bedrooms," said Lady Lithby. "You naughty girl," she admonished the dog. "You know you are not allowed upstairs."

Daisy only gazed at her blankly, tongue hanging out of the side of her mouth, with its crooked teeth. It was hard to look at her and keep a straight face.

"It's a waste of breath scolding her now," Darius said. "She's a dog. To all intents and purposes, they have no past. She wandered because she was bored. She must have been very bored to climb all those stairs."

"Ah, yes, how could I forget?" Lady Lithby said with that easy laugh of hers. "You are the animal expert."

"It doesn't want expertise," Darius said. "One need only remember that they're dogs, not children."

The boy found the courage to rise to Daisy's defense. "She's a good dog, sir," he said. "She came right away when I said, 'Come.' Didn't you, girl?" He bent and rubbed Daisy's head. She submitted happily to his attentions, tongue lolling, drool oozing out of the side of her mouth.

Darius recollected what the plasterer had told

him. "Lady Lithby is busy at the moment, Pip. Since your master doesn't want you underfoot, you shall help us by giving the dog air and exercise. I'm on my way to the stables. You and Daisy had better come with me."

Charlotte's unhappy wandering took her to Beechwood's stables. They needed a great deal of work. The sloped paving was in the process of being replaced, she saw. The window shutters and the racks were undergoing repair. The old-fashioned building was being taken care of and the horses looked to be well tended.

She hadn't come to inspect them, though.

She'd come because of the horses.

Horses, Papa said, were the animals to go to when one wanted calming. Pigs were good for reflection and talking over important matters but a horse was Nature's great tranquilizer. Some people believed this was because the animal's large eyes exuded a quieting energy. He doubted this was the proper reason. Whatever the true reason was, though, the effect was not to be denied.

Mr. Carsington's groom being elsewhere at the moment, Charlotte had the tranquilizing effects all to herself.

She stood inside the stable door, leaning against the doorpost and inhaling the familiar earthy aromas while she waited for Mr. Carsington's cattle to work their equine magic on her troubled spirit.

Her turmoil was beginning to subside when she heard his deep voice outside—and a heartbeat later, the boyish tenor, instantly recognizable. The stable offered only one way out, and that would bring her into their path. She moved farther into the building and pressed herself up against the wall, waiting for them to pass.

The voices came ever nearer, to the door itself. She edged yet more deeply inside, aiming for a shadowy corner where she might not be noticed when they entered.

"I understand you've had schooling," came Mr. Carsington's voice, so very near.

"Yes, sir. That is, not a public school, you know. Mr. Welton, the gentleman who took me in after my parents died, took pupils. He taught me along with them."

"He must have been a well-educated gentleman, then," Mr. Carsington said, "if you learned your speech from his example."

"Mrs. Tyler says it won't do me any good, talking like my betters," the young voice answered. "She says I'm not to think I'm above anyone else on account of it. And I said 'But I was in the workhouse, ma'am, and we were all the same.' And I told her I was as glad and grateful as any of the others to get a place and get out."

Charlotte pushed her fist against her mouth to keep from crying out. A *workhouse?* This child—not hers, no, he couldn't be hers, but even so—this innocent boy consigned to a workhouse with the parish homeless, jobless, hopeless?

"It was not a long time you were in that place, I understand," Mr. Carsington said.

One minute was too long, she wanted to cry. She made herself remain still, very still, looking straight ahead.

"It felt like a long time," the boy said. "It wasn't as long as some stay there, though. Mr. Welton died in the winter, and it was spring when Mr. Tyler took me on."

"I'm sorry you were there for even a few months," Mr. Carsington said. "But you had no one to take you in, I suppose, and it was that or an orphanage."

"I heard some of them are worse than any workhouse," Pips said. "Worse than prison. I know I was lucky, sir. And I got out, didn't I? Now I pretend it was a bad dream."

"That's probably best."

"All I have to do is do what I'm told," Pip said. "And do it the best I can. Mr. Welton said I must always do my best. Mrs. Tyler says I had too much schooling and speak too fine. But if I could learn from Mr. Welton, why can't I learn from Mr. Tyler? If I could learn from books, why can't I learn from doing? Why do they think I can't?"

Mr. Carsington must have heard the anxiety in the boy's voice, for he said sharply, "There's no reason you can't. There's no need for you to go back to the workhouse. If you lose your place with the Tylers, you must come to me, and I will find you a place. Do you understand?"

"Yes, sir, thank you, sir," the boy said, in a rush of relief.

"Never mind thanking me," came the gruff answer. "Take Daisy for a good run. She's getting fat from want of exercise. She needs to run and play. Unfortunately these elegant ladies don't run and play. And so the dog will only grow fatter, and stupid and lethargic besides. We can't have that."

"No, sir."

"Pip, I am charging you with running and playing with Daisy and keeping her lively—and out from underfoot of the workmen," Mr. Carsington said. "You'll see to this for me?"

Charlotte couldn't help smiling. He'd paid a good deal more attention to Daisy than one could have guessed.

He'd paid attention to an insignificant apprentice, too. She'd heard in Mr. Carsington's voice a degree of compassion and generosity that surprised her. Rakes, in her experience, were among the most selfish and self-centered of men.

"Indeed, I will, sir. You are very good to take the trouble to explain." The boy sounded as surprised as Charlotte was. "Where may I take her to play?"

"Keep to the gardens and park—such as they are—and watch where you're going. We are not yet properly civilized here, and offer a hundred ways to break your skull. Try not to trip over anything or fall into the ponds. Some of them are as thick as marshes, and you'll find falling in much easier than getting out again."

"Yes, sir. Thank you, sir."

She heard footsteps dashing away and Daisy's short bark.

Heavier footsteps came nearer. She edged farther into the shadows.

"You are the most deluded woman in the Northern Hemisphere if you think you can hide from me there, when you are wearing a light-colored dress," came the deep voice. "You were eavesdropping, Lady Charlotte. Yet one more to add to your long list of unfortunate habits."

She stepped out from the gloom. "I came here for solitude," she said, putting her chin up. "I could hardly accomplish that if I came out and joined in the conversation. Or should I say 'interrogation'?"

"It was an interrogation," Mr. Carsington said. "I spoke to Tyler. I did not want the boy to be beaten on account of someone else's error."

Her hands clenched. She made herself unclench them. "I wish you had told me," she said. "I should never permit such a thing."

"That's what a woman would say," said Mr. Carsington. "Since you are a woman, Tyler would humor you now and beat the boy later."

"And since you are not a woman, what then? Why should he not beat the boy later, whatever you said?"

"Because Tyler understood that he should have to answer to me, and because he could see that I was quite capable of beating *him*, should he disregard my wishes."

Her gaze shot to Mr. Carsington's hands. He had not yet put on his gloves but held them in one hand. It was not hard and callused. It wasn't soft, either. It was unfashionably large, the fingers long, not

thick yet sturdy and capable. She was sure that a
blow from those hands would not be a gentle one
. . . though their touch could be gentle enough when
he chose.

Devastatingly so. She remembered the light brush
of his fingers . . .

She hastily returned her gaze to his face. In the
dappled light of this corner of the stables, it was
hard to read.

"Then I thank you," she said. "It was kind of you
to take notice of such a thing and take trouble over a
boy you don't know."

"I know him now," Mr. Carsington said. "I had
only to notice his eyes to understand he'd met more
than his share of trouble."

She could not prevent the quick inhalation but
it was the tiniest of gasps, scarcely noticeable, she
hoped. "His eyes?" she said, keeping her voice non-
committal.

"You were too dizzy to note it, I don't doubt," he
said. "The boy's eyes don't match. One is blue, the
other a sort of green. Uneducated people can be su-
perstitious about such things. The devil's work or a
sign of bad luck, they call these oddities, when it is
merely an innocent quirk of nature. This combines
with other factors to make Pip's position less secure
than it ought to be."

"The Tylers seem to think him overeducated,"
she said.

"His schooling is a drawback," Mr. Carsington
said. "Yet another is his uncertain parentage."

The last sentence was a blow, and she felt as

though a heavy fist delivered it to her heart. But on the outside she was composed, as cold as ice.

"People can be . . . so unkind . . . to children with defects or without parents," she said through stiff lips. "As though . . . as though it were the child's fault."

He ducked his head to look at her more closely. "Good gad, are you crying? Well, what a softhearted creature you can be at times, to be sure."

"I am not crying," she said with a sniff. "And if I was, what of it? You are softhearted, too. I heard you assure the boy that he would not go back to the workhouse."

He would not let her lead him into the detour. He bent nearer still, and even in the uncertain light, she felt the falcon's gaze, too keen. "Something is wrong," he said. "You are not yourself. You've been behaving strangely ever since you stumbled on the water bucket."

She saw the boy's face, as sharp and clear as life, in her mind's eye.

Grief came, sudden and vast, like a rising ocean wave. She saw it sweeping toward her, threatening to swallow her as it had done ten years ago.

Utter despair. No way out.

No. Not again. If she sank into that darkness again, she'd never come out.

She brought her hands up, grasped the back of Mr. Carsington's head, and pulled him to her as a drowning man would seize a rope.

She pressed her mouth to his, and kissed him, as though she were dying in fact, and he offered life.

The small, happy lifetime he'd given her yesterday.

He wrapped his arms about her, as though he understood. He held her as though for dear life, as though he sensed the danger.

Make me forget.

As though he understood, he deepened the kiss, and sorrow melted away in the sweetness of their mingling. The taste of him was like a honeyed liqueur, cool at first on the tongue yet flooding her senses with warmth. Happiness.

This is right.

She dragged her hands down over his arms, feeling the muscles shift under the coat, under her touch. She spread her hands over his chest, broad and hard, and made it, for this moment, her own. Like a blind woman, she discovered him with her hands, and the chill of shame could not withstand the warmth of touch and the sense of belonging: she to him, he to her. Shame and grief dissolved. The past dissolved and with it the loneliness of the time since.

Only now remained. Only now mattered.

Now was his mouth, sliding from hers to mark her throat with its warm imprint. *Now* was his hands covering her breasts, molding to them as though imprinting their shape on his palms and fingers. *Now* was the movement of his fingers, over her bodice, and the tingle of her skin, under layers of clothing, as it awakened to his touch.

The warmth spread, and prickling sensations with it, swarming over her skin and under it and pooling in the pit of her belly. One moment. This moment. This happiness. To want and know she was wanted in return.

She remembered the tenderness he'd shown her and she gave it back, tracing the planes and angles of his face with her mouth. Her senses became vibrantly aware of a world of masculinity: the tickle of his neckcloth against her cheek, the light wool under her hands, and the male scents of starch and soap, the light fragrance of herbs, all mixed with the potent scent of his skin. She swam in sensations, touch and taste and smell. She was no longer drowning, except in pleasure. It was as though she'd slipped into a crystalline pool in some exotic place, far, far away from the world. The darkness of her mind now was pleasurable, not fearful. It was a summer darkness, lit with stars and a glowing moon.

She let her hands rove the way his did. She dragged her hands down over his chest and slipped them inside his coat, and let her fingers trace the sinuous lines of embroidery on his waistcoat. She was searching now, for the man under the fine cloth, and her hands moved on to the back of the waistcoat, where it gathered, then down lower still, to the edge of his waistband. She slid her fingers under it, to the fine, thin fabric—the only barrier between her hands and the skin of his back.

He made a sound as she splayed her fingers over the thin cloth, discovering the shape of his spine and the shift of muscle and the warmth of his skin. So alive, so strong, so beautiful. And she wanted him.

Now. This small lifetime, this moment.

She tugged at the shirt but there was too much of it and she grew impatient. She moved her hand to find his trouser buttons and found him instead, the most masculine part of him, large and warm and pulsing under the palm of her hand.

She held her hand there, her heart racing, with fear and excitement. She held her hand there while need built, low in her belly, throbbing, aching.

He made a growling sound and set his hand over hers. He held her so for a moment, then drew their hands away.

Still holding her hand, he said something but his voice was so thick, so deep, that her mind—or the morass that used to be her mind—couldn't make it out.

"What?" she said, in a voice that seemed to belong to someone else.

"We have to stop," he said. "Now."

She didn't understand. Her body ached, craving his. He was warm, and his body was big and hard and powerful. She wanted him. That was all she understood.

"Why?" she said.

He made another sound, a growl or a groan, she couldn't be sure.

"What?" she said.

"If we don't stop now," he said slowly, "something will happen almost immediately." A pause. "Then you will have to marry me." Another pause. "I do not believe this is what you wish to do."

The word *marry* was like a bucketful of cold water dashed in her face.

She came out of her mad paradise with a start, pulled her hand from his, and backed away from him.

"Oh, no," she said. She didn't recognize her own voice. It was low and thick, a stranger's voice. She looked at her hands, her wicked hands. She looked up at him, into the golden eyes. They were so dark now, watching her. "What am I doing? How *could* I?"

"That," he said, "was what I was about to ask you."

Chapter 9

Lady Charlotte turned away from Darius in a rustle of muslin and fluttering ruffles. She looked about her, at the horses, at the windows, the paving. At last she seemed to collect herself. He watched her shoulders settle, her spine straighten, and her chin go up.

"I was trying to distract you," she said.

"It worked," Darius said. In all his life, no one had ever distracted him as fully as she did.

Lack of practice, he told himself. Except for the brief time when he was an innocent, more or less, he'd had almost nothing to do with innocents.

No, that explanation wasn't satisfactory.

Practice or not, he was no longer a boy. He ought not to feel so shaky as he did now, like one recovering from a fever. The taste of her shouldn't linger like this. He shouldn't be so conscious of her scent. He shouldn't feel the imprint of her body on his, and his hands shouldn't tingle as they did.

Above all, he shouldn't feel as though there were more, far more to this than a torrid embrace.

What he felt for her was supposed to be lust, plain and simple. It wasn't supposed to feel like this. It *never* felt like this. He ought to know.

He spent most of his waking life desiring this woman and, after he'd had her, the next woman, and the next. Lust was reasonable and rational. It was the natural instinct of the male to copulate. This was the foundation, was it not, of the animal behavior he studied. Everything in Nature must reproduce itself. For the most part, the male of the species seemed to devote the greatest amount of time and energy to the business.

This wasn't reasonable and rational.

This was complicated. Aggravating.

Yet why should this surprise him? She was, after all, the most irritating woman he'd ever met. The irritation started with her being unwed and thus unavailable and went on to her capricious personality.

"You should not have kissed me," he said. *And definitely not like that.* "For any reason."

"I know that," she said impatiently. "It was . . . an impulse."

"Don't do it again," he said.

"Not likely," she said, brushing at her skirts with the same energy maids devoted to beating rugs, though he saw not a speck of straw or dust on the fine cloth.

"Your dress is perfectly clean," he said. "Or are you brushing off the contamination? If so, you're working on the wrong place. I never touched your skirts."

"They touched your legs," she said.

"You put your hand on my trouser front," he said. "You don't see me brushing it in that deranged manner."

"It is not deranged!"

"What is it, then?"

"I am keeping my hands busy because I want to slap you."

"That is patently unfair," he said. "You started it."

"You always say I start it," she said.

"I don't *always* say it," he said. "Only when you do start it." He paused, trying to put a name to what he'd felt—apart from surprise—when she grasped his head and kissed him so . . . fervently? Desperately? "Why did you start it?"

"Did I not tell you a moment ago?" she said. "To distract you. And you said it worked."

"But what were you distracting me from?"

She returned to brushing at nothing. "I forget."

"You have not forgotten," he said.

"I have," she said. "It could not have been very important."

"One of these days," he said, "I am going to strangle you, and when they ask why I did it, and I tell them, the jury will cry, unanimously, 'Not guilty!'"

"You are not going to strangle me," she said, "because I am going to strangle you first."

"I should like to see you try," he said. "That ought to be amusing."

"I'll be laughing, certainly, when your face turns black, and your eyes bulge out of your head."

"I see what you're trying to do," he said. "You're

trying to divert me from the point I am trying to pursue. It won't work. You said you were bored. Was that the reason you kissed me?"

She shrugged. "I don't remember."

"I understand that risk is exciting," he said.

"No, it isn't," she said. "Not with you. It is . . . boring."

He wasn't sure what she was trying to do, but he wasn't going to let her do it. He could be as tenacious as any bulldog. "It was not boring," he said. "Not for me, not for you. If it were, we wouldn't have a problem. But we do, and unless we cooperate to solve it, we'll end up in a situation neither of us wants."

"Marriage," she said. "Does it pain you so much to say the word?"

"As I recall, I said it only a moment ago, to bring you to your senses," he said. "I notice that you're not overly fond of marriage, either. Seven and twenty and not wed. It is absurd."

She stiffened. "How old are you?"

"Eight and twenty," he said.

"*You're* not married."

"I'm a *man!*"

One of the horses snorted.

"You're upsetting the horses," she said. She started to move past him, toward the door, then stopped short. Her Cupid's bow mouth shaped an *O*. She brought her hand to the back of her dress. Her eyes widened. "You undid my frock!"

"No, I didn't," he said.

"Who else do you think could have done it?" she

said, backing away into the shadows again. "It was fastened when I came in here. Do you think one of the horses did it?"

Plague take him, had he started undressing her without realizing it?

How could he not realize it?

Don't panic, he told himself. *Don't panic.*

"Oh, my goodness, someone is coming," she said in a frantic whisper. "Quick, do it up."

He heard it then, too: voices, male and female. Servants or workmen. They were everywhere, confound them.

"There isn't time," he said.

He strode to the stable door. He didn't know who the pair were, but it was clear they were a couple, for they had their arms about each other's waists. Seeing him, they hastily disengaged and changed direction.

He reentered the stable and went to her. She had retreated to the far corner once more. "Turn around," he said.

"You didn't need me to turn around when you undid it," she said.

"We stood closer then," he said. "Do you wish to plaster yourself against me as you did before?"

"I did not *plaster* myself," she said.

Still, she did turn around, and he focused on the fastenings. Though women's buttons, hooks, pins, and tapes were small and complicated, he'd had plenty of practice. They seldom gave him trouble. Yet his hands were clumsy.

Feelings, curse her.

"Talk of risks," she said. "What if they'd come in?"

"That was what they meant to do," he said. "That's why I stood in the doorway, in sight. Seeing me, they were obliged to find another private place in which to copulate." He finally got her done up. His hands were steadier now.

"Copulate?" she said, her voice choked. "*Copulate?* You cannot say 'make love'? Must you use that—that coldly rational word, as though you spoke of—of pigs."

Coldly rational. How he wished, at this moment, that were true!

"I never formed the habit of speaking in euphemisms," he said. "It is one of my numerous flaws of character. I might have used a shorter, very old English word—"

"You already used it," she said. "Last week, when I accidentally placed my knee on your privates."

"A lady is not supposed to know what that word means," he said. He frowned. "I'd always thought unwed ladies were not aware we *had* privates."

"I have boy cousins and little brothers," she said. "They think it's great fun to say shocking words and do shocking things, and well worth the whipping they get for it. You don't know very much about ladies, do you?"

"No, and I'd like to keep it that way." He stepped away from her. "There, you are done up properly. I hope you have learned your lesson. You must never assault me again."

"Put your mind at rest," she said crisply. "The

next time I want excitement, I'll shoot myself. It will be a good deal more fun."

She swept past him.

All he had to do was stick his foot out and watch her trip and fall on her face.

But that would be childish. Like saying shocking words. He wondered if she'd been shocked the first time she'd heard such words. Or if she'd thought it great fun, too.

Had she thought it great fun to see how many feelings she could stir up in Mr. Coldly Rational Carsington?

He stood where he was and watched her go out, head high, backside swaying.

She wanted him to think it meant nothing to her. She wanted him to believe she was merely toying with him.

He almost wished he could believe she was. He'd be able to dismiss it—to dismiss her—so easily.

But he didn't believe her. That kiss—there was more to it than caprice or boredom. Being such an old virgin, she might have learned a thousand ways to torment men while still preserving her virtue, technically, at least.

Yet he didn't think so, and he most certainly did not believe it explained what had happened this time.

A puzzle, another irksome puzzle.

He'd get to the bottom of it but not now. He wanted a cool head.

He pushed the puzzle aside temporarily and put his mind to the simple matter of saddling his horse.

By the time the groom Joel Rogers returned from wherever he'd been or whatever wench he'd been with, Darius was on his horse, preparing to ride to Altrincham, with far too much else on his mind to demand explanations.

Friday 28 June

All in all, it would have been wiser, perhaps, for Charlotte to keep away from Beechwood this morning.

The boy would be there, the boy whose face had haunted her all day and night. She knew that seeking him out would do neither of them any good. The odds were infinitely great that he wasn't hers. And if he was—and how could she be sure of that— what could she do? She couldn't tell him the truth, couldn't acknowledge him, couldn't take him back. She couldn't do any of those things without telling her father the truth.

Oh, he'd forgive her, but she'd never forgive herself—for the hurt she'd cause him, for the ruination of all his hopes for her. Worse than that, though, far worse, was the damage the revelation would do to Lizzie, whom Papa trusted implicitly. The truth would destroy that trust and with it, their happiness.

Charlotte knew all this.

Yet she wasn't sure she could keep away from the boy.

She wasn't sure she could stop herself from seeking out Mr. Carsington, either. She was too lonely now, too troubled by this child, too vulnerable to trust herself. Mr. Carsington made her believe in happiness, and he made her believe she could trust him. She'd already trusted him too far. She'd already stirred his curiosity, made him ask questions she'd better not answer.

In short, wherever she went at Beechwood, she was all too likely to find trouble.

But there was trouble at home, too. Everyone there was consumed with preparations for the house party.

At home she must hear the names of the gentlemen, again and again. Where they would sleep. Where they would sit at table. Which activities would allow this one to shine or that one.

At one moment, she'd tell herself she'd simply pick one gentleman's name out of a hat and have done with it.

At another time she'd tell herself she must proceed as usual, and redirect each and every would-be suitor to her cousins and friends.

But how could she perform her usual maneuvers, with Papa studying them all so closely, as though this was one of his agricultural experiments?

In the end, her father decided it. Charlotte came to Beechwood mainly so she wouldn't have to look at his loving face, practically glowing with anticipation.

At present she stood in the picture gallery that ran along one side of Beechwood's first floor. She was supervising the servants who were rehanging the paintings that had been taken down when the ceiling, floors, and walls were cleaned. This room had needed few repairs. It had not been used in a quarter century or more, having been shut up tight long before Lady Margaret's death.

Charlotte did not understand why. While Beechwood was rather ramshackle and wanted some modern conveniences, it was a handsome house, and the gallery was one of its most inviting rooms. It was neither overly large and grand nor too cramped and narrow. Filtered through the thick-paned glass, the daylight gently bathed the old portraits and softened the subjects' features.

Many needed softening, for they'd been painted in the stiffly formal style of centuries past. However, she found several more lifelike images from what she guessed was her grandparents' generation. She discovered, much to her surprise, that one strikingly beautiful young lady, wearing a richly decorated silk gown with a long waist and full skirts, was Lady Margaret, about the time of her marriage.

The painting hung at the far end of the gallery.

As Charlotte turned away from it, she caught a movement at the edge of her vision. She moved to the open window.

In one of the parterres of the formerly formal garden Daisy trotted after a boy in a cap, a thick stick in her mouth. The boy jumped and skipped in a circle round the perimeter of the barren garden, occasionally glancing back to see if the dog still followed. After a time, he began to laugh. He stopped skipping about, bent, and grasped one end of the stick. A tug of war ensued, Daisy shaking her head—drool flying, no doubt—trying to shake him off. The boy held on, but as the bulldog flung him this way and that—or he let himself be flung— his cap fell off, revealing hair the color of sunlight.

Charlotte's heart gave a lurch, and she nearly cried out. But she couldn't. Servants filled the gallery.

She folded her hands tightly at her waist and watched the boy Pip play with Lizzie's bulldog.

He let go of the stick and fell on his back onto the mat of weeds, laughing. Daisy dropped her stick, pounced on him, and started licking his face. Still laughing, he pushed her away, and she licked his hands. He sat up and, unafraid of the dangerous jaws, rubbed her wrinkly jowls and behind her ears.

It was too much, too much.

She ached to cup that young face in her hands and say, "Are you mine? Are you my beautiful lost boy?"

She had better get used to aching, she told herself. She had no right to trouble that child. Even if he was hers, he wasn't. When she'd given her baby away, she'd given up any right to him.

She must turn away from the window and turn her mind away from him. To move closer, to ask questions was asking for grief, no matter what the answers were. Even if he was hers, she couldn't have him without opening Pandora's box and bringing trouble to the lives of everyone she loved.

She tried, but she couldn't keep away.

She murmured a few last commands to the servants, put one in charge, and left the room. She could not stop. The best she could do was keep herself from running.

She was trying not to run down the stairs when she heard Lizzie's voice above her.

"Have you finished in the gallery, Charlotte?"

Charlotte took a calming breath, stopped at the landing, and looked up at her stepmother with her usual affectionate smile. "There was little enough to do," she said.

"You'd like to go home, then, and settle down to planning for our guests, I daresay."

"No, no, there's no hurry. You really ought to take a moment to look in the gallery, Lizzie. Now that we've let in the light and aired it out and removed about a century's worth of dust and grime, it's quite beautiful. I only left because I wanted to take a turn in the garden."

"Oh, dear, those gardens," Lady Lithby said with a sigh. "I wish I had time—"

"I am sure Mr. Carsington wishes you hadn't," said Charlotte.

"I fear you're right." Lizzie laughed, then turned away and started down the hall toward the gallery. She said something as she went, but Charlotte didn't stay to listen. She continued down the stairs, a little faster than before.

Minutes later she was stepping through the French doors of the conservatory onto the terrace. A clump of overgrown shrubbery obscured her view of the parterre. She didn't run but walked quickly along the neglected pathway. She heard boyish laughter and Daisy's short, eager bark.

She stepped through an opening in the shrubbery.

Daisy had the stick in her mouth once more and was teasing the boy with it. She would come close, shaking her head, then back away when the boy reached for it.

Charlotte had come to ask questions, but she found that she couldn't speak, her heart pounded so hard.

An infinity of a moment passed before the boy noticed her. He stopped short then, reached up to doff the cap that wasn't on his head, realized it wasn't there, and looked about for it.

Through the strange fog obscuring her vision, Charlotte discerned it lying on the ground but a pace from where she stood. She took the step to it, bent, and picked it up. She looked down at it, turning it over and over in her hands.

She looked at the boy.

Are you mine?

She opened her mouth to speak.

"Wrong hat," came a deep voice behind her. "I think this is the one you want."

She turned. Mr. Carsington held up her bonnet.

"I heard Lady Lithby call to you not to go out into the sun without your hat," he said. "She sent a servant after you, but I was coming in the same direction. In my bountiful munificence, I condescended to bring it to you myself." His glance fell to the cap in her hand. "Perhaps you will let Pip have his cap back."

Yes, she'd better. This was wrong of her, so wrong.

Yet her gaze returned to the cap in her hand. A few strands of fair hair clung to it. She stroked the coarse cloth as she would have stroked his hair, if he was hers and if she'd had the right and if what she'd done could be undone.

If, if, if.

"I believe Lady Charlotte fancies your cap, Pip," said Mr. Carsington. "Perhaps she's thinking of bringing it into fashion."

She turned her gaze to meet the boy's, his strange, beautiful eyes puzzled and wary now.

She made herself smile. "I was woolgathering," she said. She held out the cap. Cautiously, he approached. Cautiously, he took it, one of his fingers brushing hers in the process.

Her hands shook.

"You are very good with Daisy," she said through stiff lips.

"She's a good dog, your ladyship," the boy said. "Mr. Tyler told me to keep my distance. He says bulldogs grab your nose as though you were a bull, and then they won't let go. But she isn't like that, is she, your ladyship?"

"All the same, you'd do well to remember that she isn't a lapdog," Mr. Carsington said. "She might be young, and gentler than many of her breed, but bulldogs are bred for fighting. You'd be asking for trouble if you teased her cruelly or hurt her."

The boy looked shocked. "I wouldn't ever do that," he said. "Mr. Welton said I wasn't to hurt anybody or anything that couldn't fight back, or was smaller than I was. I asked him, 'What if a rabid dog came after me, sir? Or what if I was in the jungle and a wild animal was about to eat me?' He said it wasn't wrong to defend myself from anything or anybody trying to do me harm."

Mr. Carsington laughed. "I notice you began debating at an early age. Questioning your master? Looking for loopholes? My brother's nephew Peregrine is like that. But we keep you from your important dog work. Daisy is far from tired yet. Take her to the home farm and see if the pair of you can help my land steward, Purchase, with his rat problem. I'll pay you halfpenny a rat, the same as I'd pay anyone else."

The boy's face lit. "Oh, yes, sir. Thank you, sir." He bowed to Charlotte. "Your ladyship." He looked down at the bulldog, who was gazing up at him adoringly. "Come, Daisy. Let's catch some rats."

She watched the lad scamper away, his young mind as untroubled as that of the dog who followed so eagerly.

"I hope Tyler will not punish him for playing with the dog instead of working," she said. "It seems hard, does it not, to keep a child indoors at labor on such a day." She swallowed. "But you will say I am sentimental and irrational. Only privileged children may play on fine summer days. All the others must earn their bread, and precious little of it they get."

"You mistake me for my eldest brother if you

think I should say anything so pompous," he said. "Rathbourne is the philanthropist in the family, and the poor and the criminal classes are his special interests. Do you want your bonnet or not? You are getting red in the neck from the sun. If you don't look out, you'll break out in freckles."

She took the bonnet from him and put it on. "I never freckle," she said, tying the ribbons. "I go directly from white to red."

Did the boy sunburn? she wondered. Or did his skin simply darken to a golden tone, as Papa's did? Her gaze went to the sun-burnished features of the man beside her. He was golden, too. Nature could be so cruel. Though men were not a fraction so dependent on their looks as women, they always seemed to have the advantage, even in that. *He* would not freckle or break out in ugly red splotches. The sun loved him.

As great numbers of women must have done, she supposed. It would not be so difficult, after all, to succumb to the sweet illusion he created, the small lifetime of happiness.

She looked away in the direction the boy had gone. A wall of overgrown shrubbery shut him out from sight.

"You needn't fret about the plight of the poor apprentice," Mr. Carsington said. "I met your father in Altrincham yesterday. Among other things, we talked of the bulldog. We agreed that she was growing fat and lethargic. I mentioned Pip and how well he handled her. Lord Lithby said he'd arrange for Tyler to be paid for the boy's time."

This pulled her attention away from the wall of shrubbery. "But when?" she said. "After today, Stepmama and I shan't be here so much. We must give a little time, at least, to preparing for our guests."

"Ah, yes, the mating party," he said.

"It is not . . ."

But it was.

To her it was a nightmare, a monstrosity.

But his casually blunt assessment conjured a mental image as vivid and comical as one of Rowlandson's or Cruikshank's caricatures. Laughter bubbled up inside her, in spite of the ache that seemed to pulse with every heartbeat.

She saw the gentlemen preening and swaggering for the ladies' benefit and imagining they were so subtle when they were so obvious. How many times had she watched these proceedings? How many times had she stifled laughter, watching the males strut like peacocks, and talk too much and too loudly, showing off? How many times had she watched them hover about a current favorite, jostling for position? And what about the ladies' maneuvers, more subtle in comparison to the men's yet equally comical?

She laughed then, out loud, because she could not keep it back for the life of her. Perhaps so much bitter grief filled her heart that it must find a way out, like bad blood, or her heart would burst or break. Laughter was like bloodletting.

She heard Mr. Carsington's deep chuckle, and that made her giggle like a schoolgirl. She covered her mouth, as a little girl would do, trying to be good.

But she'd always had to try harder than most. She gave up. What was the point of stifling her mirth with such a man, who scorned euphemism and hypocrisy?

She became aware of his gaze, and of the lingering smile that softened his features and made him seem, for a moment, like someone else. Someone less cynical and not quite so coolly rational. Someone like the man she believed he was when he held her in his arms.

"There, you know I'm right," he said. "It is exactly the same as they do with bulls and horses but with more elaborate social rituals attending the process. And considerably more elaborate attire."

"Is that how Papa put it to you?" she said. "You debated the merits of breeding certain types of pigs, for instance, then went on to speak of his guests?"

Mr. Carsington nodded. "More or less."

"Then that is more or less how he presented the matter to me," she said. "My father takes the methodical approach, you see."

"To getting you fired off."

Gad, that was what it was, after all. Poor Papa, all he saw was an aging daughter in dire need of a husband.

"I believe he has hopes of getting some of my cousins *fired off*, as you so romantically put it, at the same time," she said. "When Papa puts his mind to something, he puts his heart into it, too, and proceeds with his usual enthusiasm."

"Are all those cousins as old as you?" said Mr. Carsington.

"Heavens, no," she said. "No one is as ancient as I." She started to walk, carefully avoiding the direction the child had taken.

Mr. Carsington followed her. "You are not quite ancient," he said. "Not past all hope."

"Thank you," she said. "I am relieved to learn I am not yet tottering toward my grave."

"Looking at the matter objectively," he said, "in purely reproductive terms—which is the essential purpose of marriage—one must consider a woman of seven and twenty prodigious old. You are rapidly nearing the end of your prime reproductive years. Males generally choose young females, who have many breeding years ahead of them, to increase the odds of producing male children who will survive to adulthood."

"If one looks at the matter objectively, it is hard to understand why my father goes to so much bother," she said. "I am not his son. I cannot inherit his title or the bulk of his property, which is entailed. Thus it is nothing to him whether I produce many sons or none, since my children cannot continue the line."

The pathway took them to one of the several swampy ponds that had once formed an elegant series of water features adorning the landscape. She discerned no signs of child or dog. The home farm stood a distance away. She was safe, for today, thanks to Mr. Carsington's timely interruption.

"All parents, no matter what their social position, seem to want grandchildren," he said meditatively. "It would appear that humans, being mortal, want reassurance that some part of them will continue long after they're dead. In any event, parents want to see their children settled."

"Your parents, too, it appears," she said. "In lieu of a wife they have given you a property. That is sensible. I should imagine it is harder to get a son wed than a daughter. Girls will marry practically anybody who seems agreeable. They don't know any better because they've never been allowed to learn. They've never had the freedom to discover what they truly want. They understand practically nothing of men—including their own brothers, if they have them—and base their opinions, their ideas of love, mainly on looks and charm. For some, money and position are at the top of the list."

There was a silence. She didn't care. This was not a social event, and she wasn't obliged to keep the conversation going. She watched the insects and birds darting over the water and into the surrounding trees. In the late-morning silence, the buzzing and twittering sounded like music. For a moment, at least, she could pretend she was at Beechwood in the way she always used to be, as herself. For a moment, at least, she was almost calm.

"It pains me to admit this," came his deep voice at last, "but you continue to surprise me."

She looked at him. He, too, was watching the insects and birds—no doubt with a deeper understanding than she had of what each creature was and what they were about. Though his hat brim partly shaded his face, the shadow only seemed to emphasize the strong, chiseled features. She remembered the feel of his cheek against hers, the taste of his mouth, the comfort of his strong arms. The wild longing she felt was not a memory but a current of feeling. It belonged not to yesterday but to this moment.

She wished she might touch his hand, as one might touch a friend's hand in a moment of understanding. Only that. But when could it be like that, with a man?

She pushed aside both the wish and the longing. This was not so very difficult to do. She'd had years of practice.

"You've surprised me, too," she said. "You can admit a mistake, which so many men—and women —cannot do. You can apologize, a form of speech that seems to strike even the most loquacious dumb. And you have shown compassion for an insignificant apprentice," she added, her voice almost perfectly steady.

"It is nothing to get maudlin about," he said.

"I was not maudlin," she said. "I only remarked on your kindness to the boy."

"You make too much of it," he said. "I gave him a job to do, that is all. There's nothing out of the way in hiring boys to rid the property of vermin. Your keepers pay hosts of boys to kill crows and starlings, rats and weasels and such. Your father suggested it, in fact."

"It seems you and Papa discussed Pip at length," she said.

"I sought his advice," Mr. Carsington said. "Your father's experience far surpasses mine. I wanted to give Pip something to do outside of the house. Some of the workmen have got it into their heads that he's bad luck. Every time there's an accident, it's because of him—not another's clumsiness or carelessness or simple happenstance. It's hard enough managing the multitudes at work on my house. The last thing I need is a Jonah."

"Perhaps we could find something for him to do at Lithby Hall," she said—and instantly wished the words back.

She could not have the boy about constantly. As large as her father's property was, she'd know Pip was there, and she'd be looking for him, constantly looking for him. She was demented to raise the possibility.

"Your father's vermin are under control," Mr. Carsington said. "I've more need of Pip at Beechwood. We've arranged for him to go to Lithby Hall to collect Daisy, early every morning, as soon as the servants are up. After her exercise, he'll return to work—if the other laborers will let him. Meanwhile, I'll watch how matters proceed in that regard. He seems to like the plaster work—what little he gets to do of it. Like any apprentice, he's assigned the drudge work and fetching and carrying. But Tyler admits the boy has a talent for designing patterns, some of which he's used. If Pip is suited to the trade, then it's folly to take him away. But we shall wait and see."

"And if matters do not go well?" she said. "You promised to find a place for him, and I do not think you make idle promises."

He turned and smiled at her. "Do you not? What, have I a redeeming quality?"

She lifted her chin. "Being kind to children is a redeeming quality, I believe. It seems I must mark that down in your favor."

"Are you keeping a book?" he said.

"Oh, yes," she said. "Always." She glanced up at the sun, half-obscured by a cloud. "It must be close to noon. Stepmama will be ready to go home. I had better go back."

She left him then.

He did not come after her this time, yet she could feel it, as palpable as a touch, the golden gaze following her, and she wondered if he wore that softened smile.

Chapter 10

Sunday night 30 June

"A difficult day, sir?" Kenning said as he followed his commander up the stairs. "You're later than your usual time."

"Lord Eastham had a good deal of advice for me concerning Lord Lithby's forthcoming house party," said Colonel Morrell.

The invitees to Lithby Hall included half a dozen of England's most eligible gentlemen—that was to say, the half dozen Lady Charlotte had not yet rejected out of hand.

She'd reject this lot, too, because they'd all make the same mistake. They would go directly for their target.

Lady Charlotte must be won by stealth, indirection, and slow siege.

Colonel Morrell did not explain his strategy to his uncle. Nor did he mention that the only man who worried him was Darius Carsington, who gave no

signs of courting her and had the advantage of proximity.

"The house party will mean the end of the ladies'
daily visits to Beechwood," the colonel said. "I was
in the army too long, it seems. I had no idea a gentleman would permit his wife and unwed daughter to
spend so much time in the house of an unmarried
man."

"His lordship's always let Lady Charlotte run on
a long leash," said Kenning. "On account of how
she almost died."

"Ten years ago," his commander said. "Hardly a
reason to risk her safety and reputation. In his place,
I should be all the more cautious."

She wanted a firm hand, he thought, not for the
first time.

"Speaking of those old times," said Kenning as
they entered the colonel's bedroom, "I heard something."

"Did you, indeed?"

Though Colonel Morrell did not keep a large staff,
and most of those were in bed, Kenning closed the
door. "I've been to the Axe and Cleaver," he said.

This, the colonel knew, was a tavern in Altrincham Lower Town. Like most taverns, it offered
gossip in abundance.

"To wet your whistle," Colonel Morrell said with
a thin smile.

"More to wet somebody else's," said Kenning. "A
coachman what felt ill-used and needed a sympathetic ear."

"Fewkes."

The servant's bald head bobbed up and down. "He got to talking, sir, as men will do when lubricated sufficient. He got to telling me how he'd served the family since a boy and knew things."

"I daresay he does," said his commander, "know things."

Nothing more was said until he had donned his dressing gown and was settled in his favorite chair, his nightly glass of whiskey at his elbow.

Then, in a low voice—as though they stood in a tent and Napoleon's spies might be listening outside —Kenning told his commander what the aggrieved coachman knew.

It was not much, the smallest dirty nugget of a clue. Still, as Colonel Morrell knew, sometimes small, dirty nuggets proved to contain solid gold.

Beechwood
Monday morning 1 July

On Sunday night, Darius had received a note from Lady Lithby. Her youngest, Stephen, was ill. She would return to her duties at Beechwood as soon as he recovered, which she did not expect to take long.

Though work in and on the house continued without her and Lady Charlotte, the atmosphere was not the same. Darius felt the difference, a constant awareness of something wrong. It took him a while to pinpoint it.

At first he thought he was simply out of sorts because of spending the morning in his study, attending to the stacks of bills and staring at the columns of figures in his ledgers, most of the figures being in the outgoing columns.

This did not satisfactorily account for the troubling change in atmosphere.

Being a man of uncommon intelligence, he did not require months, weeks, or even days to work out the answer.

He remembered what Lady Charlotte had said, on the evening he'd dined at Lithby Hall.

He has so much work to do, and a great deal on his mind. I should think he would want a refuge.

. . . after all, it is his house, and ought to be the way he likes it.

He remembered his brief vision of a beautiful someone making a refuge for him, a place of warmth and order, a place of his own where things were as *he* liked them to be.

He recalled the magic she'd wrought in his dairy and the advice she'd given him about bribing his grandmother with a fan. He remembered the last time they'd spoken, and his sense that a barrier between them had cracked. Listening to her then, he'd realized she was two people. One was the woman with whom he conversed so easily, the one who giggled and laughed as they stood at the edge of the marshy remnants of a fishpond, so careful not to touch each other. She was intelligent and perceptive. She had a naughty streak and a sense of humor.

This was the real Lady Charlotte.

The wrongness in the house was her absence.

He missed her.

"This is not good," he muttered to himself. He stared at the columns of the ledger. "I cannot—"

"Bugger the little bastard!" came a shout from the corridor. "He's bad luck! You keep that devil-eyed whoreson away from us, or I'll tear a strip off his hide."

Darius couldn't hear Tyler's answer and didn't wait to hear it.

He went out into the passage. "What is this noise?" he said, in a precise imitation of his father. Like his father, he did not raise his voice. Like his father, he didn't need to. No Carsington male ever had to raise his voice to obtain instant and undivided attention.

The two men looked at him.

"Well?" he said.

The noisy fellow, who turned out to be Jowett, the head carpenter, had the usual complaint. One of his men had dropped a hammer on his foot and broken a toe. Pip was at the other end of the house, but it was his fault.

Jowett refused to continue working while the boy remained on the property. He could not endanger his men, he said.

Darius was strongly tempted to tell the man to leave the property and never come back. A carpenter could be replaced easily. The trouble was, his replacement was all too likely to have the same irrational attitude about Pip.

Instead, Darius told him to go back to work. Then, feeling depressingly like his father, he summoned Tyler into the study.

The plasterer apologized for the disturbance. "I'll have to get rid of the boy," he said. "He were a mistake, like the missus says. Only ever brought bad luck to everyone he come near. He's bad luck to me if no one'll work near him."

"I told you I don't hold with superstition—or tormenting and persecuting children," Darius said.

"Sir, I can't stop folk from believing what they believe," Tyler said.

That was true enough. Darius couldn't stop them, either.

It was ignorance that bred prejudice and superstition, and ignorance was a good deal more intractable an ailment than it ought to be. It did not respond to facts or logic.

He would simply have to command.

"You may not get rid of the boy for the present," he told Tyler. "Lord Lithby needs him to exercise the dog."

"But sir—"

"I shall find other tasks for him," Darius said. "Make sure the other workmen are aware that he is now in my charge."

Exactly what he needed. Another responsibility, with complications attached. But he couldn't abandon the lad.

He told Tyler to prepare an itemized account of what he'd spent on Pip since his articles of indenture were signed. Though the amount would probably be small, it was one more expense Darius could ill afford. Very possibly, legal issues might be involved as well, either with the articles of indenture or with the parish workhouse.

Since he knew nothing about workhouses and orphans and his brother Benedict knew everything, Darius would write to him.

To Tyler, meanwhile, Darius pretended to know precisely what he was about. He asked questions about Pip, and wrote the answers down in a businesslike way.

Name: Philip Ogden.
Place of birth: Yorkshire. Possibly the West Riding.
Date of birth: Tyler unable to remember. Believes boy
  is age eleven "or thereabouts."
Mother: Unknown.
Father: Unknown.
Note: Both believed to be highborn.

"Leastways, that's what everyone said, on account of how it was a parson and his wife who adopted him," Tyler explained.

Clergyman and wife, last name Ogden, of Sheffield,
  Yorkshire, died "about four years ago" (1818?)
Second adoptive "father": Samuel Welton, widowed
  clergyman of Salford, Lancashire, and cousin of
  Mrs. Ogden. Died December 1820.
Philip Ogden given into the care of Salford parish

workhouse in late 1820 or early 1821.
Indentured to Tyler in May 1821.

A short, unhappy history. Darius found no comfort in knowing that the majority of illegitimate children endured worse.

He thought matters over after Tyler left and decided he'd better visit the Salford workhouse. He wanted to make sure he'd encounter no bureaucratic obstacles to breaking the indenture, and to fill in any other missing details he could.

But first he called in Pip and told him he would not be continuing in Tyler's employ.

The boy looked as though he'd been struck. Something in his expression nagged at Darius's mind, but he hadn't time to ponder it. The lad was blinking hard, trying not to cry.

"Come, come," Darius said bracingly. "I promised I would find a place for you, and I shall. For the present, we'll see Purchase at the home farm and find out how you can best be of use to him."

Pip nodded, but the look of utter misery remained.

Feeling unwanted and unloved was not the most agreeable sensation. Being abandoned repeatedly, though it was fate rather than the boy's doing, could not be pleasant, either.

Darius's family merely deemed him aggravating, and it bothered him more than he liked. This boy had no family, and strangers disliked him on sight.

Darius wished Lady Charlotte were here. She would know what to say to the child. She had known what to say to Darius. Hadn't she given him a completely new perspective on his father?

"Come now," Darius said. "You can do better than this, Pip. Mr. Welton must have thought so, or he wouldn't have taken such pains with your schooling."

Pip wiped his eyes with a grimy sleeve.

"You must not mind these fellows," Darius went on. "They don't know any better. William the Conqueror was a bastard. Do you know who he was?"

Pip nodded.

"There's a lot of that, among the upper orders," Darius said. "If it wasn't for bastards, we should be able to fit the entire House of Lords in a wardrobe, with room to spare."

The image of England's great lords stuffed into a wardrobe brought a shaky smile to the boy's face.

"The first Duke of Richmond," Darius said. "The first Duke of Grafton. The first Duke of St. Albans. All of them the by-blows of King Charles II."

The boy's mismatched eyes widened, and his mouth formed an O.

"The Duke of Somerset's descended from a bastard son of the Duke of Lancaster," Darius continued. "These are merely the ones who come quickly to mind."

He had the lad fully diverted from his sorrow now. "All of them were conceived in sin, sir?"

The concept of sin had never made the slightest sense to Darius. "They were conceived in the usual way," he said. "Do you know how it's done?"

Pip's face reddened. He covered his mouth, but Darius heard the stifled snigger.

Again, something nagged at the back of Darius's mind, but it must wait for another time. For now he must press his advantage.

"Then you know it's nothing to do with you, and not your fault," he went on. "There's nothing evil about your eyes, either. I've seen it before. At Eton. One of the older boys, if I remember aright. None of my schoolfellows ran away screaming from the sight, or uttered nonsense about devil's work. It's a quirk of nature, nothing more, and a very interesting one, in my opinion. Anybody can have two matching eyes. Eyes of two different colors are distinctive."

"Eton," the boy murmured. "Distinctive." He stood a little straighter.

"We've got that sorted out, then," Darius said. "We've only one other matter to settle. I must make sure there's no trouble about your indenture. For that I must go to Salford."

The boy looked alarmed at the mention of Salford, but he lifted his chin bravely, ready to trust Darius. "Yes, sir."

"You'd better play least in sight today," Darius said. "I'll take you with me. Can you ride?"

Yes, Pip could ride. Mr. Welton had taught him.

The prospect of riding one of Darius's fine horses helped quell the child's anxieties about returning to the scene of his nightmares. Not twenty minutes later, he and Darius set out for Lancashire.

Tuesday night

Colonel Morrell sipped his whiskey. "Jowett," he repeated.

"Head carpenter over at Beechwood, sir," said Kenning. "Said Mr. Carsington took an interest in the plasterer's apprentice. The one I told you about, with them odd eyes. The one who walks Lady Lithby's dog."

"Odd eyes," his commander repeated.

"One blue is what Jowett said. The other a sort of muddy green."

The colonel considered for a time. "I knew a man with eyes like that," he said. "Frederick Blaine. He was one of my officers. You remember him, Kenning?"

"Oh, him," said Kenning. "Never noticed his eyes."

"Troublesome fellow," said his commander. "Blown up at Waterloo. Always careless and impetuous, but he grew worse after his younger brother Geordie died in a duel, some years before that. That one was a rake of the worst kind. Locals complained about his leading their daughters astray. Had he been under my command, I should have had him up on misconduct charges at the first whiff of scandal." He considered again. "But his commander was notoriously lax. If my memory does not mislead me, the battalion were stationed somewhere hereabouts for a time."

Colonel Morrell's memory rarely misled him. On

the contrary, it was a prodigious memory, and it had served him well in his profession.

"The boy's one of his bastards, you think, sir? From what Jowett said, he's somebody's bastard."

There was a silence while the colonel's reliable faculty made a connection between a coachman's obscure references to events of a decade ago and the current discussion. "How old did you say the boy was?"

"Ten or thereabouts, sir."

"Ten." Colonel Morrell sipped his whiskey. "Or thereabouts. Came from the Salford workhouse."

"Previous in Sheffield."

"Sheffield, Yorkshire," said the colonel. "Ten years. Yorkshire." A possibility occurred to him. A week ago, he would have deemed it unthinkable.

Now he thought it.

"Kenning," he said. "You're going to Salford tomorrow."

Beechwood
Friday morning 5 July

"I was afraid you'd abandoned me," Mr. Carsington said, "to the hordes of servants and workmen."

He and Charlotte stood outside the open doorway of the corner guest chamber. The housekeeper, Mrs. Endicott, had told Charlotte that he'd asked to speak to her as soon as she arrived.

"We might have come sooner," she said. "Ste-

phen's fever passed quickly. But he was ill and fret-
ful afterward, and Stepmama decided he might be
allowed some coddling. Usually she leaves the children to the nursemaids—and Papa. But when the
boys are ill, she steps in. When they're especially
obnoxious, too."

"What are they?—one of them not three, as I rec-
ollect, and one four or five years old?" he said. "Can
such little ones be especially obnoxious?"

"The older ones, certainly," Charlotte said. "She
banished Richard and William to Shropshire because
they'd started bullying Georgie. In Shropshire, they
have older cousins who'll give them a dose of their
own medicine."

"Her ideas of child rearing sound like my mother's," Mr. Carsington said.

"She is unsentimental about them," Charlotte
said. "She needs to be, I think, because Papa tends
to overindulge them. She does not want the boys to
be spoiled."

"Were you spoiled, does she think?"

"I don't know what she thinks about that," Charlotte said. "I only know that she did me a great deal
of good when she came." She pushed the past to the
back of her mind, where it belonged. "You did not
summon me here to discuss the rearing of children,
I think?"

"No," he said. "The image of obnoxious infants
led my thoughts astray. I asked you to come because
I need your help."

She said nothing, but she could not conceal her
surprise. She hoped she did a better job of hiding

the foolish burst of happiness that made her heart beat erratically.

"Those last may be the most difficult four words I've ever uttered in my life," he said. "I thought I would choke saying them."

"I thought I'd faint, hearing them," she said. "In my experience, men would rather have a limb amputated than admit they need help. And to seek it from a woman is completely unheard of."

He smiled. "The pain is nearly unbearable."

"Yet you appear to be breathing normally," she said. "Your face has not turned blue."

"Perhaps there will be a delayed reaction," he said. "In the meantime, I will tell you that I am at a loss." He nodded toward the room. "I don't know where to begin."

Several pieces of furniture had been moved out of rooms in which work was being done and into this one, which would need only cleaning and perhaps a fresh coat of paint.

"Both Mrs. Endicott and Lady Lithby say this is not something for them to decide," he said. "But I have no idea how one decides what to keep and what to throw away."

Charlotte stepped into the room. It was more crowded than the last time she'd entered, to investigate the trunk. It would grow more crowded still as repairs proceeded. The trunk, she saw, was still here. It stood open on the floor. Judging by appearances, someone had thrown back into it everything she'd taken out and so carefully sorted.

He must have followed the direction of her gaze

because he said, "I gave up. I still haven't chosen a fan for my grandmother. Perhaps I should send her the lot."

"That would ruin the effect," she said. "The effect you want is of one exquisite item, carefully chosen for her and her alone. Then she will believe you are more thoughtful than she'd supposed. If you choose well, she may even decide that you have more sensitivity and feeling than she gave you credit for."

"That shouldn't be difficult," he said. "She gives me credit for having none whatsoever."

He spoke in the detached way he often adopted, but she detected the note of frustration. "Do you mind so very much what your grandmother thinks?" she said.

"I shouldn't mind," he said. "She's equally merciless to everybody, including my esteemed father." He smiled. "But I should like to astonish her. At least once in my lifetime."

He had so many smiles, and in this one she saw his younger self so clearly: the boy vexed with his provoking grandmama.

"I'm acquainted with your grandmother," she said. Compared to the Dowager Lady Hargate, Mrs. Badgely was the meekest of lambs. "I'll choose a fan. As to the rest . . ." She made a sweeping gesture. "Tell me what the rules are, and I'll make a preliminary list."

"If I had rules, I should not bother you with it," he said. "But furnishings are not my area of expertise. I'd better leave it to your judgment." He paused very briefly, then added, "If any of it will fetch money, I should like to know."

"Ah," she said, unsurprised. Restoring an estate of this size was a costly business. She'd guessed his finances were not limitless, and she was sure he'd hate asking his father for money.

What surprised her was his embarrassment. He was always so completely self-assured. Yet it was unmistakable, the darkening of the bronzed skin at the top of his cheekbones.

She ought not to let that sign of vulnerability affect her; she ought not to let him touch her heart so easily, but it was too late to protect herself. He was kind to children and dogs and to her and he fretted about his father, as any son might do. He was not always cocksure, not always coolly rational. He was human, a man she could talk to easily.

A human who happened to be a rake. But what could she do? She was human, too.

"My father expects me to make Beechwood produce income within a year," he said. "I am making progress on the agricultural side but the repairs to the house . . ." He trailed off, shrugging.

Incredulous, she stared at him. "A *year?*"

"He wants me to be able to support myself," he said.

"That is not at all unusual," she said. "Younger sons can be a severe financial drain. But only a year—"

"The alternative is marriage," he said. "To live off a wife's dowry."

"And you are averse to marriage," she said.

"Not *averse*, precisely," he said.

"Not ready, then."

He did not answer right away. He moved to the window where she'd sat the other day, trying to calm down. She remembered how he'd sat beside her, waiting, watching . . . concerned.

He gazed at the sunlit landscape beyond. Then he turned around and looked at her. "I fully understand the purpose of marriage," he said. "It is one of society's more reasonable constructs. It is grounded in natural law, and it is of both economic and social value. It theoretically provides protection to the female who bears and cares for progeny. It offers a means of securing property and ensuring its passing to the male's descendants. Even in nature, among animals, males employ methods—some quite ruthless—to ensure the continuation of their seed."

"Too, since monogamy is not required among human males," she said, "being married need not be so very different from being single."

"Exactly," he said. "In other words, matrimony, in itself, is not to me an intolerable idea."

"Yet you chose to accept an impossible challenge instead," she said.

"It isn't impossible," he said.

"Perhaps not impossible, but the very next thing," she said. "You'll have the devil's own time."

"I didn't expect it to be easy," he said. "If it were easy, my father wouldn't have proposed it."

It would be far more difficult than finding a wealthy bride, she thought. He'd have no trouble at all sweeping any girl off her feet, and his connections would allay parental concerns. Did not her own father consider Mr. Carsington matrimonial material? Her cousins, when they came, would swoon if he paid them the slightest attention.

Even she, who understood men far better than any of them ever would, couldn't help wishing her past were only a bad dream, and she might try to win his heart, truly.

If, if, if.

She turned her mind to calculating. "You have excellent timber, and the home farm is already functioning," she said briskly. "The dairy will bring in a good sum. I should not advise you to sell the silver or auction off the paintings, except as a last resort. However, there is no reason to keep all the furniture. Some of the heavy pieces especially will sell for a high price to the ironmongers and such who are building those absurd medieval castles and devising their own coats of arms." She looked about her. "You might manage it, though I suspect it will be a very near thing."

"I know what you're thinking," he said.

"I doubt it," she said.

"You're thinking it would be easier to wed an heiress," he said. "But that's the trouble, don't you see? Marriage would be the easy way out. Whether or not my father has high expectations of me, I should be a disappointment to him and to myself if I fail in this."

What argument could she give him, she who understood, acutely, painfully, the wish to live up to what was expected, to not disappoint?

"I quite understand," she said. "I shall proceed with this lot of possessions according to economic rather than aesthetic or sentimental principles."

His posture relaxed. "Except for Grandmother," he said, coming away from the window. "Nothing remotely practical for her. Beautiful. Unique."

"Yes, Mr. Carsington, I understand," she said.

She understood too much. Her heart would be so much safer now if she hadn't let herself get so close. The more she knew, the more she was drawn to him and the more she wanted to confide in him, as he confided in her.

Oh, she must be desperate indeed to come to this. Desperate, confused, and lonely.

The house party . . . the boy . . . this man.

She wished she could escape her life, if only for a short time, to clear her head and sort everything out and put things in their proper places.

She couldn't. She'd have to make do with sorting furniture. She made herself give an impatient wave of dismissal. "Leave it to me," she said. "Go on about your business."

Charlotte could have tackled the furniture first, but the trunk, with its souvenirs of a bygone era, called to her. His grandmother and Lady Margaret must have been contemporaries. Furthermore, Mr. Carsington's grandmother still showed a partiality for the fashions and manners of her youth. She often entertained guests in her boudoir, wearing her dressing gown, as ladies did in the time of King George II.

And so, after Mr. Carsington left, Charlotte once more threw a cushion on the floor. Once more she emptied the trunk, sorting its contents as she went along. This time, though, when she reached the bottom, her finger snagged on something. Peering down, she saw a loop made of ribbon. Gently, she tugged at the loop.

The bottom of the trunk came up. The false bottom.

Underneath lay packets of letters tied in faded ribbon. A little book. And a miniature of a handsome man in uniform.

She opened the book.

She began to read.

She read on, turning page after page. Then she started to cry.

Darius was at his desk, staring glumly at a ledger, when a sound made him look up. The boy Pip stood in the doorway, looking worried. The bulldog stood beside him, looking up worriedly at the boy. Or maybe that part was Darius's imagination.

"What's wrong?" Darius said. "Has someone fallen off a ladder again and blamed you?"

"No, sir. I only came in the house because Daisy chased a cat inside, and I was afraid someone would trip over her or the cat or they'd knock something over. May I come in, sir?"

Darius impatiently waved him in. Them in. Because the dog seemed to believe she was leashed to Pip's ankles.

The boy closed the door behind him and crept

toward the desk. "Sir," he said softly. "It's the lady. The younger lady."

Darius's heart raced. "Has she fallen off a ladder?"

"No, sir. She's crying."

"Crying," Darius repeated blankly. She had seemed cheerful enough when he left her. They'd had a strange conversation, true, a conversation far more deeply personal than he could recall ever having before, with anybody.

Yet he doubted she was weeping over his finances or his typically male need to prove something to his father or his views on marriage. "They do that, you know, Pip," he said. "Ladies. They can be sentimental."

"Oh," said Pip. "I wasn't sure. I had to chase Daisy up to the first floor. The cat got out a window, but Daisy stayed there, waiting. Then her head went up, like she heard something, and off she went the other way. She stopped at that room—the one where the lady tripped over the bucket. You remember?"

Darius nodded. He had no trouble remembering how ill she'd been, and how frightened *he'd* been.

This was very bad, he thought. Fretting over her. Panicking over her. Confiding in her.

He was in trouble.

"I heard a sound and thought maybe what Daisy heard was a rat," Pip said.

At the word *rat*, Daisy came to attention.

"But Daisy didn't go in," the boy continued. "She only sat there, looking at me "The door was almost closed, but I opened it a little bit and saw her—the younger lady, I mean. She was sitting on the floor, crying. I didn't know what to do. I didn't want to tell the other lady and upset her if it wasn't important. But I didn't want to do nothing if I was supposed to do something. I knew you'd know what to do."

"I'd better look into it," Darius said. "It could be simply . . . ahem." Though Pip seemed to understand the basics of mating, he probably had no notion of various related matters. Now was not the time to enlighten him. "Ladies have moods at certain times," he said. "I'll get to the bottom of it. Thank you for telling me. You were right not to upset the other women. Crying is contagious among females. They catch it from one another, and the result can be dreadful. You have discretion beyond your years, young Pip."

He rose, patted Pip on the shoulder, and, squaring his own, set off to deal with the fearsome phenomenon of a weeping female.

Now it's too late, I see what a fool I was. We might have run away. What could Papa do? He had no money to chase after us, no power to destroy us. We might have run away and wed. I could have given myself to Richard. Then Papa would have had no choice. We would have to wed. There's always a choice, as Richard said. I should have chosen. I should not have let others choose for me.

Now I am off Papa's hands. He has his money, which he will surely gamble away, as he did all the money he had before, and no one cares about me.

No one knows or cares that I had a chance for happiness.

Now it is gone, forever.

Richard is dead.

I wish I had the courage to join him, but I ever was a coward. The same coward I was then, when I had a choice and a chance, and let them browbeat me and tell me what my duty was.

Richard is dead, and I am chained for life to a man I cannot love. I never gave myself to the man I loved, and now I must give myself again and again to one for whom I feel nothing and never will. I came chaste to my marriage bed, like a good girl, and my reward is dust and ashes.

How shall I bear it?

I shall go mad, I know it.

Charlotte could scarcely see the words through her tears. She sat reading the passage over and over while the words blurred before her, while tears fell, and her chest heaved.

The mad old woman.

She had been a girl once, a beautiful, innocent girl in love with a young man who adored her: the handsome young officer in the miniature, who'd written her the most beautiful, loving, heartbreaking letters.

"I am not afraid of weeping," came a deep voice from somewhere in the watery blur.

She looked toward the sound.

"My brother Rupert is not afraid of snakes,

scorpions, or crocodiles, but he is afraid of weeping women," Mr. Carsington said as he entered the room and gently closed the door behind him. "It is a terrifying sight, calculated to unman the stoutest-hearted fellow. Yet I am not afraid. I come armed." He drew out a handkerchief.

She sobbed, helplessly.

He crossed the room to her. "Come, come," he said. "It cannot be so bad as all that." He reached down and lifted her up, as easily as if she'd been a rag doll.

She fell upon his shoulder and wept.

He put his arms around her.

"I don't know what to do," she sobbed.

"Lady Charlotte," he said.

"They're coming in a few days," she said. "What shall I do? I can't bear it. How did *she* bear it? All those years. I shall go mad, and turn into a mad old woman and make a hundred wills."

"No, you won't," he said. He stroked her hair.

"You don't understand," she said.

"No, I don't," he said. "I truly don't."

I can't live this life.

I must have some happiness, even if it lasts for only a moment.

She lifted her head from his shoulder and looked at him, into those strange golden eyes, puzzled now and so gentle.

She put her hand up and touched the place between his brows, where a faint frown line had formed. She drew her finger along the arch of his brow, then down along the chiseled line of his jaw. She smiled and touched his nose.

He smiled, too, and the puzzlement left his eyes. What she saw there seemed so very much like affection.

She brushed her finger over his lips.

I had a chance for happiness.

She had this chance, this moment.

She didn't reach for him this time. She only curved her hand, so lightly, against the side of his face. Then she stood on her toes and kissed him with all the sweetness she knew how to give.

His hand came up and covered hers, and he gave the sweetness back, in a kiss as gentle and true as a young lover's.

The past was nothing, then, no more than a bad dream from which she'd awakened.

This was real and true, the sweetness and fondness and kindness of young love.

No one else and nothing else mattered, only they two, only this moment of happiness.

She wrapped her arms about his neck.

And *yes*, her heart said. *Yes, this.*

Chapter 11

It should have been so easy to move away.

The feathery touch of her finger on his face, the gentle caress of her hand along his jaw, the light pressure of her mouth on his. So easy to escape.

He had only to turn his head, to take a step back.

Should have done it.

Couldn't.

He saw the last tears glistening on her long lashes when she lifted her head, the surprisingly fond smile curving her lips as she traced his features with her finger—the caress so like the way he'd kissed her the other day, trying to win her over.

He could have stood there forever, drinking her in: the ethereally beautiful face; the small, fond smile; the soft, caressing hand.

He could have been content with this, and with the kiss, almost painfully sweet. It was a girl's kiss, without artifice or cynicism or any trace of self-protection.

Even when she wrapped her arms about his neck he had only to remind himself that she was a maiden. He had only to lift those slender arms gently and step away and simply let it end thus: the touch, the caress, the kiss, all adding up to thanks.

She'd wanted comforting; he'd comforted. She was grateful and said it in a caress and a kiss, and that was enough.

He did lift his mouth from hers. He did lift her hands from his neck. But he kissed them, first the backs, then each knuckle. Then he set them over his heart, beating so hard but steady, still steady, and held them there.

Her scent wafted up to him, and his head filled with it, clean and light, like the scent of flowers after a rain. He bent his head and nuzzled her hair, the curls like silk against his face.

She leaned into him, her hands still upon his heart, beating harder now.

One hand still clasped over hers, he brought his arm round the back of her neck and cradled her in the crook of his elbow. She looked up at him, and he could have stood forever thus, gazing into those clear blue depths.

They didn't have forever. They had only this private moment, this quiet place amid the chaos of his crumbling house with its hordes of servants and quarreling workmen.

He bent and touched his lips to hers. He felt her mouth tremble at that light touch. His allegedly small, cold heart should have felt nothing.

Yet he felt something there, a stab of feeling, and he stopped the trembling with a kiss, firm and reassuring.

That should have been enough. Time to put an end to this.

Yet he wanted to make this kiss last a little longer. How could he hurry to end it when this was so perfect: she so warm and light in his arms, her mouth so soft, her scent everywhere, and he, dizzy, drinking it in?

She slid her hands from his chest and brought them round him. She held him tightly, as though she'd fall otherwise. He tightened his hold, gathering her close.

Her lips parted on a sigh, and he should have overlooked that as well. He couldn't. She invited, and he couldn't say no. He had to steal inside, to taste her and tease and play with her as lovers did, and discover her again, because every time he found her—in his arms or across a room or looking out of a window—he found something new.

Now he found the taste of her innocent and not innocent. He found sweetness and laughter tinged with a note of sorrow, the last vestiges of the tears she'd shed. The mixture was never the same and always full of contradictions. This time she offered a hundred mysteries in a kiss that deepened and deepened, because he was falling into dangerous waters and couldn't stop.

He brought his hands down, shaping them to her, as he discovered and rediscovered every perfect curve: the graceful arch of her neck and the slender shoulders, the full curve of her breasts, whose warmth he felt though the thin layers of her summer dress.

The warmth was inside him, too, heat snaking swiftly down. It melted his thoughts, orderly and disorderly, along with all the mysteries he wanted to solve and couldn't hope to, not all at once in this stolen moment.

What remained was only a man's simple longing for a woman.

He said, his voice rough, "We need to stop."

"I know," she said.

In a minute, then.

He trailed his fingers over the light fabric of her dress, over her belly and hips. He let his palms graze her bottom.

"We have to stop," he said.

"I know," she said.

In a minute.

He dragged his hands up, pausing at her waist. He was telling himself, *Enough*, but the word made no sense. There was no "enough" for him.

He buried his face in the curve of her shoulder and inhaled the fragrance of her skin. He kissed her smooth throat, and she let her head fall back, offering herself. The simple act of surrender made his heart beat faster, its rhythm as hard and unsteady as the drumbeat of driving rain. Like a storm, it shut out the world. Reason and Logic faded behind it. They didn't matter.

She was in his arms. This minute mattered. This world of theirs, where she needed him and he needed her and all was right while they held each other.

"Don't stop yet," she said. "Not quite yet."

"No, not yet."

He found the fastenings of her bodice and undid them one by one. He drew the bodice down and let his fingers graze the velvety swell of her breasts. He bent and followed the same path with his mouth. The warm scent of her, rich and womanly, filled his head. All the world seemed to swim in it, all of this small world of theirs.

Her hands came up and her fingers slid through his hair and she held him there, against her. He heard the hurried pounding of his heart—or hers— or both—and "Yes," she said, her voice husky.

He lifted his head to speak, but she silenced him with a kiss, ferocious this time. She moved her hands over him, taking possession fearlessly: pushing under his waistcoat, roving over the back of his shirt, then down, to cup his buttocks.

His mind thickened and darkened.

He dragged her closer, crushing her against him. He pushed his knee between her legs. She should have recoiled then and made him pause, made him think.

Instead she pressed herself against his knee. If he'd had any last, desperate hope of control, that finished it.

He groaned against her mouth, then lifted her up and set her down on something—a table, a desk— he hardly knew—and stood between her legs. All the while their lips clung in an endless kiss, darker and hotter and wilder than before.

He grasped her ankles and slid his hands up her legs.

She made a sound in her throat, and broke the

kiss. "Your hands," she whispered, reaching down to cover one, to stroke it. "Your hands. Yes, touch me."

She pressed hurried, hot kisses over his face, his neck, then she leaned back, her blue gaze heavy-lidded and dark.

"Touch me," she said. She let go of him to catch up fistfuls of her skirts and pull them up over her knees.

He touched her. Yes, of course. As she wanted. As *he* wanted. He drew his hands up over the elegant curve of her legs and up over the knot of her garters. He caressed the silken skin above her stockings. She shivered.

She put up her arms, and he let himself be caught. He let her draw him down to her. She kissed him hungrily, and he answered the same way. He gave himself up to the longing and the promise of a kiss that felt like forever. He cast aside all else and lived only in the taste and scent and feel of her. He gave way to the heat inside and to the urgency of physical need.

He kissed her while he unfastened his trouser buttons.

He kissed her while he pushed his clothes and underclothes out of the way. He felt her hand move down the front of his body, and he kept his mouth on hers, to keep from crying out when she touched him.

Unbearable touch.

Tentative, her fingers so light. The tease of it was cruel. "Charlotte, please," he growled against her mouth.

Her fingers curled round him.

Sweet Aphrodite and all the deities, major and minor.

This was . . . This was . . .

She clasped him, growing bolder. Her slim fingers slid up and down, exploring his length.

Maybe he could have stopped but for this.

He'd never know.

She stroked him, and he must do the same to her. He must arouse her to the same pitch of madness she'd brought him to.

He slid his hand to the miraculously soft triangle of down between her legs. He felt her readiness, and he stroked her, intending—if he'd any mind left for intentions—to pleasure her with his hand.

But she inhaled sharply at his touch, and squirmed against his hand. And "Yes," she said. "I want you, yes."

And there it went, his last, fragile tie to conscious thought and reality. There it went, his last, frayed bit of sanity.

I want you.

Yes.

He raised her legs, and she wrapped them about his hips. Her hands curled on his upper arms.

He caressed her, opened her, and pushed into her.

She gasped. He paused, gritting his teeth as he summoned the last vestige of his will. Her hold of him tightened.

Then she pushed against him.

Then he was done for.

He thrust, and she was warm and welcoming, her

muscles pushing against him like a beating heart. His heart beat with her, harder and faster.

This was what he wanted, all he'd ever wanted.

She, his.

He wrapped his arms about her and held her.

She was his and he wouldn't let her go. He held her while they moved together, pleasure pumping through them, driving them. He held her through the last fierce rush to the crest. He held her, tightly, so tightly, when he was spent and she still pulsed against him. He held her still, tightly, when at last she quieted and sank against him.

"That was demented."

His voice was a low rumble against Charlotte's head.

She was still floating in the afterglow.

She sat there, stupid with happiness, while he kissed her temple. Then he eased away, and his hands—his magical hands—were refastening her bodice.

Still she was dazed, stupid, floating.

"Charlotte," he said.

She looked up at him, into his golden eyes. "Yes," she said.

"We have to get dressed."

"Yes," she said.

He pushed his handkerchief into her limp hand. "Oh," she said, and came back to earth. She looked about her, and down at herself, and at him, as he pulled up his trousers and tucked in his shirt.

Face hot, she cleaned herself and pulled her skirts

down. She remembered pulling them up, offering herself like the most shameless of wantons.

"That wasn't supposed to happen," he said.

"I know," she said. "But . . ." She swallowed. "I'm not sorry. It was . . . it was . . ." She hunted for words, but she had none. "I had no idea it could be like that."

"Neither did I," he said.

She looked up, afraid to search his eyes and unable not to. "Really? No, you're saying that to make me feel better, but you don't need to because—"

"This is different," he said. "You and I. It is completely different. That much I know. I meant to stop us before it went so far. I never doubted I could. And yet, perhaps, I didn't want to, because I didn't stop us. I think . . . perhaps . . ." He frowned and she saw the flush appear, at the top of his cheekbones. "I have become . . . attached to you."

She'd wanted happiness, and he'd given it to her. She'd thought—as far as she'd thought—she'd wanted physical joy, to be touched, kissed, as other women were. But he'd given her more than she'd expected, more than she'd hoped for. This had been furtive, yes, and perhaps hurried, like her few couplings with Geordie Blaine, but this was not the same, not at all the same.

"I have become attached to you," she said. "In spite of my best intentions."

"I doubt this would have happened otherwise."

"Probably not."

"But it did," he said. "And I must speak to your father and tell him we mean to wed."

A mad flurry within her now: a leap of joy, then a crushing sense of defeat, hopelessness. "You can't," she said.

"I must," he said.

"Your father," she said. "What about your father and your determination to prove yourself? You cannot let me ruin that."

"I won't ruin *you*," he said. "Your honor is more important than my pride."

"My honor," she said, and she couldn't keep the bitterness from her voice. "What honor?"

"You are—were—the innocent, not I."

"I'm not innocent," she said. "Didn't you notice?"

"Are you saying you have no hymen?" he said. "Is that what you mean? I wasn't paying close attention."

"I'm not innocent," she said.

Don't make me say it.

"You're twenty-seven years old," he said. "The hymen can be quite fragile. And I do know that even gently bred girls do not always abide strictly by the rules."

I ever was a coward. The same coward I was then, when I had a choice and a chance . . .

Charlotte had a choice now, and a chance.

To do what? Lie? Marry this man, who was prepared to sacrifice his pride in order to protect her so-called honor? What happiness could exist in a marriage founded upon a lie?

She slid down from the desk. "I mean," she said deliberately, "you are not the first."

A silence. She made herself meet his gaze, braced herself for anger, disgust. He only tipped his head to one side and regarded her quizzically. "Was it recently?" he said.

"N-no," she said. She realized she was wringing her hands. She stilled them and held them, folded, at her waist. "It was a long time ago."

"Ah."

Another pause.

"Am I the second?" he said.

"What?"

"The second?" he said.

She could only blink at him. Good grief. He was thinking. Analyzing. "Yes," she said. "You are the second."

"Did you bury your heart in your lover's grave?"

"No, certainly not," she said.

"Or vow undying devotion, or some such?"

"No, of course not," she said.

"Then we had better marry," he said. "One may impregnate a girl who is not a virgin as easily as one who is."

She took a step back. Not that. She hadn't thought of that. She hadn't thought of it the first time. Then she was ignorant. She wasn't now. But how was she to think? She was all turmoil and confusion.

He drew closer and she saw the keen intelligence at work, the falcon gaze. "Tell me," he said. "Tell me what it is. I know it must be something dreadful, else you'd tell me straight out. We speak our mind to each other, do we not? This day I told you what I'd tell no one else."

She'd spoken to him as she'd speak to no one else, too. She'd done it not only today but so many times, perhaps from the very start. She'd tried to pretend with him as she did with others but she could never quite carry it out. With him she spoke her mind. She was easy with him, more so than she'd ever been before, with any man.

She could not be false now.

Her eyes filled nonetheless and her heart pounded and shame flooded through her, like a fever, hot and cold at the same time.

"I had a child," she said.

Never in all his life had it cost Darius so much to appear calm. Even with his father he had not felt his heart pounding as though it would break through his chest.

He was ashamed of his loss of control, ashamed of destroying her prospects. But he wanted her.

He wanted her enough to bear the prospect of facing her father.

I've despoiled your beautiful daughter.

Now she has to marry me.

Yet Darius would do it. He'd bear Lord Lithby's anger and disappointment and the loss of his esteem.

He'd bear his own father's contempt.

What he was not sure he could bear was bringing her misery, making her regret what had happened . . . for the rest of her life.

Four words made the world shift, completely.

I had a child.

He simply put his arms about her and pulled her close.

Now he understood. Everything, it seemed. With those four words, all the puzzle pieces simply fell into place.

It was an appalling burden for any woman to carry, and she would have carried it alone, for the most part. She would have had help, certainly, in concealing the matter, for it had been amazingly well concealed. He hadn't heard a whisper, and that was rare in country villages, where everybody knew everything about everybody, and the secrets of the great house were common knowledge.

Still, it was her secret, her sorrow, and a heavy burden it was.

He remembered the sketch of the mother and child, and the grief he'd sensed.

"I'm sorry," he said. "I'm sorry."

She wept, quiet, fierce sobs that shook her body.

"I'm sorry," he said. "I'm sorry."

He held her while she wept, and he held her while, gradually, she quieted.

"I'm not g-good," she said, her voice muffled against his coat. "I have no honor. I'm a hypocrite and a coward. I g-gave my baby away as soon as he was born. I shall never forgive myself."

"You said it was a long time ago," he said, stroking her back. "You were young then."

"I was s-sixteen when I met him," she said. She drew away, and fumbled at her skirts and found a handkerchief, with a great deal of lace and a very little useful cloth. She wiped her eyes, her nose.

"Geordie Blaine. He was an officer. So handsome in his uniform. So kind and understanding—or so I thought. But I was only a conquest to him. He had me and left me and eventually got himself killed. Meanwhile I was with child and I didn't even *know*, I was that naïve—I, who grew up in the country. But Molly guessed, and she told Lizzie, and I wouldn't let them tell Papa. They took me away to Yorkshire, saying I was sick and needed a change of air. I nearly died giving birth, they said. I don't remember very much, except that I wished I would die. I was sick for a long time afterward."

She'd been sick with guilt and sorrow, he was sure, which would have compounded any physical injury or illness. The so-called wasting sickness people talked of in her case was very likely melancholia.

He brushed a strand of silky hair back from her cheek.

"We need to talk more of this," he said. "A great deal more. But now is not the time. We've been alone, behind a closed door, far too long for propriety. The workmen and servants will be gossiping as it is. I will say only this to you: We cannot change the past. We can only do our best in the present. For the present, the best course is for us to wed."

"I can't," she said. "I won't have you throw away everything important to you because we were careless once."

"You are important to me," he said.

"But I'm an heiress," she said. "I have pots of money. You said before—"

"That was before."

"But I want you to do what you meant to do," she said. "I want you to restore Beechwood. I was so excited when I understood what a great challenge you'd accepted. I was so . . . proud. You cannot marry me—not at least until you've done what you set out to do."

"This is absurd," he said. "What if you're breeding?"

"I shall know in a fortnight," she said. "If I am—" She stiffened then.

He heard it, too. Voices, drawing closer now, recognizable. Lady Lithby. The housekeeper.

Darius hurried to the door and opened it. Then he said, making sure his voice carried the length of the corridor, "Upon consideration, Lady Charlotte, I prefer to keep the desk. I've developed a sentimental attachment to it."

He needed another opportunity to talk to Lady Charlotte, but he wouldn't find it at Beechwood this day. Now that Mrs. Endicott was installed as housekeeper, Lady Lithby rarely stayed past noon. They had a house party to prepare for, and though she made light of it, Darius was well aware that this was no ordinary house party. Lady Lithby must give it more than her usual attention. She and Lord Lithby were counting on this party to settle Lady Charlotte's future.

The cream of Great Britain's bachelordom would

attend. Darius had not given this much thought until today. He had had Lady Charlotte more or less all to himself. The only rival he'd been aware of was Morrell, and since she seemed unaware he was a rival, Darius had given the colonel little more thought than he'd given the others. In any event, marriage was the last thing on Darius's mind.

That was before.

Now there was a chance she would bear his child. If he'd impregnated her, she must marry him, like it or not.

If he had not, she must marry him anyway.

He was an intelligent man. He didn't need days, weeks, months to comprehend the obvious: She was different, and he had feelings for her, strong feelings.

The challenge was to get her to marry him, and to make sure she liked the idea. The challenge was proving to her that marrying him would not be a mistake. He must give her time—and he could make good use of that time as well.

By the time the ladies' carriage had arrived, he'd analyzed the problem and decided upon a course of action.

He accompanied them to the carriage. As he was about to close the door after them, he said, "I must call upon Lord Lithby soon."

Lady Charlotte's eyes widened.

"Goats," Darius said. "I was thinking of getting goats, and I wanted his advice."

"Then come to dinner this evening," said Lady Lithby. "He'll be more than happy to talk about goats instead of listening to us debating seating and sleeping arrangements. Mr. and Mrs. Badgely will be there, too. You would be doing him a kindness."

Lithby Hall, that evening

Darius soon understood that Lady Lithby had uttered no more than the truth. Dinner that night was definitely a trial, and even Lord Lithby's genial smile seemed forced. Mr. Badgely prosed on and on about one of the house party invitees—a naval officer who happened to have served with his nephew—and Mrs. Badgely was even more tiresome, offering endless unsought advice about the correct way to conduct a house party.

This, no doubt, was why Lord Lithby did not hurry back to join the ladies as he usually did. Instead, the men lingered over their port. Ordinarily, Darius preferred this phase of dinner. Male conversation, even drunken male conversation, was usually more stimulating than women's talk. Tonight, though, he was impatient to join the women in the drawing room, and perhaps did not pay as close attention as he ought to Lord Lithby's observations about goats.

Once there, though, Darius's opportunity came, more quickly and easily than he'd expected.

"Let us have some music, Charlotte, please," said Lady Lithby. "I'm sure the gentlemen have had quite enough of decorations and flower arrangements and whose feelings will be hurt by what."

"Gladly, Stepmama," said Lady Charlotte. "Mr.

Carsington, perhaps you would help me choose
something to soothe the gentlemen's delicate
nerves."

"I should be delighted." He joined her at the pianoforte.

"You stayed in the dining room for a long time,"
she whispered as she began leafing through music. "Please do not tell me Mr. Badgely fell asleep
over his port and you took the opportunity to speak
about us to Papa."

"You are overwrought, or you'd never imagine
such a thing," Darius said. "I've thought over what
you told me. Your concerns are more than reasonable, and I've decided it would be best to let the
mating party proceed as planned."

Her blue eyes widened. "You have? It would?"

"For two reasons," he said. "Firstly, by the end of
the party, you will know for certain whether or not
you are . . ." He glanced about, but the others seemed
engrossed in their own conversations. "Breeding.
Secondly—in the event you are not—and I have
failed by then to persuade you that I shall suit you
best, then I must accept defeat."

She looked at him as though she was not at all
sure what to make of him. "How neatly you've sorted it out."

"We cannot both be emotional," he said. "One of
us must be calm and objective."

"But where is our music?" Mrs. Badgely called.
"How difficult is it to choose?"

"I agree, Mr. Carsington," Lady Charlotte said
more audibly. "Beethoven is too . . . ferocious for a

small after-dinner gathering. My talents are not up
to him, at any rate. By the way, we shall have some
fine musicians playing for the house party. From
London."

"I should keep a close watch on them if I were
you, Lord Lithby," said Mrs. Badgely. "With so many
impressionable young ladies in the house."

"I have tried to consider your father's feelings
as well," Darius said under cover of Mrs. Badgely's
lecture about professional performers and their pen-
chant for leading innocent young ladies astray. "It
will please him to believe his scheme worked. Too,
in this way, if we become engaged, it won't seem
suspiciously hasty. Furthermore, the house party
will give me an opportunity to court you properly."

"Does that not strike you as farcical?" she said.

"On the contrary, it strikes me as crucial," he
said. "I have gone about this backward—seducing
first instead of wooing first. But I didn't know, you
see—"

"You can never go wrong with Handel," Mrs.
Badgely called out.

"I hate Handel," Lady Charlotte said under her
breath.

"I hate Handel," Darius muttered at the same
time.

They looked at each other, their lips tight to keep
back the laughter.

"Thank you, Mrs. Badgely," Lady Charlotte said.
"An excellent suggestion."

"She likes anything that sounds like church music," she whispered. "She dozes the way she does in

church. As soon as it's over, she starts talking."

Lady Charlotte played the Handel, and Mrs. Badgely behaved as predicted.

When it was over, the rector's wife was once again loudly monopolizing the conversation.

"You are right," Lady Charlotte murmured while she pretended to look for more music. "One of us must be sensible, and I cannot be. I am too . . . emotional. Thank you. It is most kind."

He had not been nearly kind enough. There was so much he had to say. But he could not say it now, in between interruptions, in sight of everybody. He'd have to make another opportunity.

Sunday 7 July

"I cannot believe you are doing this," Charlotte said.

"Nor can I," Mr. Carsington said. "I cannot remember when I last darkened the door of a church. I have never understood the logic of religion."

"Yet you came," she said.

"We must talk privately," he said. "This was the first opportunity."

She and Lizzie had not gone to Beechwood yesterday because Saturday was the day Lizzie reserved for reviewing accounts with the housekeeper, approving menus for the coming week, and attending to her correspondence.

Charlotte had not expected to see Mr. Carsington until Monday. She'd spent two restless nights, debating whether she'd done the right thing in not simply saying yes.

But now, as he walked beside her, so calm and completely confident, she was sure she'd been right.

She'd cried herself to sleep on Friday night, thinking of his kindness, of the comfort and relief she'd felt after she'd confessed, and he simply held her in his arms.

She couldn't repay that kindness at the expense of his pride and reputation.

If they married in haste, people would talk. He mightn't mind, but she would, on his account. She couldn't bear for anyone to think him a fortune hunter. She couldn't bear for his father to suppose he'd taken the easy way out.

Now, though, it seemed he was determined to set tongues wagging.

Since the church was a short distance from Lithby Hall, Lord and Lady Lithby preferred to walk there, weather permitting. At present they walked home, far enough ahead of Charlotte and Mr. Carsington to be in sight while out of earshot.

"I hope you realize you've put ideas in Papa's head," she said. "I hope you realize the whole village will be talking of this. It is as good as a declaration to walk with a lady after church."

"I know," he said. "Though I haven't spent a great deal of time among the fashionable set, I'm well aware of courtship practices. I've heard endlessly how they did it in my grandmother's day, and how my parents courted, and this relative and that. I hear all the gossip."

"Then why did you not wait for a less public opportunity?" she said.

"Because I *am* courting you," he said. "I see no logical reason to make a secret of it. That was not my main reason for coming here today, however. You said yesterday that you would never forgive yourself. You said many harsh words about your behavior. It is a cruel burden to bear. I cannot feel what you do. I am not a woman. I've never borne a child. But because I am not, I have, I hope, something to offer that a woman cannot. Another viewpoint, perhaps. I do not know exactly what needs to be done, but I mean to try, in every way that I can, to help you find peace." He looked away from her, to the couple ahead of them. Lizzie glanced back, smiling. "I mean to court you, yes," he went on. "But in these coming days I am determined as well to find a way to ease your heart."

It took her a moment to answer, because the heart he spoke of was so full. "You're a shockingly good man," she said at last. She mustered a smile. "Perhaps I'd better say yes and have done with it. I've never had any trouble resisting men's lures—at least not since that first time—but so much kindness is beyond me."

"No, I want a hearty yes," he said. "No questions, no doubts. I am determined to make you believe your life will be a desert—utterly unlivable without me."

She laughed then, how could she help it?

She didn't see her father look back then, and look to her stepmother, and exchange knowing smiles with her.

She didn't see the villagers exchange knowing glances, either, and she didn't hear the talk. She'd known tongues would wag, and she had an idea what they'd say.

She had no inkling of the danger.

She saw only the tall, powerful man beside her, and all she understood was the lightness of her heart as she walked beside him.

Sunday night

"He *what*?" Colonel Morrell said, his hand tightening on the whiskey glass.

"Walked with Lady Charlotte after church today," said Kenning.

Colonel Morrell threw the glass into the grate. It shattered.

Kenning didn't blink.

"Get me another," his master said quietly.

The manservant did as ordered. "I couldn't hardly believe it myself, sir, when I heard it," he said. "Everyone was talking about it. There was wagers on it. People saying they'll be calling the banns next Sunday, and the house party'll end in a wedding, if it don't start with one."

All this time—nearly a year—of watching her, studying her, planning, so carefully planning how to win her trust. All this time, enduring his uncle's sarcasm and criticism and nagging: *What's taking so long? Keep dawdling and a bolder and cleverer fellow will snatch her out from under your nose. You'd better find a gal easier to please; you ain't up to this one.*

Now she'd as good as declared she'd marry Lord Hargate's worthless Don Juan of a son.

She was not to be blamed. This sort of thing happened, unfortunately, all the time.

She'd taken leave of her senses, that was all.

Not for the first time.

But it was not her fault. She was a woman. Even she, remarkable as she was, had a woman's weaknesses.

He was not angry with her.

She was in danger, grave danger.

Colonel Morrell would have to save her from herself.

Chapter 12

Monday 8 July

Darius stared at the paper in his hand. It was neatly ruled, the handwriting clear and square, the figures all too easy to read.

It was the list of expenses he'd told Tyler to provide.

"It would have been cheaper to send the boy to Eton," Darius said.

Tyler twisted his cap in his hands. "The missus keeps the tally, sir," he said. "Tells me the lad grows out of his clothes as fast as she can make them. The girls pass on their things from one to the next, so it don't cost much more to dress six of 'em as one. But he been growing at a great rate, and he can't wear the girls' things now, can he? Not that he could wear any of their shoes anyway, what with his feet bigger even than my oldest gal's. I wish you could see how he eats. Going to be a big one, my missus says."

His missus had a good head for figures, apparently. She certainly had no trouble with large numbers.

The sum, Darius supposed, was not exorbitant. The trouble was, he didn't know where he'd find ready money at present, as "the missus" demanded.

"What of the money Pip earns catching rats?" Darius said. "Purchase tells me the boy's earned as much as ten pence in a day."

"Yes, sir, but while he's catching rats for you, I'm losing his help. Then I'll have to train up a new boy, won't I? And no telling how long it'll take to find one. I been looking, but as you know, sir, the most of 'em's worthless. Not to mention the missus must say aye or nay—on account the girls, you know. Don't want no thieves and ruffians and such living in the house with my girls."

Healthy and willing orphans were not thick on the ground, Darius knew. Still, he was sure the Tylers were making matters more expensive and complicated simply because they saw an opportunity to do so. Or the "missus," did, at any rate.

"I shall speak to my man of business," Darius said. While he was in Altrincham, he'd pay a visit to Mrs. Tyler as well.

Darius returned to Beechwood late in the day, nursing a headache. His visit had upset Mrs. Tyler, and when she was upset, her voice rose to a screech. Since he was a gentleman as well as her husband's employer, she couldn't shriek at him, so she shrieked at her daughters instead.

"Stop that coughing, Sally! Watch what you're doing with them greens, Annie! Mind that pail, Joan! You're splashing water everywhere!" And so on.

The girls shrieked back, defending themselves. She screeched at them not to talk back to their elders.

It was amazing that Tyler still had his hearing.

Screeching notwithstanding, it was not, all in all, a bad place for an orphan boy. Pip ate with the family instead of waiting for their table scraps, as was the case for many in a similar position. He slept in the kitchen, not a cupboard or a dank cellar. They did not dress him in rags. Whatever Mrs. Tyler's faults, she took great pride in her housewifery. Everyone under her roof—including the lowly apprentice— was "fed and clothed proper and knew what soap was," she told Darius.

Still, it represented a steep descent from Mr. Welton's household. Life with the Tylers meant no more schooling and that, Darius had discovered during last week's ride to Salford, distressed the boy, though he made a brave show of not minding.

I shall have to send him to school, Darius thought, as he rode home. It was that or take on Mr. Welton's role and tutor the boy himself.

School was better. A boy ought to be with other boys. The trouble was, one must pay for it. As it was, Darius still needed to find the ready money to reimburse the Tylers for Pip's upkeep. Mrs. Tyler might deem the boy bad luck, but she wasn't about to let the articles of indenture be broken until she was compensated—in hard coin—for every last scrap they'd provided him and every minute they'd spent on him.

Darius was analyzing his finances for the hundredth time as he neared his stables. A series of shouts and shrieks brought him out of the mathematical reverie.

He hurried toward the noise. A short distance from the stables, he found two boys rolling in the dirt, pummeling each other.

"You queer-eyed little bastard!"

"You'll look queer when I break your nose!"

"Your ma's a whore!"

"Your father buggers sheep!"

"Your pa's prick fell off from pox!"

"Your grandmother poxed the Royal Navy!"

Darius swiftly dismounted, strode to the combatants, grabbed them, and pulled them apart.

They continued to swing ineffectually at each other while breathlessly trading insults.

Darius lifted them off the ground and gave them both a shake. "Enough!" he said.

He didn't raise his voice. He never had to raise his voice.

The boys fell silent.

He let them down but didn't let them go.

He looked at Pip, who sported a bloody nose and would soon boast a black eye as well. "He never heard of William the Conqueror," Pip said. "He's an ignorant bloody buggering sod of an arsehole."

"That's enough," Darius said. He looked at the other boy, whose nose was bleeding as well. "Who are you?"

"Rob Jowett. Sir."

Rob looked to have suffered the worst of the battle. Not only was his eye promising to turn colorful, but his jaw was starting to swell. Darius released him. "Go home, Rob ," he said.

"He said the House of Lords is all bastards like him, sir," Rob said indignantly. "That's treason, ain't it?"

"It isn't, and I didn't say *all* of them," Pip said scornfully. "I said *some* of them *were*. Past tense. I suppose you can't hear any better than you can hit."

"That's enough," Darius said. "Rob, go home. Pip, I want to speak to you."

Rob went off, making hideous faces at Pip over his shoulder until he was out of sight.

When he was out of sight, and Pip had no one to make hideous faces back at, Darius said, "What was that all about?"

"He's as big as I am, sir," Pip said. "It's not wrong to hit someone as big as you are."

"What was it about?"

"He's so *ignorant*," Pip said, looking in the direction Rob had gone. "He said Daisy was ugly." He wiped his bloody nose on his coat sleeve.

Oh, Mrs. Tyler was going to love that.

"Where is Daisy?" Darius said.

"I brought her back. They like to have her home at Lithby Hall when Lady Lithby gets back from here, and these days the ladies go home near noon."

"Then Rob didn't try to hurt the dog," Darius said. "He merely found fault with her looks. And you hit him for that?"

Pip shook his head. "Oh, no, sir. First I tried to reason with him. First I said that she's a bulldog and that's how they're supposed to look. Besides, how could you say whether an animal was ugly or not, unless it was deformed? And he said I was deformed, and I said I wasn't—like you said. I said my eyes were *distinctive*. And he said I gave myself airs because I was a pet with the Lithby Hall ladies, exactly like the dog. And I said the ladies were only polite to me because that's how ladies are—polite, not that I expected him to know anything about what was polite any more than what was present and what was past tense. And he said my eyes were queer and it was because my mother was a poxy whore. And *then* I hit him." He looked toward where Rob had gone and smiled an unmistakably self-satisfied smile.

That smile.

Darius knew that smile.

But no.

It vanished as the boy's gaze came back, all earnestness now, to Darius. "I had to defend her honor, didn't I, sir?" he said.

His mother's honor.

The mother he'd never seen because she'd given him up when he was an infant.

A *newborn* infant?

Perhaps, but not the same newborn.

A coincidence, that was all.

"Sir?" said Pip. "Am I in trouble?"

"You'll be in a great deal of trouble if you return to Mrs. Tyler looking like that," Darius said. "You'd better put your head under the pump. And your coat sleeve as well. Where's your cap?"

The boy looked about, found it, and snatched it up.

The cap.

Darius remembered the way Lady Charlotte had held that same cap in her hand, the dazed look on her beautiful face.

He remembered her odd behavior when she'd tripped over the bucket. He remembered Pip standing in front of her, wide-eyed . . .

. . . wearing an expression much like the one she wore.

Had she wondered what Darius wondered now?

Staring at the boy's hair—filthy and tangled at present—Darius saw in his mind's eye Lady Charlotte on the day they'd tussled on the gravel: the Botticelli Venus bedraggled and dirty.

He saw the same contradiction: the angelic beauty and the grimy belligerence.

Coincidence. She must have thought so, too. What were the chances, after all?

Yet when he returned to the house, the first thing Darius did was review the notes he'd made over the course of the last week, about Philip Ogden.

He thought about it for the rest of the day.

Even when he lay in bed, aggravating himself imagining the time when Lady Charlotte would be lying with him, in his arms, his mind reverted to the puzzle.

By the time he fell asleep, he'd decided he must

travel to Yorkshire and try to get to the bottom of this. But first he'd better talk to her.

Tuesday 9 July

Darius was adding notes to those he'd already made when Mrs. Endicott appeared in the doorway of his study. "If you please, sir, the ladies are here," she said. "Lady Lithby wishes to speak to you."

He had not yet decided how to raise the subject of Pip with Charlotte. He knew he had no tact. He didn't want to upset her. He needed to think. What he didn't need was to have to make decisions about furnishings.

"It isn't about wall coverings, is it?" Darius said. "She does understand that I can't be asked about wall coverings. Or curtains."

"I can't say, sir," said Mrs. Endicott said. "All I know is—"

"Oh, come, Mr. Carsington, you are not afraid of curtains, I hope," said a light, laughing voice.

Mrs. Endicott hastily moved away from the door, and Lady Lithby sailed in, Lady Charlotte behind her, looking utterly angelic in a fluffy white dress.

Darius remembered her sitting on the desk upstairs and pulling up her pristine skirts, unabashed, uninhibited.

He took a calming breath and rose from his chair, casually pushing the papers under a ledger.

"I am deeply afraid of curtains," he said. "I say

I want red curtains. You ask whether I mean crimson or scarlet. You ask whether I prefer brocade or embroidered. Fringed or unfringed. Then you ask about *tassels,*" he added darkly. "It is a quick route to dementia."

Lady Lithby laughed.

"There's nothing to be frightened of," Lady Charlotte said. "It's only about the laundry."

"I know nothing about laundry, either," he said.

"We refer to the building on your property where the washing used to be done," Lady Lithby said patiently. "The dirty linen is accumulating there."

"I thought Goodbody sent my things out," he said.

"That may be, but a household requires household linens," said Lady Lithby. "Bed linens. Kitchen linens. The servants' smocks and aprons and such. As a single gentleman, you may feel it is more practical to send your laundry out or to have a wash maid come in once a week. However, if you plan any change in your circumstances . . ." She paused very briefly. ". . . or if you plan to entertain often, you may find it more convenient to hire live-in laundry maids."

Where the devil was he to find money to pay laundry maids? He needed money for Pip first.

He must have looked panicked because Lady Charlotte said, "Your laundry needs almost no repair. We've had it cleaned. The maids can begin working as soon as you please."

"I have a great deal of business to see to," he said.

"I'll stop and look at it as soon as I finish here. Then I'll weigh the pros and cons on my way to the home farm."

"That seems a most logical and efficient use of your time," Lady Charlotte said, looking mightily amused.

"Indeed, I dare not keep Mr. Carsington any longer from his work," Lady Lithby said. She turned away and left the room.

Darius joined Lady Charlotte as she started after her stepmother. He touched her arm to slow her down. "Meet me at the laundry in half an hour," he whispered.

"What shall I tell her?" she said.

"Anything but the truth," he said.

It took Charlotte more than half an hour to escape to the laundry because, naturally, this must be one of the days Molly accompanied her to Beechwood. The maid had plenty to do at home, tending to her mistress's clothing and overseeing the servants who looked after Charlotte's rooms. Like Lizzie's maid, she had precious little time to spare for following her mistress about at Beechwood, where one certainly didn't need her, with servants swarming about like flies.

But Molly came today, and getting rid of her wasn't easy. Finally, Charlotte sent the maid to consult with the housekeeper about a heap of Lady Margaret's gowns they'd found stuffed into a window seat. The consultation would involve tea, Charlotte knew, because Mrs. Endicott would be eager to establish a good relationship with the upper servants of the great house next door. As lady's maid to Lord Lithby's daughter, Molly stood near the top of the female staff hierarchy, only a very little below Lizzie's maid.

Amid all the bustle—workmen and servants going to and fro, hammering, scraping, cleaning, and so on—it was easy enough to slip out of the house. Sneaking to the laundry was more difficult. It had been built farther away from the house than other service areas because it could be very smelly, especially in the old days, when lye was the main cleansing agent.

Still, Charlotte knew the place well enough by now to work out a path that would keep her out of view for the most part. If caught, she could manufacture an excuse on the spur of the moment. She'd had plenty of practice lying.

She didn't have to lie to Mr. Carsington.

No pretending. No concealing. Freedom, to be herself.

The thought made her dizzy.

Or maybe that was simply happiness.

She came to the laundry at last and reached for the door handle. At the same instant, the door flew open and a large hand grabbed hers and pulled her inside.

He shut the door and pulled her into his arms and kissed her.

Her knees instantly gave way. She clutched the front of his coat and hung on and kissed him back as hard as she could. She didn't know how to hold back, with him. She didn't want to hold back. She only wanted to hold on.

He smelled of outdoors. His coat held the sun's warmth, and his kiss was warm, too, and so wonderfully familiar. She could have stayed forever like this, pressed against his big, hard body, letting her mind swirl, giddy as a girl's, while they kissed, endlessly.

But it ended as abruptly as it had begun. He broke the kiss and put her away from him.

"We must talk," he said.

It was the tone, the serious tone that drained away the warmth, as much as the distance he'd made between them.

Then it came back to her in a vivid flash of recollection: Geordie's voice on that last day, so grave. *We cannot see each other so often,* he'd said. *People will talk. I'd better go away for a time.*

"I may need to go away for a time," Mr. Carsington said.

She shook her head, unable to comprehend. Too much noise in her head, and too much noise in her pounding heart. Why had he kissed her, only to put her away from him and say he was going away?

He frowned. "Are you ill?"

"No," she said. "No. Only tell me straight out. Don't break it to me gently."

His frown deepened. "When have you ever known me to break anything gently? I scarcely know how. That's the difficulty with . . ." He trailed off. "But tell me what's troubling you."

"I don't know," she said. *Be sensible*, she told herself. *This isn't Geordie.*

"It's your face," she said. "You look so serious. I wondered if you'd changed your mind . . . about me."

"Would you mind very much if I changed my mind?" he said. He bent his head and peered into her eyes. "Would you mind very much if I set you free to marry a duke's son, or an officer covered with medals or any other of those paragons your father's chosen for his mating party?"

She nodded. "I should mind very much. I think," she began, and paused because she saw the smile then, so very faint, curving the corners of his mouth. She saw it more distinctly, a glint in his eyes. "I think," she said, taking heart, "I would choke you if you changed your mind. I have so looked forward to your courting me. Properly. As you promised."

"Properly?" He quirked an eyebrow. "I walked with you after church yesterday. How much more wooing do you want?"

"More than *that*," she said. "I was looking forward to a long, slow courtship. Instead, you barged into it. Though he's much too discreet to say so, Papa has taken the hint already, I am quite sure."

"I should be vastly surprised if he hadn't," he said. "The village idiot has taken the hint, I daresay. I am not sure how I could have made my intentions plainer."

"Oh, you," she said. She went to him again and butted her head against his chest. He brought his arms about her, and she looked up into his laughing eyes. "You cheated," she said. "I thought you said the mating party would go on as planned, and you were going to persuade me of all your perfections and how unlivable my life will be without you."

"I said I'd participate," he said. "I said I'd do a great many things, and I mean to. I never said I wouldn't cheat."

"Very well," she said. "You didn't say that. What else didn't you say that I ought to know about?"

"Nothing," he said. "At any rate, it isn't cheating, precisely," he said.

"Then what is it, precisely?"

"I'm simply stealing a march on my rivals," he said. "Colonel Morrell will understand, certainly, though he won't like it. I have no dashing uniform, no medals, no—"

"Colonel Morrell?" Charlotte said. "How does he come into it?"

"Ah, yes." Mr. Carsington studied her face. "I'd forgotten. You have no idea. Not surprising. He isn't at all obvious. In most cases, that would be a great disadvantage, but he's no fool, and I'll wager—"

"What are you talking about?"

"He wants you," Mr. Carsington said.

She would have laughed, but she could tell he wasn't teasing her now. Uneasy, she said, "He doesn't. He can't. He's a good friend, no more. I think you see a rival where there isn't one. I know he's been invited to join the house party, but that's because he's a neighbor."

"Colonel Morrell has spent most of his life in the military," Mr. Carsington said. "He did not rise as rapidly as he did by being a fool. He has a strategy, you may be sure. I daresay he's observed you as carefully as he might observe a town he means to capture. Having observed you, he must have decided that camouflage was in order."

What had Colonel Morrell seen? Charlotte wondered. And how had she failed to see?

"I should have noticed," she said.

"Then what?"

"Then I should have done something," she said.

"Such as?"

"I should have got him to not marry me," she said. "I'm quite good at not getting married."

"Are you, indeed?" he said. "I wondered how you managed it for so long. I shall be interested to hear your technique. The question has puzzled me no end."

She was more concerned with the other puzzle. "Colonel Morrell was in London during the Season," she said. "He attended many of the same affairs. If he observed me so closely, he must have found me out. Still, I don't—"

"Don't fret about him," Mr. Carsington said. "He'll understand *my* strategy easily enough. I'm the youngest of a nobleman's five sons. I have no profession, no source of income apart from my father, and no assets except for a dilapidated estate. My main advantage is proximity to the object of desire. He can hardly blame me for exploiting the advantage. He would do the same in my place. Males will do whatever is necessary in these situations, and they are not overly scrupulous about their methods."

"You greatly underestimate yourself," she said.

"Not as a marital prospect," he said. "I have considered the subject with ruthless objectivity."

"You have overlooked several other assets," she said. "For instance, there is your considerable intelligence."

"Intellect is not necessarily an advantage," he said. "Many women prefer men stupider than they are, because dolts are easier to manage."

"That's true," she said. "But remember, most women have a keen aesthetic sense, too, as well as a desire to produce strong, beautiful offspring. Consequently, they prefer men who are tall, strong, and attractive. We must add your prodigious good looks to your list of assets."

"That is not where a man wants most to be prodigious," he said. "Good looks are common enough. We suitors will be more concerned about the prodigious size of our rival's procreative organs."

"That's ridiculous," she said. "It's not as though we can see them and make comparisons."

"Ridiculous or not," he said, "it is true. We all behave as though this is something the average young lady, with limited or no experience of such matters, will take into consideration. As though the girls would take out their rulers or measuring tapes and make comparisons."

Instantly she saw her young cousins, innocents, all of them, with dressmaker's tapes in hands, soberly assessing the gentlemen's assets. She let out a whoop of laughter, and hastily covered her mouth.

How on earth was she to behave herself for the

next month, pretending to allow him to court her? Properly. She wondered if he knew what *proper* was.

"You've made me forget what I meant to say," he said. "We need to—" He broke off and clamped his hand over her mouth.

Then she heard the voices outside.

She didn't have time to hear the conversation. Mr. Carsington pulled and pushed her into a far corner of the room, onto a heap of sheets. He picked up a large basket of laundry and dumped its contents onto her. "Don't move," he whispered. "Try not to breathe too much."

She heard him walk quickly away.

Darius had hoped the voices belonged to servants, either coming to deliver more dirty linen or simply passing by. But as soon as he neared the door he recognized the stentorian tones of Mrs. Badgely and the lighter notes of Lady Lithby.

Grimly he opened the door.

"Ah, there you are," said Mrs. Badgely. "This will not do, sir, you know."

He did not let his gaze stray to the heap of laundry at the other end of the room. He merely regarded the rector's wife with an expression of polite inquiry.

"He is a single gentleman, Mrs. Badgely, " Lady Lithby said. "Single gentlemen often find it simpler to send their things to one of the local laundresses."

"Mr. Carsington is not a single gentleman in lodgings in *London*," Mrs. Badgely answered. She turned to him. "You are a gentleman of property, sir—a not-inconsiderable property. You will set a bad example, to leave your laundry standing vacant and unused. In doing so, you encourage immoral behavior among the servants. Their sneaking about the stables is difficult enough to suppress. When one leaves buildings unattended, one extends an open invitation to fornicate."

Let them, Darius thought. It was a natural instinct, and one of the two main pleasures the lower orders had in their lives: copulation and intoxication.

Normally, he would have said as much, thereby enhancing his reputation for being aggravating. That was not the way to get rid of Mrs. Badgely in a hurry, though.

The way to get rid of her was to use the Lithbys' method: Appear to listen attentively, then do as one pleased.

He said, "Those are excellent points, Mrs. Badgely. I shall certainly take them into consideration. If it is not too much trouble, perhaps you would look about you as you make your rounds of the parish, and advise me as to any superior candidates for the position. Mrs. Endicott is not familiar with the local families, and I'm sure she'll be grateful to have the benefits of your knowledge."

"She would, indeed," said Lady Lithby. "In fact, I wonder if I might prevail on you to help us determine what to do with some ancient gowns of Lady Margaret's we've found here. I think we might keep one or two for fancy dress. But what to do with the rest is the question. There is a great deal of usable cloth in the collection, yet I fear it is too fine for the servants, let alone the poor."

"Gowns, really?" Mrs. Badgely was intrigued. "I always heard that Lady Margaret was a leader of fashion in her day."

Mrs. Badgely might be a tiresome scold, but she was a woman, too, and Darius saw her eyes light up when Lady Lithby mentioned the gowns.

In a moment, the two women were gone, the laundry forgotten. He waited until they were out of earshot, then closed the door.

He hastened to the heap of dirty linen in the corner.

An apron caught him in the face.

He saw Lady Charlotte's upflung hand before he saw the rest of her.

The household linens and items of attire became a writhing mass as she struggled to extricate herself.

She sat up, sputtering, a pair of his drawers on her head. "You," she said. "*You.*"

He bit his lip. He coughed. He snickered. And finally, he let it out, a great whoop of laughter.

She scowled at him. "I was afraid to breathe," she said. "Then my nose itched, and I dared not scratch it. Then—"

She broke off, glaring at him—no doubt because he must be grinning like an idiot.

"What?" she said. "What?"

"On your head," he said. "My drawers."

She looked up.

"You have my drawers on your head," he said.

A pause.

Then, "Oh, that," she said. "Yes. I do that sometimes. Wear drawers on my head. It's one of those interesting habits one gets to know about the other person as one gets to know the other person."

"I should not wear them outside if I were you," he said.

"Oh, very well." She sighed. "I suppose you want them back."

"Well, they are mine."

She lifted them off with two fingers and threw them at him.

Seeing her sprawled among rumpled bedclothes, he could easily picture a future involving pillow fights . . . and underwear flung hither and yon . . .

The thought warmed him.

It warmed him quite a bit.

"I'd better go back," she said. "If they're going to talk to Mrs. Endicott, Molly might decide she isn't wanted and will come looking for me."

She started to get up, then paused, a comically baffled look on her beautiful face. She twisted to one side, her hand searching among the linens. "I've lost my shoe," she said.

She turned about onto all fours, and started crawling about over the sheets and pillowcases. "I can't believe this," she said. She turned her head to throw him an exasperated look. "Don't just stand there. Help me. I can't leave without my shoe."

He knelt upon the tangle of laundry. He began looking for the shoe.

This would have been easier if she hadn't been crawling over piles of bed things and bath things and kitchen things and stray underwear, her derri-ère swaying as she moved.

Don't look, he told himself.

He tried not to look but he couldn't shut out the teasing rustle of movement nearby.

"I cannot believe I lost my shoe," she muttered. "The curst things *tie!*"

He tried not to look but he could see, out of the corner of his eye, the light muslin dress with its feminine froth of ruffles. He recalled then, vividly, her sitting upon the desk last Friday, in her too-innocently feminine dress. He saw her hands pulling the skirts up to her knees and telling him to touch her.

"I thought you sent your laundry out," she said. "I cannot believe your valet would let your drawers be jumbled among the bed linens."

Darius could almost feel the slope of her insteps under his hands, the slender ankles, the elegant curve of her legs.

"Charlotte," he said, "you have to get up. Now. And go to the other end of the laundry."

She looked over her shoulder at him. "Why?"

"Because," he said.

"Because . . . ?" She waited for clarification.

"Because Mrs. Badgely is right. Laundries are dens of iniquity."

She started to get up. Then she sank back onto her haunches. "Did she put indecent thoughts in your head?" she said.

"No," he said. "*You* put indecent thoughts in my head. And it won't do. I made up my mind to woo you properly. I made up my mind that the next time we made love it would not be furtive and hasty. The next time we made love, we would be wed, and have all the time in the world, and we would take all the time we needed. I would undress you, slowly, and learn every inch of you."

He heard her breath coming faster, as his did.

She folded her hands against her stomach, as though she must hold herself back. "I love when you touch me," she said. That was all.

He remembered how she had touched him. His body remembered, in a rush of heat that thickened his mind.

"We'd better find your shoe," he said.

"Yes," she said. "You're right."

She never moved, though, only sat looking at him, her folded hands tight against her belly.

He crawled to her, over the discarded sheets and towels and aprons and underwear.

"I think about you all the time," she said. "I can't help it. Last night, I lay in bed—"

He put two fingers against her lips. "Don't tell me."

She took his fingers away. "Is it wrong?" she said. "Am I a hopeless wanton? Am I too bold?"

"No," he said. "Oh, no. Not for me. With me you need never hold back."

"Then I won't," she said. She put her hands up and cupped his face and kissed him, sweetly, lingeringly.

His arms went around her, helplessly.

He leaned in, and she fell back, and he with her, onto the heap of laundry.

He felt her laughter against his lips, and he was laughing inside, and laughter should have been enough to keep desire at bay.

But the laughter was pleasure, and from one pleasure to the next was all too easy.

Her hands moved over his coat, then under, and
under again. Heat rippled wherever she touched
him.

Your hands, your hands.

It was the same for him: At the touch of her hands,
feeling stirred and built and roiled through him,
wave after wave. He couldn't name what it was she
awoke in him. It didn't need a name.

Call it hunger.

He kissed her throat and dragged his hands over
her. She sighed and squirmed under his touch. He
let his body sink onto hers, and their legs tangled.
They kissed, rolling over mounds of bedclothes, until she was on top of him, straddling him, her core
pressing against his arousal.

He dragged his hands up under her skirts and
petticoats. She tugged at his trouser buttons, quickly, impatiently. Her hair was tumbling about her
shoulders.

Wild and so beautiful.

"I want you," she said. "I want you inside me."

"I'm yours," he said raggedly.

She pushed his clothes away, setting him free.
Her gaze locked with his, she caressed him. "Like
this?" she said. "Is this right?"

"Whatever you do is right," he said. He brought
his hand to her core, brushing over the downy
curls. He was awash in pure hot pleasure, simply
touching that warm cloud of femininity.

"Your hands," she said. "Oh, your hands."

"Come to me," he said.

She understood, and rose a little. He guided himself into her, and she gasped. "Oh," she said. "Oh, this is . . . good."

"Yes," he said. It was good, so good.

He reached up and cupped her face and brought her lips to his.

A long, aching kiss, while their bodies joined in simple, primitive rhythm. He felt her pleasure peak, her body vibrating. He rolled with her onto his side, and she pulsed with every movement, yielding utterly to him, to herself, to feeling, pure feeling.

Yes, this was right and good.

She was right and good.

He pressed his mouth against her neck to muffle his groans as his body pumped with hers, and fiery happiness coursed through him. He heard her muffled cries, too, as she went with him this time to the pinnacle of all the human body could give in pleasure.

Then, when at last they began to quiet, he wrapped his arms about her and kissed her neck, again and again.

He kissed her and laughed, for delight—of her, of the two of them, joined, the two of them as one.

It was so easy then, to understand what was in his heart, and easy, too, to say it. He murmured the words against her silky skin: "I do love you, I do."

Chapter 13

Of course she couldn't believe her ears.

A wise woman would not seek confirmation.

A wise woman would hold her tongue, and not risk spoiling the fantasy.

Charlotte wasn't wise.

"Say that again," she said.

He lifted his mouth from her neck. "Say what?"

"What you just said."

"I didn't say anything."

She heard laughter in his voice. "Yes, you did," she said.

"No, I didn't."

"Yes, you did."

A long pause. "*Must* I say it again?" he said.

"Yes," she said.

"I forget," he said.

"Say it," she said.

He chuckled softly.

"Say it," she said.

He put his mouth close to her ear. "I love you," he said. "Now are you happy?"

"Yes," she said. "I am very happy."

This lovemaking was even better than the previous, and that had been a sort of miracle. She hadn't thought she could be happier. She'd been unaware of the weight remaining on her heart until he uttered the words, and it lifted.

"Now you may say it," he said.

"Say what?" she said.

"I know you better than you think," he said. "You act upon feeling, and you would not make love without feeling it. Or something close. Say something."

"If we stay like this for too long, will we be stuck?" she said. "Dogs get stuck sometimes, I know."

"You are an abominable tease," he said.

"Yes," she said. "And sometimes I wear underwear on my head."

"Come, Charlotte," he said, "Say something."

She gave a soft laugh, dislodging him slightly.

"Be kind to your besotted lover," he said.

She drew in a long breath and let it out. "I love you," she said.

He gazed at her, his golden eyes glowing like candlelight. "Do you, indeed?"

"I can't seem to help it," she said. "You have become another habit."

"I don't mind being one of your habits," he said. "And I think you are charming wearing my drawers on your head." He kissed her. "But we had better separate. I'm too excitable today, and I can't become aroused again. We haven't time, curse it."

Gently, he eased away from her.

"I am not sure this long courtship idea is going to

work," he said. "If we keep on like this, we're going to set off a scandal. It's amazing we haven't been caught yet."

"Oh, you're right," she said. "It is so easy to be foolish. No wonder long engagements are not encouraged. If you care for someone, it is very difficult to keep a proper distance."

She found a towel and cleaned herself. He did the same, with a brisk efficiency that made her smile.

"Mrs. Badgely was right," she said. "Laundries are practically Sodom and Gomorrah. It's too easy to be tempted. Heaps of soft things to lie or kneel or sit on. Then all the towels and such to clean with afterward."

"We'd better not come here again," he said. "At least not until after the wedding."

"We should have to chase the laundry maids out first," she said.

He growled. "Laundry maids," he said. "Don't remind me. Laundry maids and milkmaids—but I shall do it."

The estate, she thought. She'd let herself forget why he'd come here in the first place.

"Mr. Carsington," she said.

While they spoke, he'd put his clothing back into order and helped with hers, all with the same smooth economy of movement. Now he stood and helped her up. Hauled her up, rather. The lovemaking had left her limp as well as stupid.

"Darius," he said. "In the circumstances, I think we may be a bit more informal together."

"Darius," she tried softly. She shook her head.

"Not yet. That makes it even harder to keep a proper distance—and I am sure to slip and say it in public. I'd better wait. After we're officially engaged, perhaps. Or after we're married. And as to that—the courtship, the wedding—"

"I know," he said. "I'm not sure we can wait a year. I seem unable to exercise even a modicum of restraint."

"It takes two," she said. "And I seem to be the instigator."

He smiled. "I like that about you," he said. "The way you instigate."

"Perhaps we need to reconsider our plan," she said.

"Yes," he said. "But that will have to wait. Once again, we have lost all sense of time as well as restraint. You'd better get back before—"

"My shoe," she said. "I forgot about my shoe. I can't go back wearing one shoe." She started to kneel, to look for it.

"*No*," he said. "That's how the trouble started. You must stay exactly where you are and let me look for it."

He knelt and systematically went through the linens, tossing them into a separate heap as he went along. Near the bottom of the mass, the shoe appeared, its ties tangled, as she had guessed, with the button of one of his shirts.

He quickly untangled it, his big hands swift and capable. Those hands.

"Give me your foot," he said.

She braced her hand on his shoulder and slipped

her foot into the shoe. He quickly tied it. Then he patted the shoe. "Good shoe," he said. "If you had not gone missing, this would not have happened." He looked up at her. "It was foolish but it was good."

Charlotte lifted her hand to his head, and dragged her fingers through his thick, sun-kissed hair. "Yes," she said. "It was good."

"You'd better get back," he said. "We'll have to find a time tomorrow to talk."

She shook off the remaining afterglow of love-making.

The house. She must get back. Yes. Soon.

Good grief. *Mrs. Badgely* was there.

That meant closer inquiries about her whereabouts than usual.

"Oh, my goodness," she said. "The crocodile." She ruffled his hair, then hurried away from him and out of the building, her mind so busy formulating an explanation for her absence that she utterly forgot about asking him where he needed to go and why.

Lady Margaret's magnificent old gowns proved so fascinating that the ladies hadn't noticed Charlotte's extended absence.

Molly noticed her return, though, and promptly devised an urgent question for Charlotte to answer in another part of the house.

"Oh, your ladyship, your hair," she said, as she pushed Charlotte into a chair and quickly set about restoring it to rights. "I was frantic when you came through the door. If Mrs. Badgely had looked up from those gowns—well, I'm afraid to think what she would have said. Oh, you're all wrinkled, too, and what am I to do about that? Shall I say you're feeling poorly and need to go straight home?"

"I don't want to worry Stepmama," Charlotte said. "Is it that bad?"

"It's dreadful," Molly said. "I'm sure Lady Lithby noticed, and I expect she'll be talking to you later. But meanwhile, *you can't go back in that room with them.*"

"Very well. Tell them one of the shoulder straps of my stays has given way," Charlotte said. "Or the busk has snapped. A dress emergency of some kind."

Lizzie, bless her, led Mrs. Badgely to speculate about Lady Margaret. Charlotte escaped without an interrogation.

One would come later, from Lizzie, but Charlotte would deal with that when the time came.

They soon returned to Lithby Hall, and while Molly stripped off the wrinkled dress, she told Charlotte the latest servants' gossip: The footman had reported that Pip had sported a black eye this morning when he came to collect the dog.

Charlotte froze where she was, her hand over her fast-beating heart. "Someone's been beating him?" she said.

"More like he beat someone else," Molly said. "He got into a fight with one of the carpenter's sons over to Beechwood, I heard. Rob Jowett. Stouter than Pip but got the worst of it. They say Rob's face is swelled up like a balloon, and his own mother wouldn't recognize him. Everyone here says young Jowett had it coming for provoking Pip. But they say the Tylers say it's the last straw, and the boy's going back to the workhouse."

"That's absurd," Charlotte said tightly. "Mr. Carsington wouldn't permit it. He's taken an interest in the child. Was he not the one who found a job for Pip when the workmen were making trouble about him at Beechwood?"

"Mr. Carsington will have to get the boy back from the workhouse, is what I heard," Molly said. "Something to do with the articles of indenture. I don't understand it, but they say the boy has to go back to the workhouse first, then Mr. Carsington must go to the law about it."

Charlotte knew nothing about the legal details regarding apprentices. But some official arrangement must be made, she was aware. For a journeyman, an apprentice was an investment of time as well as money.

She didn't care what the law said. She remembered the tone of Pip's voice when he spoke of the workhouse. He could not go back there, even for an hour. It was too cruel.

She shook her head at the frock Molly had taken from the wardrobe. "I must go to Beechwood," she said. "Find me a habit—and have someone ready my horse, right away."

Though Molly looked worried, she did as Charlotte commanded, and the horse was ready by the time Charlotte was dressed. Tom Jenkins was there, too, which surprised her. He was head coachman now, and accompanying the ladies was a task given to lower-ranking grooms. At her look of inquiry he said, "I heard it had to do with Pip, your ladyship, and I knew his lordship wouldn't be wanting me at present. I wanted to let Mr. Carsington and the rest of 'em know the lad was provoked. I heard Jowett's boy and the others plaguing Pip, calling him names, time and again."

She doubted Mr. Carsington needed a character reference for Pip, but she was glad of Jenkins's company.

She had not yet left the park when she encountered Colonel Morrell.

She had to struggle to keep her greeting cordial and not impatient. "I'm sorry I can't stay to talk," she said. "I have an errand at Beechwood that can't wait. But my father is expected home soon, and Lady Lithby arrived a little while ago."

Charlotte had hurried out while Lizzie was changing into afternoon dress.

"It was you I wished to see," he said. "I had hoped to speak to you privately. Perhaps you would be so good as to spare me a moment of your time."

Charlotte remembered what Mr. Carsington had said, and her heart sank.

She had rarely allowed men to reach the point where they'd make her an offer. She did not relish rejecting them. She much preferred to deflect them before matters reached that stage.

Still, she could read the signs as well as any other woman. If a gentleman who was not a rake wanted a word in private, he wanted to make an offer of matrimony.

Oh, why now, of all times? she thought. Why couldn't he have given her some warning and spared them an unpleasant conversation?

It couldn't be helped. She nodded, then glanced at Jenkins. He frowned but dutifully dropped behind them, out of earshot.

"I shall come quickly to the point," Colonel Morrell said. "I am a plain soldier and an unpolished sort of fellow, I suppose, by Society's standards. Yet I am not without sensibilities, and mine were touched, deeply, from the moment I met you."

She said nothing. He had a speech prepared, and the kind and proper thing to do was to let him say it, and do him the courtesy of considering it. Or at least pretending to consider it.

Oh, how she hated this! How she hated to disappoint them, hurt them.

"I cannot make flowery speeches," he went on. "It were absurd to feign to be other than the plain fellow I am. I shall not bore you with my accomplishments or prospects. You know them already and have formed your own judgment. You know I can keep you in the style to which you are accustomed, that my position in the world is not low and in time shall be higher. There is no need to expand upon these matters. What I wish to say, simply, is that I admire and love you exceedingly. I want nothing more than to protect and cherish you. I hope you will allow me to do so by doing me the great honor of becoming my wife."

If he had made a flowery speech or boasted of his

accomplishments and prospects, it would have been easier for her. As it was, she was grieved to disappoint him.

Oh, why had he not given her some warning!

She took time to try to calm herself and assemble the words she must say. She took a deep breath and let it out again. "Colonel Morrell, you do me a great honor," she said. "I hold you in high esteem, and I have been grateful for your friendship, but I cannot offer more than that. I cannot accept your offer."

He let out a sigh. "Ah, well, I expected as much," he said. "I had better not keep you any longer from your errand. May I accompany you as far as the gates?"

She nodded, relieved that the matter was disposed of so easily, that he took it so well.

He was a soldier, after all, as both he and Mr. Carsington had pointed out.

She gave her horse leave to walk on, and the colonel did likewise.

"I collect your business at Beechwood is important, to take you back so soon," he said.

"It is rather important," she said. "I heard that the boy Pip—the one who walks Lady Lithby's dog—got into a fight with another boy and is to be sent back to the workhouse. I'm not sure that Mr. Carsington has been informed of this turn of events. I wanted to warn him."

"Ah, yes, the apprentice boy in whom Mr. Carsington has taken so much interest," the colonel said. "Does he know that Pip is your son?"

* * *

Darius sat at his desk, regarding Tyler through narrowed eyes. "This had better not be a trick," he said. "I will not be made a game of."

"It ain't no game, sir," Tyler said. "Pip's bolted."

"That makes no sense at all," Darius said.

"He took the dog back to Lithby Hall afore noon," Tyler said. "He was to come straight back and do an errand for me. It's two hours now, and he ain't back."

"He's a boy," Darius said. "They're easily distracted. What would make you think he's run away?"

Tyler shuffled and looked everywhere but at Darius. "That fight yesterday, with Jowett's boy. My missus had a deal of work cleaning and mending Pip's coat and breeches. She said he was an ungrateful boy, and deserved to be sent back to the workhouse." Tyler wrung the cap in his hands. "She didn't mean it, sir. She was vexed was all."

Darius did not believe Pip was foolish enough to run away. Had Darius not told the child to come to him if he lost his place? Surely he trusted Darius to keep his word?

Still, he was a boy, and they were not the most logical beings.

"I'll look for him," Darius said. "I doubt he's gone far."

Your son.

Long practice kept Charlotte firmly in her saddle. Years of self-discipline kept her countenance calm while within she reeled from the blow, so sudden, so utterly unexpected.

The cold came first, a chill so deep that she might have believed, for an instant, that her heart had given way and she was dying.

"You didn't know, then," Colonel Morrell said. "I wasn't sure. I'm sorry to distress you but it cannot be helped. I learned of it. Others might."

She found her voice. "You cannot be serious," she said.

"I wish I were not," he said. "But one cannot change the facts. Philip Ogden was born in the year 1812 on the twenty-fourth of May near Halifax, in the West Riding of Yorkshire."

Halifax. Twenty-fourth of May. Born at four o'clock in the morning. Gone out of her life within an hour.

"He was the son of Captain George Blaine," Colonel Morrell went on. "The captain was killed in a duel the previous November. The mother, reputed to have died in childbed, did not die, though she was gravely ill for a long time afterward. Her name was—is—Lady Charlotte Hayward."

Pip. Her son. Alive.

She'd known. Of course she'd known, the instant she'd seen the child. She had known in a deep, secret place in her heart. Everything else she'd thought and told herself since that moment was pretending, as she'd always done. Trying to follow the rules. Trying to be sensible. Trying not to upset anybody. Trying to live up to her father's love and Lizzie's, too. Trying to be a good girl.

She wasn't a good girl. Never had been. Never would be.

"It was his eyes, you see," Colonel Morrell said. "Frederick Blaine served under me. I knew his brother George's reputation, and I remembered that he'd been stationed near here not many months before his death. About the time of his death, you fell ill suddenly and were taken to Yorkshire. But you were not ill then. You were pregnant with his child."

He went on to describe Pip's early life: the death of the Ogdens, the two years with Mr. Welton before he, too, died, then the time in the workhouse.

"The facts were all readily available but scattered and apparently unrelated," Colonel Morrell said. "It was an odd happenstance that I had more facts at hand than most people. This made it relatively easy for me to piece together the story."

"You sound as though you have no doubt you've pieced it together correctly," she said.

"No doubt whatsoever," he said. "Last week I made sure to be traveling the road to Altrincham at the same hour Mr. Tyler and his apprentice walked to work," he said. "The boy has the Blaine eyes. Everything else . . ." He paused and smiled faintly. "Everything else seems to be his mother's."

Mine, she thought. *Everything else is mine.*

"I would rather not have to tell you this," he said.

"Yet you have," she said.

"The charade cannot continue for much longer," he said. "You had a discontented former coachman at large. Though he knew next to nothing, he made a great deal of it, and dropped obscure hints about skeletons in the family closet. If I hit upon the kernel of truth in his drunken maunderings, others could do the same."

Fewkes, she thought. He'd been a groom ten years ago. Was he the one Geordie had bribed to get near her?

"Fewkes is on his way to foreign parts," Colonel Morrell went on. "This is but one of many precautions that ought to be taken. I can do a great deal more. Something must be done about the boy, certainly. Buying his articles of indenture is only the first step, no trouble at all. While it is impossible to acknowledge him, one must see that he's raised in a good home and given a gentleman's education. This can be arranged discreetly. Your honor—and that of your family—must be protected. This trouble must not burden your father. Among other things, he must not learn of your stepmother's role in the deception. Naturally, I should feel it my responsibility to see to all this and more . . . for my wife."

What had Mr. Carsington said? *Males will do whatever is necessary . . . and they are not overly scrupulous . . .*

"I see," she said.

She saw clearly: no way out.

"You need only reconsider the answer you gave a moment ago to my proposal of marriage," Colonel Morrell said. "You need only give me a different answer, and I shall serve you as I serve my king—to the utmost of my ability."

There's always a choice, poor mad old Lady Margaret had written.

No, there wasn't, not always.

Chapter 14

"No," said Lady Charlotte.

Colonel Morrell had prepared himself for everything. He had all his facts in order. He had gauged this meeting to a nicety.

He was not prepared for *no*, and he couldn't believe his ears.

"I beg your pardon," he said. "I thought you said no."

"That is what I said," she said. "No the first time and no again. I can hardly believe you would use these tactics. But yes, I must believe it, because I know men can be unscrupulous in such matters."

He was not unscrupulous. He was trying to save her from her own folly!

"Lady Charlotte, I think you are letting your emotions get the better of your sense," he said.

"I'm done being sensible," she said. "Ten years of it have brought me nothing but regret."

He saw her slipping through his hands, after all these months of making her feel safe in his company, all this time getting her used to having him about.

This was not supposed to happen. She was supposed to see that he was the steady one, the man she could rely upon. He'd found out her secret and not breathed a hint of censure. He was prepared to do whatever was necessary to keep it, to protect her. He was her knight in shining armor. Why couldn't she see that?

Because Carsington stood in the way.

"Lady Charlotte, I heard about the walk after church with Mr. Carsington," he said. "You think his intentions are honorable. They may be. For the moment. But to some men, marriage means nothing."

"I'll take my chances," she said.

"For God's sake, don't be a fool!" he said. "Don't risk everything—your honor, your family's honor—to throw your life away on a man who won't stand by you. Don't make the same mistake you made when you were sixteen."

"It's not the same mistake," she said. "This is a completely different one."

"Lady Charlotte."

"Thank you for telling me about my son," she said.

She rode away.

Darius had mounted his horse and was about to set out for Altrincham when two riders entered the stable yard, one male, one female.

One, Lady Charlotte. The other, Tom Jenkins.

She wore a blue habit, which Darius supposed was plain and practical compared to her other attire. Yet ribbons sprouted gaily from her hat, a lacy ruff encircled her throat, and puffs jutted out from the shoulders of the riding dress, whose absurdly long sleeves were festooned with braids. She was braided up the front, too, in a deranged imitation of a military fashion.

The attire was pure feminine froth. But as she neared, Darius saw nothing light or frivolous in the way she carried herself. Something was very, very wrong.

He looked into her taut, white face. "What is it?" he said. "What's wrong?"

She glanced back at Tom Jenkins, who withdrew to another corner of the yard.

"It's Pip," she said.

"Yes, he's gone missing," Darius said. "But don't worry. He can't have gone far."

"He's mine," she said. Her eyes filled. "He's mine, and it is—" She broke off, swallowing hard.

"Well, yes, I surmised as much," Darius said, wishing he could take her in his arms. At the moment, that was not only indiscreet but impractical. He ached for her, but emotion would not solve any problems. They needed to be rational. "He's deuced expensive, too," he said. "You would not believe the sum the Tylers want for him. But I'll find the money. You needn't worry about that."

"The Tylers," she repeated. "Good grief. The money. His articles. You said he's gone missing. The colonel said— Oh, dear God, we must find him."

"Charlotte, you must try to calm yourself," he said, handing over a handkerchief. "What is this about the colonel?"

She wiped her eyes, her nose. "It was Colonel Morrell who told me about Pip," she said. "He knew everything: the date my baby was born and where and the couple who adopted him. Everything. But I knew. Even before the colonel told me, I knew Pip was mine. But I wouldn't let myself believe it. I wouldn't let myself look for him or talk to him. I was afraid. A great coward, as I told you. My whole life has been a lie. A house of cards. If I faced the truth, told the truth, everything would fall to pieces."

Darius saw it in an instant: the scandal, the end of respect for her . . . shame for her family . . . heartache for her father. Endless repercussions.

"You are not a coward," he said firmly. "You were facing catastrophe."

"I should have faced it," she said. "Now I don't know what Colonel Morrell will do. He may be angry enough to tell my father. I don't know. I don't know him at all, I realize. But I think—I'm afraid, truly afraid he'll take Pip away. For all I know, he's sent him away already. He said the articles were easy enough to buy."

Darius swore, quietly but fervently. "No one will take Pip away," he said.

"I knew you'd say that—or something like that," she said. "He said I couldn't count on you, but I knew I could."

"I'm sorry," he said. "I could have spared you this trouble if I had not been such an idiot yesterday. I had been wondering if you knew—or guessed," he said. "I meant to ask you about it yesterday, but I'm not good at broaching delicate subjects delicately and then I was distracted by the drawers on your head and the fornication and such."

She tried to smile. Her mouth trembled with the effort and a teardrop made its way along the side of her nose. "I don't know what to do," she said. "I only knew I couldn't agree to Colonel Morrell's proposal. I want you. I want my son. I came to you because I didn't know what else to do. I cannot think clearly. You are so—so logical. I knew you would sort it out."

And he knew he would do anything for her. She was his to love, to protect. He'd never guessed how good it could make him feel, to be needed, and to know he was capable of doing what needed to be done.

"Of course I will," he said. "Wipe your nose."

They must first go to the Tylers' place in Altrincham, Mr. Carsington told her. That was where he was already planning to go when Charlotte arrived, he said. He'd found it hard to believe Pip would run away for the reason given, and he suspected this was a ploy of some kind.

"I doubt Mrs. Tyler would give up Pip easily, in any event," he said, as they rode out of the stable yard. "If she thinks she has two parties interested in him, she's likely to play one against the other, hoping to raise the price. She seems to believe that all aristocrats have bottomless purses."

But Mrs. Tyler wasn't at home when Charlotte and Mr. Carsington arrived. The eldest daughter, Annie, said her mother had left for Manchester in

the morning, leaving Annie in charge. Mrs. Tyler
wasn't expected back until tomorrow. In response
to further questioning, the girl said, yes, a man had
come about Pip this morning. Not a gentleman. A
bald man who talked a long time with her mother.
No, Pip hadn't come home yet. Annie thought the
bald man had gone looking for him, but she couldn't
say for certain.

"Do you recall the bald man's name?" Charlotte
asked. "Was it Kenning, by chance?"

Kenning had been with Colonel Morrell in the
army, she knew. He was the one the colonel would
trust with a secret, or something underhand.

The girl thought, then shrugged. "Might've been,
your ladyship. I don't remember. I've seen him before. Goes to the tavern regular. I don't like him, always nosing about."

Annie seemed genuinely baffled at the idea of
Pip's running away. "But he'd got nowhere to go
to," she said. "Anyway, Ma always screams like that.
She don't mean half what she says. She's always
saying she's going back to Manchester and leaving
us, as we're so ungrateful and troublesome. She's
only cross, you know. Even when she does go, she
always comes back. She didn't want to leave there
and come here, but Pa said we had to, for the work
and because we can live cheaper here. Pip knows
how she is. He's very clever, is Pip."

When they left the cottage, Mr. Carsington did
not lead Charlotte back to Jenkins and the horses
but in the other direction, not many steps away, to a
quiet corner of the churchyard.

"I doubt Mrs. Tyler has taken Pip to Manchester," he said. "Annie would have said so. She did not seem concerned about keeping any secrets. She was more than happy to express her opinions. Now at least we understand why Mrs. Tyler is so short-tempered and greedy. She doesn't want to live here. If foolish aristocrats are willing to pay a high price for Pip, she'll take it—and move back to Manchester."

"But if she hasn't got Pip, what if Kenning has?" Charlotte said. "He might have offered more money than she could resist. And if Kenning has Pip, where would he take him? Colonel Morrell said he sent Fewkes abroad." The nearest port was Liverpool, not forty miles away: a journey of a few hours. "What if Pip is on his way to Liverpool?"

"Wherever he is, we'll find him," he said. "We'll need more resources than I have, though, if matters have gone as far as that." He paused. "Whether they have or they haven't, it's long past time to speak to your father. The day is getting on, and he needs to know the truth. It would be better if he heard it from you than from Morrell."

She looked away toward the church. "The colonel's probably told him already."

"Possibly. On the other hand, Morrell might be giving you a chance to have second thoughts, to come to your senses. He may be waiting, as men often do, for the woman to recover from the emotional storm and look at matters more practically."

"That is possible," she said. "He did seem thoroughly flummoxed when I said no. And it was clear he thought he was saving me from myself."

"We'd better go to Lithby Hall now," Mr. Carsington said. "The sooner you speak to your father,
the better."

"I know." That's what her brain told her. Meanwhile, her heart raced, and the inner cold came and
went.

"He won't reject you," Mr. Carsington said. "He
loves you too much."

"I know!" she cried. "That's the trouble. He'll be
hurt—for me. He'll grieve—for me. So much love
for his perfect daughter, the apple of his eye. I know
he won't love me any less, but it is so . . . *hard,* knowing I'm not what he believes me to be, knowing I'm
unworthy of so much love."

"Shall we trade fathers?" he said. "Yours thinks
you perfection. Mine thinks me hopeless."

"I should find it easier to face your father than
mine," she said. "Lord Hargate would tell me my
behavior was disgraceful as well as idiotic. He
would tell me how ashamed of me he was and how
I ought to be ashamed of myself for all the trouble
I was causing the family—and I think it would be a
relief to hear that."

"You think so now," Mr. Carsington said. "I should
like to hear what you'd have to say after spending
an hour or more in the Inquisition Chamber, having your character, tastes, principles, intellect, and
life's work torn to shreds. Then he takes all the little
bits remaining and scatters them to the wind with a
wave of his hand."

"It would be a *relief,*" she said. "But it's no good
debating which is worse. I'm only putting off the in-

evitable. I'm trying to be calm and sensible, but I am so frightened. Oh, and Lizzie—to betray her, after all she's done. That may be worst of all."

He took her hand. "It's going to be hard, very hard. But you won't be alone. You know I'll be with you."

They found Charlotte's father and Lizzie in the library. Both looked very interested indeed when Charlotte entered with Mr. Carsington. Papa came forward, shook Mr. Carsington's hand, then, smiling, moved to stand behind Lizzie's chair.

Mr. Carsington closed the door.

Since no one closed doors to rooms in the public part of the house, Lizzie and Papa looked at each other knowingly. Then they looked expectantly at Charlotte and Mr. Carsington.

She could guess what they thought they knew and what they were expecting to hear. Already they probably heard wedding bells in their heads.

They could never guess what they were about to hear.

"Perhaps, after all, you'd better let me introduce the subject," said Mr. Carsington.

"I can tell them," Charlotte said. Her hands were shaking. She folded them tightly against her waist.

"My dear," said Lizzie. "You are as white as a sheet. Is anything wrong? Molly told me there was some trouble about Pip. The child is not hurt, I hope? Those dreadful Tylers did not send him back to the workhouse?"

"We shall come to that subject in a moment," said

Mr. Carsington. "First, however, I wish to address Lord Lithby. Sir, Lady Charlotte and I would like your permission to be married."

"Mr. Carsington," Charlotte said. "I appreciate that you are trying to soften them—"

"I never softened anyone in my life," he said. "I thought, first things first. First we make it plain why I am here. Lord Lithby, I have made no secret of my intentions. As soon as I understood my feelings for Lady Charlotte, and received indications that she returned them, I commenced the rigmarole Society requires in courtship. However, in recent days it has become plain—"

"Papa, Lizzie, I have something to tell you," Charlotte cut in determinedly.

"Good heavens, you do look ill, my dear," Papa said. "You had better sit down."

"I cannot sit down, Papa," Charlotte said. "I am not ill, only sorry, so very sorry."

"My dear, it seems that you are engaged to wed— or near enough to it as makes no matter," he said. "There is nothing to be sorry about. I have a high regard for the gentleman who stands beside you. I shall be sorry to lose you, naturally. Yet I am not at all uneasy about relinquishing you to his care."

It was harder than even she had imagined, looking into his genial, loving countenance.

She dragged in air, let it out. Tried once more.

"I made a mistake, Papa," she said. "A long time ago." She looked at Lizzie, who had gone very still. "I'm sorry, Lizzie. You've done everything for me. You saved my life, and you made me strong, stronger than I'd been before. I love you dearly, and I should give anything not to cause you trouble. But I . . ." She paused, trying to collect her thoughts.

"My dear love," Lizzie began.

"No, please," Charlotte said, holding up her hand. "Let me say it." She folded her hands again, tight against her belly. "You asked about Pip. He's . . . he's the baby we gave away. He came back and . . . f-found me." She made herself look at her father then. "He's *my* baby, Papa."

There was a short, excruciating silence.

"Pip?" said Lizzie. "Oh, my love, are you quite sure? You are not imagining—"

"What is she imagining?" Papa said. "What is this about a baby? You never had a baby, Charlotte. Are you delirious?"

"I had a baby, Papa," Charlotte said. "Ten years ago."

She saw her father's grip tighten on the back of her stepmother's chair. He looked down at Lizzie, who was looking up at him. "What is she saying, Lizzie?"

Lizzie laid her hand over the one so tightly gripping the back of her chair. "Ten years ago when I took her to Yorkshire, she was pregnant," she said gently.

"I don't believe it," Papa said. "I cannot believe it. You said she was ill."

"She was," Lizzie said. "She was so distraught that I feared she'd do herself an injury."

"She didn't dare to tell you, Papa," Charlotte said.

"Didn't dare?" he said. "Didn't *dare?*"

"Please don't blame her," Charlotte said. "It was my fault. I couldn't bear for you to know. I was so ashamed and—and so wretched, I should have killed myself, if not for her. Lizzie saved my life, Papa. Never forget that, please."

"How could I forget?" he demanded. "My God, Charlotte, what do you think of me? How could you not tell me? What could you possibly fear—from me? When did I become a monster in your eyes?"

"Never," she said. "I was ashamed. I couldn't bear for you to know what I'd done. I could scarcely bear knowing it."

"You didn't have to bear it," he said. "I'm your father. You come to me when you are in trouble, and I bear it for you. Why did you not come to me? What have I done?" He looked down at Lizzie. "She should have come to me, Lizzie. What did I do that she didn't come to me?"

"I was sixteen years old," Charlotte said. "You were all my world. I was . . . afraid when you married Lizzie, and . . . I did this dreadful thing. Then I realized what I'd done—and it was too late. I knew you'd forgive me. You love me so much, you will forgive everything. But I couldn't bear it. I couldn't bear for you to know I wasn't pure and—and good. I couldn't bear for you to know I'd thrown away my innocence—for nothing, not even for love—on a worthless man. I wanted to *be* the wonderful daughter your love painted me to be. That's what I've wanted for ten years, and it's wrong. For ten years I've been thinking like a sixteen-year-old girl.

For ten years I have not grown up. And for all those ten years, my little boy has been growing up without me."

There it was, so simple: She'd given up her son for her father—the father who'd never dream of asking such a sacrifice of her.

Her heart broke then. She could feel it. Everything she'd locked up, all those wishes and longings. The stories she'd made up about her baby, and the way she'd imagined her little boy growing up. The dreams of all she might have shared with him. The fears were shut up in there, too—that he'd never had a chance to grow into a little boy. It was all locked in there, ten years' grief she'd never let herself feel fully. Ten years' grief, allowed only a few tears now and again, late at night, on her pillow.

The tears fell now, thick and fast, and she turned to Mr. Carsington. He drew her into his arms and held her tight. He said nothing but she could feel his heart beating, so hard. "It's all right," he said gently. "It's done now."

Morrell might have his medals, Darius thought, but Lady Charlotte had all his courage and more.

She had faced the father she adored, and only Darius, who stood so close, knew that she had been shaking from head to foot. Looking from father to daughter, Darius had ached for her, for her father. He'd prepared to step in, to support her at any moment, but she had spoken from her heart, and his own heart wouldn't let him diminish her words by adding to them.

She'd done her part bravely.

The rest was up to Darius, as he'd promised.

He looked over her head toward her parents. Lord Lithby stood behind his wife's chair, his hands once more clamped upon the back, as though he would strangle it if he could. Lady Lithby's hand lay on one of his, holding him there, Darius supposed, with that light touch.

"No one blames anybody, Charlotte," she said. "You must stop blaming yourself. I am sorry you have kept this inside you. If I had known . . ." She shook her head. "But never mind my *ifs*. It is a terrible circumstance of nature that one might give birth to a child while a child oneself. We did what we believed was best at the time, in the circumstances. What is important now is to make matters right as best we can."

"Make them right, yes," Lord Lithby said. But his eyes were red and all the light seemed to have gone out of him and he looked old, suddenly, though he was a man in his prime.

"I think we'd best start by finding Pip," Darius said. He quickly explained the situation: the boy's disappearance, Morrell's revelations. "Since Pip travels to and from Lithby Hall, I thought we might begin here, by asking the staff about him. Then, if necessary, perhaps you would be so good as to organize a search party, sir."

"Yes, yes, of course," Lord Lithby said, his mind clearly elsewhere. "Whatever you like. The child. Yes, certainly. Pip, is it? The boy who exercises Daisy. I saw him once, early in the morning. I saw him from a window. That is—he is—Good God, I cannot believe this. I should have known. My daughter. My grandson." He brought his hand to his forehead, shielding his eyes as though from a painfully bright light. "Forgive me, Charlotte, but I am . . . I am . . . I don't know what I am. Ten years." His countenance darkened. "It was Blaine, then, of course. Who else could it have been?"

"It was," his daughter said.

"I thought I'd dealt with him," Lord Lithby said. He took his hand away from his eyes. "I had him sent abroad—to a desert island, I hoped. But he'd got to you first, the bloody damned cur. And you blame yourself, Charlotte? I should never have blamed you. I knew what he was."

"I'm sorry, Papa," she said.

"You were young, you were young," he said. "Ah, well." He made a visible effort to collect himself. "Never mind. We must find the boy, as Mr. Carsington so wisely says. I shall be glad to help. But I must beg your indulgence, sir. A moment, if you please. My lady will act in my stead for the present. But I must have some air. And I think . . . I believe I must . . . kick something." He stalked across the room to the French windows and stepped out onto the terrace and walked rapidly away, into the garden.

Charlotte started to pull away from Darius to go after her father. "Don't," Darius said.

"Mr. Carsington is right," said Lady Lithby. "Your father only wants some time to collect himself. He would spare you every hurt, as you know, and he is understandably distressed because he could not spare you this. He must feel thoroughly bewildered and helpless. Give him a little time, my dear. Even I am having trouble taking it in. I saw that child time and again and had no inkling who he was."

"I knew," said Charlotte. "I knew the instant I saw him, the instant I looked into his eyes. But I wouldn't let myself believe it."

"I noticed his unusual eyes," Lady Lithby said, "but it meant nothing to me. I never met Captain Blaine. Even if I had, I'm not sure I would have believed it, either." She smiled, and Darius clearly saw then the warmth that had won the hearts of both stepdaughter and spouse. "How sweetly you put it, my love: that your son had found you, after all this time." She rose from her chair. "Well, let us try to make a start at finding him. Tell me again what Colonel Morrell said, exactly."

Lord Lithby stormed through the gardens for a time. He stomped on a herbaceous border. He threw an ornamental urn against a stone wall, shattering it.

He paced one of the bridges across the moat, back and forth, back and forth.

Then he made his way to a shaded avenue, flung himself onto a stone bench and sat there, his head in his hands.

He didn't know how long he sat there, grieving for his daughter. A long time, perhaps. He had a great deal to grieve.

A sound made him look up.

The bulldog Daisy stood before him, holding

what appeared to be a piece of a tree trunk in her jaws.

"You ridiculous dog," he said. "Who let you out to tear apart my gardens? Or did you come to help me do it?"

The bulldog shook her head, trying to shake the log to death, apparently.

"Lizzie sent you, didn't she?"

Drool flew as Daisy tried to kill the log.

"I can't play with you now, you silly creature," he said. "I'm trying to collect my wits. Trying to calm myself. One is no good to anybody in an excitable state, and they need me to help—to find my *grandson*. My grandson. Pip."

Daisy dropped the piece of tree trunk at his feet— narrowly missing crushing his toes—and bounded away. When Lord Lithby didn't follow, she came back and repeated the performance.

"Ah, yes, Pip is your friend," said Lord Lithby. "How many sticks do you kill for him, I wonder? But it's rats, isn't it? Good God. My *grandson*, earning his keep by killing rats at a halfpenny apiece."

Daisy barked.

The average bulldog was fearless, determined, and persistent to a phenomenal degree, but it was also inscrutable. Other dogs made a noise about every little thing. A bulldog could remain stolidly mute in the face of the most extreme provocation.

When Daisy barked, therefore, she must be in a state of unbearable excitement.

Lord Lithby realized he'd said two unbearably exciting words. *Rats* and *Pip*.

"Where's Pip?" he said.

Daisy trotted away from him, paused, and looked back.

Lord Lithby rose from the stone bench. "Very well, I'll follow you—and you had better not be taking me to the nearest rathole."

Meanwhile in the library

After closely interrogating both Darius and Charlotte about the day's events, Lady Lithby disappeared for a time. When she returned, she had her bonnet on and her carriage ordered.

Darius had been afraid of this: everyone going off in several directions and no plan in place.

"I think it would be best if we approached the search in an orderly way," he said.

"That is what I am doing," said Lady Lithby. "If Colonel Morrell has the boy or knows where he is, I shall oblige him to give him back."

"I can do that," said Darius. "In fact, I should like nothing better than *obliging* him to do something."

"I know you would like to break his nose," said Lady Lithby.

"No, I should like to break every bone in his body," said Darius. "Then I should like to throw him out of a high window."

"That is irrational," said Charlotte.

"It is perfectly rational for a male to try to kill another male," said Darius, "especially when the other male threatens those he cares about."

"It is gallant of you to want to smash Colonel Morrell to pieces," said Lady Lithby, "but that course would not be productive. You will only get his back up. You will act like men, daring and daunting each other. He will deem it a matter of pride not to tell you anything. He will not behave that way with *me*. In any case, whether or not he can help us find Pip, I must speak to him—and you must let me, sir, like it or not. You must allow me to do *something*."

"And what are we to do, Lizzie?" said Charlotte.

"You might try looking for Daisy," said Lady Lithby. "I let her out. I thought that if Pip is nearby, she'll be the one to find him. And Pip, in turn, will know she oughtn't to be running loose and will bring her back."

Colonel Morrell reviewed his speech over and over as he rode home, trying to ascertain where he'd gone astray. He should not have called Lady Charlotte a fool—that much was obvious. Her refusal had floored him, and he'd spoken without thinking.

One mustn't do that with women. Even he knew that.

Women were so difficult. Life was so much easier in the army. Rank and rules. One followed orders. One gave orders, and others followed them. If one failed to follow the rules, one suffered the consequences, and those were perfectly clear. Everything was clear, even when one dealt with muddleheaded superiors.

It was clear, at any rate, compared to civilian life.

But women . . .

He'd rather face artillery fire.

"Damn me to hell," he muttered. "I cannot leave it like this. She'll think—God only knows what she'll think."

He turned his horse around and started back for Lithby Hall.

He was surprised—but not completely, when he thought about it—when he saw Lady Lithby's carriage coming toward him.

He saluted as she went by.

The carriage passed, slowed, then came to a halt. A gloved hand signaled from the open window.

Oh, no, he thought.

He rode back to the carriage.

"How lucky," said Lady Lithby after they'd exchanged greetings. "I was coming to speak with you. Perhaps you would be so good as to walk with me for a moment or two."

This is not going to be good, he thought.

How could he expect it to be good? He had insulted the daughter of the Marchioness of Lithby. He had called her a fool—and he was not sure what else he'd said in the heat of the moment, the heat of anger and disappointment.

He quickly dismounted, opened the carriage door, and offered his arm.

They walked on until they were well out of earshot of both the maid inside the coach and the coachman on the box outside.

"I wished to speak with you about your conversation with Charlotte," Lady Lithby said.

"I guessed as much," he said. "I assure you, Lady

Lithby, it was not the conversation I'd intended to have. When you stopped me, I was on my way, in fact, to beg her pardon for anything I said that was out of order."

"I am glad to hear it," said Lady Lithby. "I suspected that Charlotte heard a threat where there was none."

"A threat?" he said. He reviewed what he'd said—for the twentieth time. "Good gad, you cannot mean she thinks I threatened to expose her. I told her quite clearly that my intention was completely the opposite."

"She seemed to think your assurances applied only on condition of her becoming your wife."

Women.

He did not grind his teeth. If he could restrain himself when with his uncle, he could restrain himself now.

"I made no conditions," he said stiffly. "No gentleman would. If it sounded that way, I can only blame the heat of the moment. I did express myself badly, I am all too well aware."

"I wished to make everything clear," said Lady Lithby. "Some remarks you made might be misconstrued. I am concerned, for instance, that in your zeal to protect her, you made arrangements for the child."

"Of course I have," he said. "This morning I sent my servant Kenning to release him from his articles of indenture. I know it is an unhappy accident of fate, but the child's present situation is an outrage. He is the son of a lady and a gentleman—a cad but a gentleman by birth. The boy shall have a proper home and an education befitting his station. I have everything in hand. You need not trouble yourself about it."

"I must trouble about it," said Lady Lithby. "We want the child."

"You cannot be serious," he said. "It will be impossible to suppress the matter if that boy remains nearby."

"Charlotte does not want it suppressed."

For the second time that day, he could not believe his ears. Had Society gone mad while he was abroad? Or was it only the Hayward segment of it? "She cannot admit to bearing a child out of wedlock," he said. "I cannot believe you will let her do it. Your influence may prevent every door being shut to her, but she will be treated differently. Women far inferior to her on every count will look down on her. Perhaps few will dare to insult her openly, but you well know that Society has a thousand ways of cutting while wearing a politely smiling face. The idea of her being subjected to such indignities—No, it is unthinkable. Lady Lithby, you must dissuade her from taking this step."

"She wants her child," said Lady Lithby. "You must recall your servant from his errand."

"Even if this were not completely mad, I could not call him off," said the colonel. "Kenning has his orders. Everything has been arranged. He ought to be in Liverpool by now, if not on his way to Ireland."

Chapter 15

Daisy did not lead his lordship to the nearest rathole but to his home farm and the pigsty.

They were still a good distance away when Lord Lithby discerned the small, lonely figure sitting atop the sty fence. Some of the men working in the farmyard glanced that way from time to time, but that was all. Apparently, they were used to the lad's comings and goings.

Once upon a time, Lord Lithby recalled, before Hyacinth's time, he used to hoist his daughter up onto that very fence. They would contemplate the pigs and converse.

Lord Lithby's throat tightened.

The dog reached the boy first, and though she was her usual silently inscrutable self, Pip must have sensed her presence because he turned and looked round.

Lord Lithby composed himself, squared his shoulders, and approached the pigsty. The boy's gaze shifted to him.

As he neared, Lord Lithby saw that one eye was

bruised and swollen, making the child look like a
little gargoyle.

He joined Pip and folded his arms on the fence,
in the same way he'd done so many times when his
daughter sat there next to him.

"You must be Daisy's friend Pip," said his lordship.

Pip nodded. "Yes, sir."

"I am . . . Lithby," said his lordship.

Pip's eyes widened. Well, one of them did, at
any rate. "I beg your pardon, your lordship." He
snatched off his cap and made to climb down.

"No, no, you are perfectly all right there," said
his lordship, gazing at the blond head. The pale hair
displayed a tendency to curl and an unmistakable
cowlick.

This was Charlotte's hair, as it was when she was
a child, when she wore it loose, when no pins tamed
the cowlick and artfully arranged the curls.

"You are welcome to admire Hyacinth," Lord
Lithby said, as he would say to anyone who seemed
to appreciate his favorite sow. "She is a fine pig, is
she not?"

"I've never seen such a pig before, your lordship," said Pip. "Everyone says she's the biggest pig
in the world. But I don't know how they can know,
when most of them have never traveled as far as
Manchester. But they think Manchester's the ends
of the earth, practically, and Salford is on the other
side of the moon. Actually it's very close. It took Mr.
Carsington and me only a few hours to get there,
and we never went faster than a canter."

Lord Lithby recalled what Mr. Carsington had said about the Salford workhouse. His *grandson*—in a workhouse! It was not to be borne. He wanted to kick the fence to pieces. He told himself not to be an idiot.

"That is a prodigy of a black eye you have," he said.

"I got in a fight," said Pip.

"It often happens that way, I find."

"Mrs. Tyler is very upset about it," said Pip.

"Women often make a fuss about such things."

"She said she'd send me back to the workhouse, but I think she was speaking in anger," the child said. "Even if she meant it, Mr. Carsington said he wouldn't let me go back to the workhouse, and a gentleman's word is his bond."

"This is true," said his lordship.

A silence.

"I know I oughtn't to be here, your lordship," the boy said. "I was supposed to go back to help Mr. Tyler today, but I needed to think. Pigs are good for thinking."

"This is where I usually come," said his lordship, "when I need to think."

This is where your mother and I have always talked over important matters, he could have added.

The most significant matter, the one they hadn't talked about, sat inches away from Lord Lithby's elbow.

"I still haven't sorted it out," Pip said. "Mrs. Tyler told me it was wrong to fight, and I said my mother was dead, and it's wrong to speak ill of the dead, isn't it? And she said it was, but that wasn't any reason to go about blacking people's eyes and knocking their teeth loose. And I said what if she had a boy and another boy said something bad about her? Shouldn't her boy defend her honor? And she said honor was for ladies and gentlemen. She said ordinary folks need to think about getting their living. She said, What if I broke my arm or leg or jaw and couldn't work?"

"She has a point," his lordship said. His face worked, but the child was looking at the sow while he talked and didn't notice.

"But I can't let people say mean things about my mother," Pip went on. "Who's going to defend her honor if I don't? I *have* to. And if I have to do that, then I can't be an ordinary person. But I can't be a gentleman, either." He frowned. "It's a conundrum, sir, isn't it?"

"No, it isn't," said his lordship, his voice not quite steady. "Women don't see things the same way men do. You were right to defend your mother's honor."

He patted the boy on the shoulder. No one would ever know what it cost him to do that and nothing more. No one would ever know what it cost him to hold back, because Pip's mother ought to be the first to hold him in her arms.

"Women don't appreciate the finer points of fighting," said Lord Lithby. "What happened, exactly?"

According to the outdoor servants, Daisy had found Charlotte's father, and they were headed to the home farm.

"Of course he would come here," she told Mr. Carsington as they made their way to the end of the yard where the pigs were kept. "This is where Papa always comes when he needs to—"

She broke off as they came round a building, and she spotted them: her father, leaning on the fence as he always did . . . and Pip, who, judging by his gestures, seemed to be reenacting his fight with Rob Jowett—and threatening to fall into the pigsty.

She'd fallen in more than once, she remembered.

Papa would shake his head, and say, *One of these days, you'll learn, Charlotte. I hope.*

"It appears that Pip has found your father, too," said Mr. Carsington.

She would have run to them, but he held her back.

"You must collect yourself," he said. "You can't start blubbering. Pip becomes anxious when you cry." He told her how Pip had come to him the other day, worried because "the younger lady" was weeping.

"Did he?" she said, her throat aching. "But he is a good boy. In spite of everything that's happened to him. A good boy, and a gentleman."

She peeped over his broad shoulder at Pip, who had turned his head and was watching them. Had he any idea? Had he sensed her in the same way she'd sensed him? Had her voice remained with him somehow, in his heart? Was it there, perhaps without his quite realizing: the broken little speech she'd whispered before she gave him away?

I love you. I'll always love you. Please forgive me.

But how could he remember? He was merely regarding her with curiosity—though it was hard to tell at this distance, given the black eye.

Papa turned to look at her, too. He smiled as he always did.

The dog was her usual self, busy shaking a stick into submission.

Charlotte's eyes filled.

"I knew this would happen," Mr. Carsington said. "You'd better get it out of your system first."

"His eye, his poor eye."

"He's proud of it," Mr. Carsington told her. "He got it defending your honor."

"Oh," she said. "Good grief. Defending the mother who abandoned him. How am I to bear it?"

"You must stop thinking that way," he said. "Society makes a grievous shame of such things for women. If you had been a man, you should have boasted of your by-blows. But a woman is supposed to be ashamed, to hate herself, and to hide. If she does not hide her so-called sin, she is made a leper." He peered down at her. "There, that lecture was pompous enough to dry your eyes, I hope. Are you recovering your composure?"

"Yes," she said. "But it is harder than one would expect."

"I know this is an emotional time," Mr. Carsington said. "But you must consider Pip's feelings. You are about to upset his universe, and though it is a happy kind of upset, it is going to take some getting used to. He needs us both to be calm and steady for him. Take your example from your father. I am sure he wants to seize the boy and take him home, but he restrains himself."

She looked at her father, who was smiling at Pip now, the reassuring smile she knew so well.

"He hasn't told Pip," she said. "He wouldn't. He'd leave it to me."

"I take back what I said before about your father," Mr. Carsington said. "My father merely infuriates me. Yours should make me feel ashamed of myself all the time."

"He doesn't mean to," she said. "There is no mathematical formula for being a parent. I suppose they are only doing the best they can."

"We shall, too," said Mr. Carsington, "and blunder horribly, as everyone else does, I daresay. Well, are you ready?"

She had calmed while they talked. He'd done it on purpose, she thought. He'd found a way to lead her through the emotional storm. "Yes, I'm ready, thanks to you." She stood on tiptoe and daringly kissed his cheek. In front of everybody.

"Very well, then," he said. "But remember: no waterworks. Later you can sob over him. For now, though, you need to be strong and calm, for his sake."

"I will," she said.

"I know you will." He led her to the pair at the fence.

"I wonder if we might interrupt, Lord Lithby," Mr. Carsington said. "The lady wishes to speak to Pip."

The boy looked to Papa. He nodded, and Pip

leapt down from the fence and came to her, his cap in his hand.

She hastily wiped her eyes with the back of her glove, gave a little sniff, straightened her posture, and smiled.

"My goodness, that is a prodigy of a black eye," she said.

"I got in a fight, your ladyship," Pip said.

"Did you, indeed? Mr. Carsington tells me you were defending your mother's honor."

"Lord Lithby said it wasn't wrong," Pip said. "He said women don't understand, but it was the right thing to do."

"I understand," she said. "I'm very, very proud of you." She crouched down to bring herself eye to eye with him. She put her hands on his shoulders and smiled, and she thought perhaps there wasn't a large enough smile in the world for what she felt. She thought her heart would burst with happiness.

She said, "I'm your mother."

Chapter 16

Lithby Hall library, that evening

Darius knew better than to suggest taking Pip home with him. Charlotte's son would stay at Lithby Hall, the boy's mother and grandparents said, until after the wedding.

They had wanted to discuss the wedding after dinner, but Darius had already made up his mind what must be done.

What must be done was not agreeable. Given a choice, he'd rather spend a week talking about nothing but curtains. But it was necessary, for his wife-to-be, and for Pip.

"We must marry in the local church, and all of my family must be here," he told them. "That includes Grandmother. We must show a united front."

"Good heavens, not your grandmother," Charlotte cried. "I should never ask that of you."

"It's the only way to assure that you won't be treated unkindly," Darius said. "A great many people will not wish to offend Lord and Lady Lithby or lose the chance of enjoying their famous hospitality. A great many will not wish to offend my parents, either. Still, my grandmother represents the one certain way to strike terror into the hearts of the hypocrites and moral zealots. Our united front will be most effective if she's at the head of it."

"If you think snubs will hurt my feelings, you ought to think again," Charlotte said. "I have my family. That's all that matters. Losing my place in Society is no great loss. The Beau Monde can be suffocating at times. While I might miss some aspects of it, I can live well enough without it."

"So can I," he said. "Easily. Happily. I should not miss Mrs. Badgely's company a jot. But that is not the point. The point is, you should be treated no differently for having had a child out of wedlock than a man would be."

"That is a radical view, Mr. Carsington," said Lord Lithby. "I am not at all sure I would wish to encourage women to behave, generally, as men do. We should revert to barbarism, I fear. It is the women who keep us civilized."

"Then let us think of my grandmother as a civilizing influence," Darius said. "And let us try not to let the thought give us nightmares."

Though he doubted Pip would have nightmares, Darius went upstairs to say good night before returning to Beechwood.

Pip was in bed but broad awake, looking at a book, when Darius entered.

In the candlelight, with that spectacular black eye, he looked like a little hobgoblin.

A very serious little hobgoblin. He set the book to one side and regarded Darius gravely. "Have they stopped crying yet?" he asked.

"Yes," Darius said. "They are arguing about the wedding breakfast."

"Then am I to come live at Beechwood, sir? After the wedding?"

"Yes. Don't you like it here?"

Pip gazed about him. "It's very . . . large. There are a great many servants. Nobody screams." He considered. "I like it, but it's strange."

"This has been a very strange day for you," Darius said.

The boy nodded.

"It's not every day one discovers a brand-new mother and a set of grandparents. You bore the upheaval well, I thought."

"I thought she—my mother—was funning me at first," Pip said. He frowned. "Maybe I shouldn't have laughed."

He'd not only laughed but said to his mother, "Go on, pull the other one, your ladyship."

"She didn't mind," Darius said.

"No, she didn't." A pause. "She's very beautiful."

"She is, indeed."

"I thought, if she wants to be my mother, I'm not arguing with her."

"She really is, you know."

"I expect she is, but I was used to the idea of her being dead," said Pip. "It's a bit of a shock. I knew my mother was a lady but she was supposed to be dead and if she wasn't, I never expected her to be so beautiful and grand. Did you ever see so many ribbons on a hat? What good is a little hat like that with all those ribbons?"

Darius remembered the frivolous hat Lady Charlotte had been not wearing at their first encounter. He smiled. "It's for decoration," he said.

Following his conversation with Lady Lithby, an alarmed Colonel Morrell rode posthaste to Altrincham, to the Tylers' cottage. Mr. Tyler was not yet back from work, a daughter reported. Mrs. Tyler was in Manchester.

"The boy," said the colonel. "Where is he?"

"Everyone asks about Pip," the girl said. "I don't know where he's got to. He went to work with Pa like he always does."

Colonel Morrell rode back the way he'd come. He met Tyler, heading home on the Lithby Road, and asked about Pip.

"Like I told Mr. Carsington, the last I knew, Pip was taking the dog back to Lithby Hall," said Tyler. "He was to come straight back. I had some errands for him to do, for my missus. But he never come back. I reckon he run away, sir."

The colonel did not draw a sigh of relief until he'd traveled another quarter mile down the road.

Kenning had done his work, then. Pip was on his way to Ireland.

Colonel Morrell had saved Lady Charlotte from herself.

To a point and for a time, at any rate.

One must simply hope that, given time to calm down and think, she would see the folly of her decision . . . about the boy, if not about Carsington.

The colonel's relief lasted until late in the evening, when Kenning came home.

"I'm sorry, sir," he said. "I had it all arranged with Mrs. Tyler. She made up errands for the boy, like I told her to. It was for after he'd delivered the dog, like you told me we should do, so as not to cause a stir at the Hall until we was well out of the way. But he never came out where he was supposed to. I been back and forth, between Beechwood and Altrincham. I looked everywhere. Then I heard he was still on Lord Lithby's property. I don't know whether the boy got the wind up or what it was, sir, but there he was, the one place I couldn't get at him, and he never came out. Shall I try again tomorrow, sir?"

"No," said Colonel Morrell. "It's too late."

After Mr. Carsington had gone, Charlotte went up to her son's room. She'd already kissed him good night, but she couldn't stay away.

Though his candle had been put out, the moonlight streaming through the window showed her his face, the great black eye stark against his pale skin.

She bent over him, and lightly stroked his forehead. A tear trickled down her cheek. She couldn't help it. She'd ten years of tears to spend, and it seemed she wasn't quite done yet. The tear fell upon his cheek, and his hand came up to brush at it. He came awake, blinking.

"I'm sorry," she whispered. "I didn't mean to wake you up."

"It's all right," he said. "Don't cry."

"I'm not usually a watering pot," she said. "You needn't worry that I'll be blubbering over you all the time."

"Mr. Carsington said you were emotional," he said.

"Yes," she said. "Yes, I am."

The boy rose up on his elbows. "You don't scream," he said. "That's good in a mother."

"You've overcome your skepticism, then," she said. "I am your mother, after all."

He nodded. "I'm sorry I laughed. I hope I didn't hurt your feelings."

"My feelings," she said. "Oh, Pip."

"Don't cry," he said.

"I'll try not to," she said. "I'm just so glad I found you. And so sorry I ever let you go."

He stared at her for the longest time. Then, "Why?" he said. "Why didn't you keep me? Was it because of my eyes?"

Why. The question she'd dreaded. Hearing the question hurt even more than she'd expected, more than the hurt of telling her father the truth.

She wasn't sure how to answer, but she must try.

"Girls aren't supposed to have babies when they're not married," she said. "I was afraid of all the trouble. People would be disappointed in me and hurt and—"

"Crying," he said. "There would be a lot of crying, I expect."

"Yes," she said. "It wasn't a good reason, Pip, I know. I was sorry afterward, but I was sick for a long time."

"But you didn't die," he said. "I'm glad you didn't die."

She wouldn't cry again, but she would brush his hair back from his face. Mothers were permitted to do that. "No, I didn't die," she said. "And by the time I was well, and wishing I hadn't let you go, you belonged to Mr. and Mrs. Ogden. Even if I dared, it would have been unkind to take you away from them. You were their child, and they loved you. I did believe you'd be better off with them. I wish I'd done it all differently, love. I wish I'd been braver, but I wasn't."

He considered. "I don't know," he said. "I don't know about these things. I don't remember when I was a baby. I hardly remember my father and mother—the other father and mother. I remember Mr. Welton. That was good."

"The workhouse wasn't good," she said.

"I pretend it was a bad dream," he said.

"It's going to be good from now on," she said.

"I know," he said. He settled back on the pillows. "Maybe you should pretend those other things—the ones that make you cry—pretend that's all part of a bad dream."

She smiled and stroked his cheek. "You're right," she said. "I'll do that."

LORETTA CHASE

338

"Maybe you could kiss me good night again, too." He grinned. "I like that very well."

She laughed and kissed her son good night.

Darius went himself to his family, to request their attendance at his wedding. As one might expect, they were all at Hargate Hall in Derbyshire—all but Rupert and his wife, who were still in Egypt, along with Benedict's nephew Peregrine.

What Darius didn't expect was to find his grandmother there, too. She rarely left London. Her friends the Harpies lived there year-round, and even in summer London was more entertaining. The country, she said, bored her witless.

Yet this summer she'd come with her offspring to Hargate Hall.

She wasn't in the drawing room when Darius announced his betrothal. His parents and assorted family members were there, though. They bore the news of his coming nuptials with straight faces for the most part. He went on to explain how and why he was going to begin wedded life with a ten-year-old son.

They bore this stoically, too. None of the ladies present fainted. None of the brothers present commented. They all looked to Lord Hargate for his reaction.

He said, "Darius, I shall expect you in my study in a quarter hour."

A quarter hour later, Darius stood in the study, an almost exact replica of the Inquisition Chamber at Hargate House in London.

The meeting began, as one would expect, in the usual infuriating way.

"Couldn't make a go of the property, I see," said his father.

"My year isn't up," Darius said, drawing on all his willpower to remain unruffled—outwardly at least.

"But it hardly matters now, does it?" said his sire. "The prize was not having to marry. Since you are now engaged to be married, what is the point?"

"The point is, I can revive Beechwood, and I shall," Darius said. "Now, thanks to my wife's immense dowry, I shall have the wherewithal to do it quickly and efficiently. I am confident of recovering the investment and more within the time we set. It *can* be done, Father, and I shall do it."

"I don't doubt you will," said his father.

Darius blinked. Twice.

"Lady Charlotte is a good girl," his father said. "A good girl and a brave one. I am glad you had the wisdom to see this. I am proud of you."

Darius did not faint.

He did open and close his mouth several times, to no audible effect.

"You'd better see your grandmother now," said Lord Hargate. He waved his hand, dismissing his bewildered son.

Darius went up to his grandmother's apartments with about the same level of happy anticipation King Louis XVI must have felt as he climbed the steps of the guillotine scaffold.

He found her as one usually found her, in her boudoir. This room, like its counterpart in London, was decorated in the style of her youth, reputedly, though he'd always thought it resembled a brothel.

Her person, too, was adorned in the style fashionable many years ago. She sat among her numerous pillows, dripping lace and jewels.

He placed a dutiful kiss on her wrinkled cheek and gave her the fan.

"What is this, a bribe?" she said, wasting no more breath than he would on preliminaries. "You want me to lend countenance to your soiled dove, is that it?"

Though she hadn't been present for the announcement, Darius wasn't surprised she'd heard the news so quickly. It was more than possible she'd known all along about Charlotte's secret since Grandmama knew everything about everybody.

He wasn't at all surprised, merely irritated.

"It is a bribe, but she is not a soiled dove," said Darius. "I cannot believe you of all people would use that hackneyed phrase. And talk of the pot calling the kettle black. I've lost count of your lovers."

"I waited until I was a widow," she said.

"What nonsense," he said. "You did it after you'd been married, and Charlotte did it before. There isn't a bit of difference, and you know it. Come, Grandmama, you must appear at my wedding."

"Ah, well," she said. "If my grandson says I must, I must. What say has a feeble old lady in such matters?"

Darius rolled his eyes.

She examined the fan. "This is one of Lady Margaret's fans, I see. No one ever could match her for taste. She was exquisite, poor thing. I, too, was married young to a man twenty years my senior. But Hargate knew how to make a woman happy. Mind you do that, sir. Make your lady happy—or she'll make you live to regret it." She waved the fan at him, much in the way his father had waved his dismissal. "Go away now. I have letters to write, and I must decide what to wear to the wedding."

On the nineteenth of July, at ten o'clock in the forenoon, Lady Charlotte Hayward and Darius Carsington were married by common license in the church at Lithby before an unusually large crowd of witnesses.

Mr. Badgely performed the ceremony. Mrs. Badgely was in attendance as well, after a hard battle with her moral principles.

She did not condone the practice of bearing children out of wedlock, naturally, and she was not at all sure that allowances ought to be made, even for one's cousins.

The trouble was, she did not get to London often, especially now that her daughters were all wed and she had no good excuse and ought to have more important things to do than indulge in extravagant frivolity. Starved for fashion, she was desperate to study the latest modes the London ladies would wear, and she wanted to be able to drop the names of all the attendees. And so, in the end, like everybody else, she set her scruples aside in favor of enjoying a party that would be talked about for months afterward.

The festivities had been planned weeks earlier as part of the house party events. The Lithbys had only to make room for more guests.

Among other members of the Carsington family in attendance was the Dowager Lady Hargate's great-granddaughter, Olivia Wingate-Carsington, age thirteen.

Following the solemnities, Pip took Olivia to meet the pig. He fell into the sty. She fished him out. They returned to Lithby Hall covered in muck and reeking. They received a sharp scolding from their great-grandmother, followed by baths and a change of clothes. After this, they adjourned to the schoolroom, where Olivia taught Pip card tricks and the thimble rig until her mother, Lady Rathbourne, came in and put a stop to it.

"But Mama, how can Pip know he's being gulled unless he understands the cheat?" said Olivia, all wide-eyed innocence.

"You'll be teaching him how to pawn his mother's jewelry next," said Lady Rathbourne. "You will desist at once, Olivia, or you will not be allowed to watch the fireworks."

Her new husband stood behind Charlotte, his arms wrapped about her, his chin resting on her head while they watched the fireworks from a quiet corner of the garden.

"Are you thinking what I'm thinking?" he said.

"I'm not thinking," she said. "I'm simply . . . happy."

"It is quite a spectacle," he said. "The sort of thing one would expect for, say, a son's coming of age or a king's coronation."

"Or the marriage—at last—of an only daughter."

"Or the marriage—at last—of that last troublesome younger son."

"Papa and Lizzie do love to entertain," she said. "They are like children when it comes to parties."

"I think they are most unchildlike," Darius said. "I suspect a family conspiracy. No one was in the least surprised when I announced that we were going to be wed. I cannot help wondering what brought my grandmother to Derbyshire. She hates the country."

"Last year, they all wanted me to marry Lord Rathbourne," she said.

"Ridiculous," he said. "Anyone with a grain of sense could see you'd never suit. You are not half-shocking enough for him. Lady Rathbourne is a descendant of the Dreadful DeLuceys. Compared to them, you are a model of purity and virtue."

"In any event, your brother thought me a great bore," she said. "And so I reckon Papa and Lizzie decided to make do with you. They were desperate, after all." She laughed.

"Of course they were desperate," he said. "You are practically in your dotage. You are nearly at the end of your prime reproductive years—if you are not already past them." He drew her more tightly to him. "Perhaps we'd better get started on the reproduction business without further loss of time."

"We already started," she said.

"I mean, in a methodical manner," he said.

"Now?" she said. "Here?" The thought was not without its appeal. What a strumpet she was!

"Not here," he said. "And not now, furtively and hurriedly, as we've done before. This time, we shall do it in a proper bed, in a proper way."

"Methodically," she said.

"Don't mock the methodical approach until you've tried it," he said. "Let's go home, Charlotte."

My home, she thought, as the bridegroom carried her over the threshold she'd crossed so many times before.

She'd even had a hand in making a home of Lady Margaret's neglected house. Not that the work was finished. Far from it. A great deal remained to be done.

Still, while one might have to dodge scaffolding and ladders elsewhere, Lizzie had made sure the master bedroom was completed before the wedding.

The newlyweds could spend the night there without worrying about pieces of the ceiling falling on their heads, she assured them.

Tonight they had the luxury of complete privacy. The servants were all at the Lithby estate, along with most of the village. Pip was staying one last night with his grandparents, becoming acquainted with his new families. When last Charlotte saw him, Pip was with the Dowager Lady Hargate and his cousin Olivia, learning to play whist.

Within, Beechwood House was quiet but for their footsteps and the odd sounds old houses make.

Outside, the noise of the fireworks had died away, leaving the insects and night birds to their summer concert.

Though only the candle Darius had carried up from the ground floor lit the room, Charlotte could see that Lizzie had performed her usual magic. The big room was simply but beautifully decorated, comfortable, and clean.

"This is a good house," Charlotte said. "Lady Margaret was unhappy here, but the house was here long before she came, and I think it wants to be a happy house." She turned to her husband. "You have made me so happy. Have I told you?"

"Yes, I believe you have," he said. He unwrapped his neckcloth and threw it onto a chair. "I'm going to make you happier. Grandmother says I must, or there will be the devil to pay."

Charlotte moved nearer to him. She brought her hand up to his cheek. He turned his head to kiss her palm.

Then he took her hand and led her to the bed. It was large and ornate, and probably dated to the time of the Stuarts. He lifted her up as though she weighed nothing at all and tossed her onto the middle of the mattress. She laughed.

"I've imagined doing that," he said, "from the time you were explaining stoved feathers to me. In the library at Lithby Hall."

"I had a feeling you weren't really attending," she said.

"I was." He took off his coat. It was snug, deceptively simple, exquisitely tailored. She watched the play of his muscles under his formfitting attire as he worked his way out of the coat, lithe as a cat. His waistcoat came next.

She lay where he'd thrown her, her head resting on the pillows while she drank in the strong, beautiful torso his shirt so thinly veiled. They'd made love yet she'd never seen him—well, not more than the crucial part of him. This was a true wedding night, she thought, a night to discover each other.

How lucky she was! Everyone made mistakes, sometimes terrible ones. Not everyone got a second chance.

He knelt on the bed and crawled toward her. He straddled her. "I hung on your every word that night," he said, "all the while wishing I was hanging on your lips." He bent and his mouth hovered over hers, a mere breath away. "Like a bee drawn to a flower." He kissed her lightly, as though her lips were the most delicate of flower petals.

"I remember," she said. "You stood improperly close."

"I almost kissed you." He brushed his lips over hers.

"I almost kissed you back," she said, doing the same to him.

He kissed her deeply, so tenderly. She answered in the same way, giving with all her heart all the love he'd reawakened in her. She gave and felt it returned to her, in the taste of him and the sweetness of the kiss. She felt it in a surge of warmth and happiness and a strange peace she hadn't known since her girlhood, along with a girlish excitement she thought she'd outgrown.

"I want to see you," he said. "All of you."

"Yes," she said. "I want to see you, too."

He lifted his head, smiling. "Where to begin unwrapping this wondrous gift?"

"Wherever you like," she said. "I place myself entirely in your hands." She looked at his hands, so large and deft. Those hands, oh, those hands.

He studied her for a long moment in that intent way of his. Then he bent and cupped her face and kissed her. He slid his hands down over her naked shoulders, making her shiver. He found the fastenings of her bodice and loosened it. He brushed his mouth over the skin he'd exposed. "Women's clothes," he murmured. "Complicated mechanisms."

But he had no trouble ascertaining how her gown functioned. He easily located the drawstrings and hooks. Then, while she giggled, he drew the gown up, and she lifted herself enough so that he could pull it over her head. She saw amusement in his candlelit face as he threw the gown aside.

In a moment he was serious again, studying her underthings with the same absolute concentration he might apply to a chemical experiment. She watched him, aware of her blood taking fire merely at his looking at her. Then his hands moved over her, caressing her through layers of fine fabric, as though what touched her was dear to him, too. And she was dear to him, yes. She had no doubt of that. She saw it in his face and heard it in his low voice.

She closed her eyes and let herself swim in the

warmth and sweetness. The petticoat came away, and the short corset, and she let out a long, shuddering breath as her chemise fell open, and she felt his mouth trail over her shoulders, her breasts, slowly, so slowly. As her clothes fell away, his caresses were there, long and slow, as though she were the most precious object in all the world, as though they had all the time in the world.

They did. This was the beginning of their world, their life together.

She brought her hands up and stroked over his shirt with the same tenderness and wonder, letting her touch tell him how precious he was to her, a gift she'd never looked for, never dared to hope for.

He unfastened the buttons of his shirt, pulled it over his head, and tossed it over his shoulder. She caught her breath. She'd seen magnificent sculptures of athletes and pagan gods, and he might have modeled for them. But he was real and warm and alive, his skin golden in the candlelight. She lifted her hand to his chest and let it rest there. Under her palm his heart beat hard and steady.

He laid his hand over hers, lifted her hand to his lips. "I can't wait much longer," he said. "I've been putting it off, but I must get to those ridiculous bits of silk you call shoes."

He edged back to the foot of the bed. He untied one shoe, slipped it from her foot, and sent it the way of the rest of her things. His warm hand closed over her foot. He slid his hand up to the top of her stocking. He untied the garter. He drew the stocking down a little ways. He made a path of kisses over the skin he'd exposed. He drew the stocking down another few inches and kissed her leg again. She began to tremble.

He continued down, to her ankles, then slowly to her instep. Finally, he drew the stocking down over her toes and tossed it aside.

She sank into bliss.

But he wasn't done yet, far from it.

He did the same, slowly, oh so slowly, with the other stocking.

By then she was aching everywhere.

"Happy, Charlotte?" he said, his voice so low. It felt like the strings of a bass viol thrumming through her.

"Yes," she said.

She felt the last of her garments slide away.

"Happier?" he said.

"Yes." Could she bear any more happiness? Yes, if she had to.

He moved away, and through eyes half-shuttered with the stupor of pleasure, she watched him strip away the last of his garments, too. She watched him come to her, his big body looming over her. His mouth met hers and the kiss was deep but slow, so slow as though it was the last kiss in the world, the only one in the world.

Then he was caressing her, rousing her, and she had no words, no thoughts. She could only let her hands move over him, let her touch tell him how she longed for him, how she longed to be his, utterly.

And then at last he was inside her, filling her, and he loved her, unhurriedly and completely, as though they had all the time in the world. And by slow, aching degrees, he took her to the one perfect moment, when there was no more "I" or "thou" but only one love, carrying them to a place of magical joy. When they came to the peak, and her body vibrated and pleasure rushed through her like liquid fire—when *he* was the vibration and the pleasure and she didn't know which was she and which was he—she laughed once, and, "Oh, my love," she said. Then she buried her face in his neck and gave herself up to peace, at long last, peace.

Turn the page for a sneak peak at
Lord Perfect by Loretta Chase ...

Also available from Piatkus Books

Chapter 1

HE LEANT AGAINST THE WINDOW FRAME, OFFERING those within the exhibition hall a fine rear view of a long, well-proportioned frame, expensively garbed. He seemed to have his arms folded and his attention upon the window, though the thick glass could show him no more than a blurred image of Piccadilly.

It was clear in any case that the exhibition within—of the marvels Giovanni Belzoni had discovered in Egypt—had failed to hold his interest.

The woman surreptitiously studying him decided he would make the perfect model of the bored aristocrat.

Supremely assured. Perfectly poised. Immaculately dressed. Tall. Dark.

He turned his head, presenting the expected patrician profile.

It wasn't what she expected.

She couldn't breathe.

BENEDICT CARSINGTON, VISCOUNT Rathbourne, turned away from the thick-paned window and the distorted view it offered of the lively scene outside—of horses, vehicles, and pedestrians in Piccadilly. With an inner sigh, he directed his dark gaze into the exhibition hall, where Death was on display.

"Belzoni's Tomb," exhibiting the explorer's discoveries in Egypt a few years ago, had proved a rousing success since its debut on the first of May. Against his better judgment, Benedict had formed one of the nineteen hundred attendees on opening day. This was his third visit, and once again, he had much rather be elsewhere.

Ancient Egypt did not exert over him the hold it did over so many of his relatives. Even his numskull brother Rupert had fallen under its spell, perhaps because the present-day place offered so many opportunities for head-breaking and hairsbreadth escapes from death. But Rupert was most certainly not the reason for Lord Rathbourne's spending another long afternoon in the Egyptian Hall.

The reason sat at the far end of the room: Benedict's thirteen-year-old nephew and godson Peregrine Dalmay, Earl of Lisle and sole issue of Benedict's brother-in-law, the Marquess of Atherton. The boy was diligently copying Belzoni's model of the interior of the famous Second Pyramid, whose entrance the explorer had discovered three years ago.

Diligence, Peregrime's schoolmasters would have told anyone—and had told his father, repeatedly—was not one of Lord Lisle's more noticeable character traits.

When it came to things Egyptian, however, Peregrine was persevering to a fault. They had arrived two hours ago, and his interest showed no signs of flagging. Any other boy would have been wild to be out and engaging in physical activity one and three-quarters of an hour ago.

But then, had this been any other boy, Benedict would not have had to come himself to the Egyptian Hall. He would have sent a servant to play nursemaid.

Peregrine wasn't any other boy.

He looked like an angel. A fair, open countenance. Flaxen hair. Clear, grey, utterly guileless eyes.

A group of boxers under "Gentleman" Jackson's supervision

had been employed to keep Queen Caroline and her sympa-
thizers out of the king's coronation in July. These fellows, if
they stuck together, might have contrived to keep the peace
while Lord Atherton's heir was about.

Other than these—or a large military force—the only mortal with any real influence over the young Lord Lisle was
Benedict—the only one, that is, apart from Benedict's father,
the Earl of Hargate. But Lord Hargate could intimidate anybody—except for his wife—and he certainly would not
stoop to looking after troublesome boys.

I should have brought a book, Benedict thought. Stifling a
yawn, he directed his gaze to Belzoni's reproduction of a
bas-relief from a pharaoh's tomb and tried to understand
what Peregrine, along with so many other people, found so
stimulating.

Benedict saw three rows of primitively drawn figures. A
line of men whose beards curled up at the end, all leaning
forward, arms pressed together. Lone hieroglyphic signs
between the figures. Columns of hieroglyphs above their
heads.

In the middle row, four figures towed a boat bearing three
other figures. Some very long snakes played a part in the
scene. More columns of hieroglyphs over the heads. Perhaps
these figures were all talking? Were the signs the Egyptian
version of the bubbles over caricatures' heads in today's
satirical prints?

On the bottom, another line of figures marched under
columns of hieroglyphs. These had different features and
hairstyles. They must be foreigners. At the end of the line
was a god Benedict recognized: Thoth, the ibis-headed one,
the god of learning. Even Rupert, upon whom an expensive
education had been utterly wasted—Lord Hargate might
have fed the money to goats with the same result—could
recognize Thoth.

What the rest of it meant was work for the imagination,
and Benedict kept his imagination, along with a great deal
else, under rigorous control.

He turned his attention to the opposite side of the room.

He had an unobstructed view. For most of the Beau Monde, the exhibition's novelty had worn off. Even their inferiors would rather spend this fine afternoon outdoors than among the contents of ancient tombs.

Benedict saw her clearly.

Too clearly.

For a moment he was blinded by the clarity, like one stepping out of a cave into a blazing noonday.

She stood in profile, like the figures on the wall behind her. She was studying a statue.

Benedict saw black curls under the rim of a pale blue bonnet. Long black lashes against pearly skin. A ripe plum of a mouth.

His gaze skimmed down.

A weight pressed on his chest.

He couldn't breathe.

Rule: The ill-bred, the vulgar, and the ignorant stare.

He made himself look away.

THE GIRL STOOD at Peregrine's shoulder. He tried to ignore her but she was standing in his light. He glanced up and quickly back at his sketchbook—enough to see that she had her arms folded and her lips pursed as she stared at his drawing. He knew that look. It was a schoolmaster look.

She must have taken the glance as an invitation because she started talking. "I wondered why you chose the model of the pyramid," she said. "It is all angles and lines. So uninteresting to draw. The mummy in the sarcophagus would be more fun. But now I understand the trouble. Your draughtsmanship is not very good."

Very slowly and deliberately Peregrine turned his head and looked up at her. He was startled at first, when he got a good look. She had eyes so blue, they looked like doll eyes, not real ones.

"I beg your pardon?" he said in the icily polite voice he'd learnt from his uncle. His father was a marquess, a peer of the realm, and his uncle had only the courtesy title of

Viscount Rathbourne at present, but Uncle Benedict administered far more devastating set-downs. He was famous for it. At his most excessively polite, it was said, Lord Rathbourne could freeze boiling oil at fifty paces.

The icy politeness didn't work so well for Peregrine.

"There's a perfectly good cross section of the pyramid in Signor Belzoni's book," she said quite as though he'd begged her to rattle on. "Wouldn't you rather have a souvenir of one of the mummies? Or the goddess with the lion head? My mother could make you a superlative copy. She's a brilliant draughtsman."

"I don't want a *souvenir*," Peregrine said witheringly. "I'm going to be an explorer, and one day I shall bring home heaps of such things."

The girl stopped pursing her lips. The severe look went away. "An explorer like Signor Belzoni, do you mean?" she said. "Oh, that would be something grand to do."

Try as he might, Peregrine could not tamp down his enthusiasm in the proper Lord Rathbourne fashion. "Nothing could be grander," he said. "There are more than a thousand miles along the Nile to explore, and people who've been say that what you see is like the tip of an iceberg, because most of the wonderful things are buried under the sand. And once we learn to read the hieroglyphs, we'll know who built what and when they did it. At present, you see, ancient Egypt is like the Dark Ages: a great mystery. But I'm going to be one of the ones who finds out its secrets. It'll be like discovering a whole new world."

The girl's blue doll eyes opened wider. "Oh, then it's a *noble quest*. You're going to shed light on the Dark Ages of Egypt. I'm going on quests, too. When I grow up, I'm going to be a knight."

Peregrine almost stuck his finger in his ear to be sure it was in working order. He rememberd his uncle was in the vicinity, though, and picturing the look Lord Rathbourne would give him, resisted the impulse. Instead he said, "Sorry. Say again? I thought you said you were going to be a knight—as in shining armor and such."

"That's what I said," she said. "Like the Knights of the Round Table. The gallant Sir Olivia, that's who I'll be, setting out on perilous quests, performing noble deeds, righting wrongs—"

"That's ridiculous," Peregrine said.

"No, it isn't," she said.

"Of course it is," Peregrine said—patiently, because she was a girl and probably had no notion of logic. "In the first place, all that King Arthur and the Knights of the Round Table folderol is a myth. It has about as much basis in fact or history as the Egyptians had for their sphinxes and gods with ibis heads."

"A myth!" The great blue eyes opened wider still. "What about the Crusades?"

"I didn't say knights never existed," Peregrine said. "They did and do. But the magic, monsters, and miracles are nothing more than myths. The Venerable Bede doesn't even mention Arthur."

He went on, citing historical references to the simple warrior leader who might or might not have been the source of the legendary Arthur. Peregrine explained how, over the centuries, a romantic tale developed, and along the way, mythical creatures, miracles, and various other religious associations got stuck onto the story, because the Church was the great power and stuck religion onto everything.

He then offered his views on religion, the same views that had led to his being chucked out of one school after another. Out of consideration for her weaker and less amply educated feminine brain, though, he gave a simpler shorter version.

When he paused for breath, she said scornfully, "That's only your opinion. You don't *know*. There *might* have been a Holy Grail. There *might* have been a Camelot."

"I know there weren't any dragons," he said. "So you can't slay any. Even if there were dragons, you couldn't."

"There were knights!" she cried. "I can still be a knight!"

"No, you can't," he said, more patient than ever, because she was so sadly confused. "You're a girl. Girls can't be knights."

She snatched the sketchbook from his hands and swung it at his head.

DISASTER WOULD NOT have occurred had Bathsheba Wingate been paying full attention to her daughter.

She was not paying attention.

She was trying desperately to keep her gaze from straying to the bored aristocrat ... to the long legs whose muscles the costly wool trousers lovingly outlined ... the boots whose dark gleam matched his eyes ... the miles of shoulders bracing up the window frame ... the haughty jaw and insolent nose ... the dark, dangerously bored eyes.

Bathsheba might as well have been a giddy sixteen-year-old miss when in fact she was a sober matron twice that age, and she might as well have never seen a handsome aristocrat before in all her life when in fact she'd met any number and even married one. She was not herself and she didn't know or care who she was.

She only stood for a long time, trying to pay attention to the Egyptians instead of him, and oblivious of the minutes passing during which Olivia might easily re-create some of the more harrowing scenes from the Book of Revelation.

Bathsheba forgot she even had a daughter while she stood as though trapped, her heart beating so fast that it left no time or room to breathe.

This was why she failed to notice the signs of trouble before it was too late.

The crash, the outraged yelp, and the familiar voice crying, "You great blockhead!" told her it was too late at the same time they broke the spell. She hurried toward the noise and snatched the sketchbook from Olivia's hands before she could throw it across the room—and break a priceless object, beyond doubt.

"Olivia Wingate," Bathsheba said, careful to keep her voice low, in hopes of attracting as small an audience as possible. "I am shocked, deeply shocked." This was a hideous lie. Bathsheba would be shocked only if Olivia contrived to

spend half an hour among civilized beings without making a
spectacle of herself.

She turned toward the flaxen-haired boy, her daughter's
latest victim. He shifted up into a sitting position on the floor
near his overturned stool, but that was as far as he came. He
watched them, grey eyes wary.

"I said I was going to be a knight when I grew up and *he*
said girls couldn't be knights," Olivia said, her voice shaking
with rage.

"Lisle, I am astonished at your flagrant disregard of a fun-
damental rule of human survival," came an impossibly deep
voice from somewhere nearby and to Bathsheba's right. The
sound shot down to the base of her spine then up again to
vibrate against an acutely sensitive place in her neck. "I am
sure I have told you more than once," the voice went on. "A
gentleman *never* contradicts a lady."

Bathsheba turned her head toward the voice.

Ah, of course.

Of all the boys in all of the world, Olivia had to assault the
one belonging to *him*.